MY CRY for NIGERIA:
Challenge to Essence

C. C. Aningo

C. C. Aningo's multiple proposals in *My Cry for Nigeria* are the result of his extensive observation, research, and love of country. His analysis is amazing, in both depth and breath. Instead of focusing only on problems, the author presents well-thought-out solutions, such as top-notch education, unselfish leadership, and reliable infrastructure. His invention of Uhuru Hut friends from different Nigerian tribes is imaginative and a cry to the country to unite.

Engineer Aningo has written a compelling allegory that might one day be a great influence, especially if it becomes required reading on the university level, where future Nigerian leaders are being developed. This is an excellent read and one that I highly recommend for anyone who advocates success for Nigeria.

Portia Tewogbade
Author of *During a Dry Season* and *Red Was the Midnight:* Novels

—Foreword

Aningo is a scientist who writes with the flair of a celebrated literary artist. His language is draped in immense colour and appeal and his descriptive powers are only fit for the classical masters . . .

I recommend My Cry for Nigeria to every Nigerian who is truly eager for the ultimate transformation of our fatherland in disposition and in character. I recommend it for use in universities and colleges. And I recommend it to the general reader.

Prof. Richard C. Okafor
Enugu State University of Science and Technology,
Enugu, Nigeria.

C. C. Aningo is a hard driving, persistent Nigerian of uncompromising professionalism and patriotism. A man of candour and uncommon fervour in causes he believes in . . . authored *My Cry for Nigeria* . . . to nucleate deep thinking about using systemic rather than reactive approaches in solving our problems . . .

Onyedika Agbedo
"The Guardian (Nigeria)"

DEDICATION

To the Nigerian youths and others who now "jump ship," this work is dedicated to your consideration of the other option—joining sincere actions on mending Nigeria. Pioneers cultivated, and residents foster, those alluring, greener pastures elsewhere, while tying their futures to them.

To all Nigerian youths at home or abroad, from whose language Nigeria understandably became "Naija," this book brings the following messages. Some in my generation and in generations older or younger targeted your well-being even as they did not fully succeed in its delivery. The mind supervises the heart. You are the final focus of this book.

May your future and those of generations following you be very much improved, unique, and well-synchronised to your world.

I equally dedicate this unnerving writing project about improving Nigeria to my family, true friends, and all who similarly cherish me.

PREFACE

Wholesome elitism comes from presence in community. This presence includes leadership that brings security and progress to all. I believe that Nigeria has enough of such elites and well-wishers who, collaborating, can lead Nigerians to change Nigeria to positively endure. It is all a matter of making the right choices and having the will to act. Then, sound knowledge base effectively drives choice and will.

This book presents possible solutions for Nigeria, using a narrative woven from reality, personal opinion, and fiction. Its content is the sole responsibility of the author. Names, characters, businesses, places, events, and incidents are either derived from the author's imagination or used in a fictional manner. Any resemblance to actual persons, living or dead, or actual events is purely coincidental. If, per chance, this coincidence causes any discomfort, it is not intended, and I truly apologise.

The first thirteen chapters focus on a few global issues and the contradictions that challenge Nigeria. Some of these challenges arise from little-mentioned, but powerful, internal events and conditions. The closing chapters present a set of dreamy solutions, which engage a reader's imagination, creativity, and attitude. There is a mind-tickler for nearly every thoughtful reader.

If, finally, you identify all the regenerative leverages stated or implied, add some more, and then catch a touch of the "fever," pass on the "heat."

Your company, dear reader, is very delightful.

Thank you!

Chukwuajalike

FOREWORD

My Cry for Nigeria is a curious treatise, a dream projection of how Nigeria metamorphoses into Naija, and Nigerians into Naijans. In an imaginative literary scheme that contests his engineering training and background, the author, engineer Chukwuajalike C. Aningo, delivers a powerful message to his country, using a subtle, light-hearted approach. He assembles a choice team of restless enquirers, "a close group of seven distilled from similar exposures, orientations, and perspectives (and who) flourish on shared values, understanding, and accommodation" (to use his own words), to brainstorm over those trite challenges that have continually afflicted Nigeria and Nigerians with avoidable adversity. Shrewdly guided and moderated by Chiamalu, whom they affectionately call Professador (Professor and Ambassador), they identify these challenges as corruption, damage of the economy by political leaders, rubbishing entrepreneurship, ethnic hostilities, poor work ethics, and unattractive work environments, resulting in unending brain drain, among others.

The seven friends, symbolically drawn from the three major tribes of Nigeria (Hausa, Igbo, and Yoruba) meet on Sunday afternoons at a tasty resort called *Uhuru Hut,* which is located between Independence Layout and New Haven in Enugu, capital of Enugu state of Nigeria. Here, they hatch a proposal to enlighten Nigerians on the challenges that beset them. Under the auspices of *Okwukwe Afrika,* a popular public relations outfit, the inimitable Chiamalu leads his colleagues to address a large crowd of Nigerians. His address draws the ire of security agencies, and the group is hounded underground. But because of the public enthusiasm for the message delivered, an organization code-named TANNA (Turn Around Nigeria Now and Associates) is quickly created to drive the demand for a peoples' national conference. Enthusiastic volunteers from all parts of the country swarm to TANNA to help.

My Cry for Nigeria is Aningo's touching lament over the horrifying rot and decay that have afflicted Nigeria and its institutions and public life, and his passionate plea that all Nigerians, irrespective of tribe and situation, should come together to look for viable solutions. The composition of the *Uhuru Hut* thinkers (Chiamalu and Nduka from the East, Danladi and Gumut from the North, Olu and Osagie from the West) carries his unshakeable conviction that the battle for Nigeria's recovery is a battle that must involve all stakeholders to the Nigerian project. Aningo does not believe in a fire-brigade approach to the solution, but in a carefully planned and executed countrywide conference in which all shades of opinion will be given the opportunity of articulation in an atmosphere free from undue pressures and harassment. He suggests that the product of this conference will be appreciated, not only in a change in the people's attitudes and practices, but also in the change of our country's corporate name. Thus, 'Naija' replaces 'Nigeria,' which has been abused as a seedbed for corruption and other social vices.

When Aningo refers to "a close group of seven distilled from similar exposures," he names only six of his co-travellers, himself being the unnamed seventh complement. What Aningo is showing by the device is that he personally stands to be counted in any programs or actions aimed at giving Nigeria a reformed personality and image, and not just leave it to "them" to actualise.

Aningo is a scientist who writes with the flair of a celebrated literary artist. His language is draped in immense colour and appeal, and his descriptive powers are only fit for the classical masters. His description of the *Uhuru Hut,* for instance, is capable of taking people's breath away—"A multi-purpose social centre, and an architectural rendition of a master's manipulation of space and culture for comfort, *Uhuru Hut* boasted of tropical ambience with intensely fragrant flowers that bloom through the year." What a poetic prose!

I recommend *My Cry for Nigeria* to every Nigerian who is truly eager for the ultimate transformation of Nigeria in character and in disposition. I recommend it for use in universities and colleges. And I recommend it to the general reader.

Prof. Richard C. Okafor
Enugu State University of Science and Technology
Enugu.

Contents

Preface vii

Foreword ix

Prologue 1

1 Global Round Up 3

2 Entrepreneurship And Job Creation In Nigeria 13

3 Analyses 27

4 Rural Echoes 41

5 Ripples Of Rural Echoes 59

6 Upscale Countrywide Dialogue 70

7 The Splash 80

8 The Splash Backwash 91

9 The Rash Flash 104

10 Counter Strategies 119

11 The Hornet's Nest 126

12 Cremating The Big Bad Monster 139

13 Hibernation 151

14 The Surge 165

15 Fast Forward 182

16 Back On Track 194

17 Priceless Conference 207

18 Convergence 221

19 Priceless Exchanges 242

Acknowledgement 249

About The Author 251

PROLOGUE

"Your 'twin brother' is not home." I still hear Chiamalu's mother as she steps towards me, head slightly tilted to the left, face broadened by a white, toothy smile. I catch a whiff of that calming scent as she pulls me into a side hug.

She often added, "He didn't say when he'll be back. Come in and have something to eat."

I liked the sound of that, particularly the special, nearly teasing, but encouraging, stress on 'twin brother.'

Chiamalu and I belong to the same age grade of Oyofo Oghe community in Ezeagu Local Government Area of now Enugu state, Nigeria. An age grade consists of people born within a three-year interval who are collectively given community service assignments. Each age grade has a mentor called "Father" of the Age Grade, selected from competing community stalwarts. Individual accomplishments often became powerful yardsticks for encouraging or assessing age grade members and their Fathers.

"Let Chiamalu talk!" was a regular chorus whenever the age grade had some explaining to make to our Father, an elder, or other community authority. His enduring, boyish, round face held high above others in the age grade and adorned with dimpled smiles—magnet to eyes—made it easy for him to communicate. A great manipulator of the decibels, Chiamalu spoke in measured sentences, tone, and tempo for the greatest effects by his controlled baritone voice.

"Was Chuks there? He must have started it all," was the result of my reputation whenever there was trouble among the age grade. I was the rabble-rousing roughrider whose informality singed weak nerves, but as age outstrips every edge, I've mellowed some.

I once thrashed an age grade peer in a fight; I didn't like him much. Our Father, who was very upset, summoned us. I feared the outcome. Everyone expected the boom to fall hard on me, but before our Father delivered judgement, after hearing us out, Chiamalu spoke.

"Father, you know we are all young and sometimes prone to small, play-frays. It was a little misunderstanding from not listening well, as you've heard. Perhaps we can sort it all out ourselves and make sure there's no bitterness between them? You know we always do our utmost to make you the best Father in the community. Please, let us settle the matter."

The boom turned into a dried, thin, hollow twig.

As classmates in primary and secondary school, Chiamalu and I were drilled in leadership through student administration and sports. We shared a passion for mathematics, science, and the common good. We always felt gifted and destined for distinction, an ambition that made the world oppose us.

We were not alone, however. This was the mid-1950s; the foreshadowing clouds of political independence from the British energised activities everywhere in Nigeria.

"The qualified will replace departing colonial administrators," was the persisting mantra.

We eventually earned scholarships to study engineering abroad—he in Europe and I in America. After our studies, we worked for some years abroad, earned professional pedigrees, before returning home. Not being able to fit well into civil service, we started our own individual consultancy practices. We never spoke about merging our businesses, though I thought about it occasionally, and I am sure he did too.

1

GLOBAL ROUND UP

In those early days following our return in the mid-1980s, we discovered what was known as Uhuru Hut located on a border hill somewhere between the highbrow Independence Layout and the mostly young professionals' New Haven in Enugu, capital of now Enugu state, Nigeria. A multi-purpose social centre and an architectural rendition of a master's manipulation of space and culture for comfort, Uhuru Hut boasted of tropical ambience with intensely fragrant flowers that bloomed through the year. There were international restaurants, bars, party rooms, dance halls, an auditorium, meeting rooms, limited shopping and lodging, outdoors facilities, and more. And, of course, "Uhuru" means "Freedom" in Swahili, and "Hut" calls up Afrika to the limited mind.

"LEVEL GROUND!" the bold amber sign over the reception desk warned.

Different kinds of people came to Uhuru Hut—it was a sort of equaliser. You could find yourself seated next to, or across from, that obstructionist bureaucrat who had ruined your past week. Tradition forbade the reopening of the matter. Uhuru Hut offered the place and time to unwind. An open mind at Uhuru Hut could lead you into a world full of stories: the exploits of football stars; the affairs between personalities and others' wives, concubines, or girlfriends; the hot corruption scandals; the shenanigans of politicians; wisecracks of activists; prophesies delivered with the passion of defence attorneys… anything was possible. The stories of Uhuru Hut were what best-selling novels are made from, only here, the characters could walk out of the novel and pass in front of your table.

"Oga sirs, good afternoon sirs." The ebony-beauty receptionist flashed white teeth as she greeted Chiamalu and me this May Sunday afternoon.

She ushered us to our normal location. Chiamalu spotted the party of five that made a full house of the regulars and waved, smiling happily at them, as they approached us.

"C & C Twins!" shouted Danladi, referring to us.

"The inseparable duo!" bellowed massive Osagie.

Our intimate group of seven was distilled from similar exposures, orientations, and perspectives, and flourished on shared values. Over time, business and socials brought us together—especially business, because we were all in engineering and technology. If we were all from Oyofo Oghe, we would be in the same age grade.

"Oga sirs. Good afternoon, sirs. Welcome to Uhuru Hut," the waitress greeted us, after her nifty tugs adjusted her skirt waistline.

Normally, "Oga" is a word used to refer to someone of a higher class. However, it could also be pregnant with meaning, a sneer masked as respect or the first shot of a hustler seeking your dropped guards.

Osagie set the topic. "The rains refuse to fall. My vegetable gardening being set back. The seasons, definitely changing patterns; have you all noticed?"

"Yep. It's happening all over the world—where have you been, heh?" Gumut said, his round, dark chocolate face creased with a mocking smile.

"What do you expect, Osagie?" Olu asked. "Half a century of continuous oil-well gas flaring must eventually affect our climate somehow, especially in the Niger Delta where the oil now comes from."

"I remember those days in Los Angeles. The smog, so thick you couldn't see a few metres ahead. Mid-afternoon, the thing would descend into near-darkness like an eclipse." Nduka raised both hands like an umbrella, then dropped them onto the table with a thud, his mid-size frame stumped.

"But I hear all the restrictions are helping," he added.

"The discipline to take remedial actions by a good number of the people, that's the difference," Chiamalu said.

"That's nothing compared to my experiences while working for a company that serviced steel mills. Steel… pollution; houses bleached out. You paint your house, within weeks, change of colour. The odour in the air, haba… unbearable!" Danladi's face skewed in disgust and he shifted in his seat. "You wouldn't believe that some mills blew their stacks at night, until the environmental agencies caught up with them – sledgehammers. The mountains of ores, where did they all come from? I imagined gaping canyons, natural settings fouled up. But well, there are the jobs for many, many families over time at mill sites, and products for everyone."

"I knew you would rationalise it all, Danladi. But you have to do so over the very long term," Gumut said, squinting.

Nduka quipped, "We all get long jail sentences, heh, Gumut?"

Olu adjusted his headgear. "Oh yes, it's right that we balance out pros and cons, but we must be realistic. Most of us don't have the patience to consider all details for such appraisals."

"That's the bogey!" Gumut said, chest expanded, glaring eyes emphasising his face.

Olu said, "My globetrotting shifts with a refinery start-up outfit exposed me to so much. I've been flown in helicopters over gaping holes left by mining all over the globe, particularly in the Third World. Abandoned structures, gullies, left by poorly handled extraction and early beneficiation."

Osagie, hands rising from the table, said, "Footprints of economies of this civilisation."

Olu continued, "My company once organised a retreat on a cruise boat on the Rhine in Germany as a treat for field people. The Rhine, with all that history, was so dead. If someone had fallen overboard, especially with all the drinking that went on, all we could have fished out would have been bare skeleton; the rest of the body would have been etched out."

Our orders arrived.

"One moment, please," Nduka shouted at the departing waitresses, his frame twisted around. "Is this the shark-fin pepper soup? For far too long, they've been terrorising and eating people. I want to contribute to eating sharks."

After the laughter, a waitress replied, "Oga, yes sir, it is. They trim off the fins first."

More laughter and a long pause during which we sampled our orders to the usual approvals.

Olu wiped his mouth. "I once flew into Chicago from London and, as we descended into the city across Lake Michigan, we observed silvery reflections from near the shores—dead fish floating belly-up. My drive through Lakeshore Drive to my friend's residence confirmed it; a strong fishy odour in the air. However, on my way out, five days later, the dead fish were all gone. Quick actions, but questions remained. Isn't nature talking to us?"

Osagie said, "Talking about O'Hare airport, my wife and I just returned from visiting her folks in Jamaica. We flew into Chicago via Miami. On descending into Chicago, we went through layers of clouds of various colours. First, the normal creamy stuff, then the dirty grey, the layer with orange tinge, the creamy stuff again, and suddenly, skyscrapers. Their sudden appearance jolted me and, boy, was I ever grateful for automated aircraft landing."

Nduka hardly let him finish. "Osagie, you were just chicken. What happened to all that Afrikan-Jamaican voodoo, heh? You couldn't trust it anymore? You didn't say how you fared with Immigration in Miami; your papers must have read: Nigeria-Jamaica, Jamaica-Nigeria."

Osagie jumped to his feet, clenched fists pumping. His tall frame cast a shadow over the table under which Nduka quickly ducked. Our laughter attracted attention.

"Yes, come to think of it," Osagie said, "there are scars in Jamaica too, left by the bauxite, railroad, and other actions, but far from the tourist trails. People like Nduka will never see those areas; they would have been dazed by the 'weeds of wisdom' just outside the airport."

Danladi leaned back, the light played up his light complexion. "This environment thing; it's global—Africa, Asia, Australia, all Europe, the Americas, you name it. The West is not the only culprit. I once flew to Australia, my seat next to this fellow from around the place nuclear power plant exploded in the former USSR—Chernobyl, in the Ukraine. First meals, drinks evaporated stiff politeness. Amazing that your interests can tally so well with those of someone from so far away and with whom you may first think you don't share much. We really took off together."

Nduka, eyebrows raised, said, "He tasked air hostesses with requests for "tuwo" and "kuka" soup, plus "brukutu" drink, heh?"

Danladi said, "Okay, Nduka. Skip details, it happened in mid-1986. First, the International Atomic Energy Agency, I think it was, and others had warned, 'those plants pose dangers because of their shutdown sequences.' No one listened in the USSR, which gained notice from spectaculars, propaganda, without paying enough attention to the needs of her people. 'To each according to his need and from each according to his ability' was beyond them. They attempted to hide the accident. Immediate global help, not sought; damage got worse. Countries that depend on nuclear energy for electricity bear such risk; other sources of risks are increasing."

"Ukraine will remain of interest to Russia as a buffer zone," Osagie interrupted.

Danladi continued, "A lot more evidence has been exposed; much more damage to nature took place in the fifty years of Soviet Union. The abuse of nature is all over; the West is not guilty alone."

Gumut told Danladi, "Yes, 'Mr. West,' but you forgot Windscale of 1957 in the UK and Three Mile Island of 1979 in the US."

Danladi lashed back, "Fellows, Gumut forgets Kyshtym in 1958 in Russia. Of all these accidents, Chernobyl/Pripyat is the worst in magnitude and its handling."

I only attended to my goat-meat pepper soup and delicious palm wine. Chiamalu hadn't spoken either. He downed his mouthful of "isi ewu," a delicacy prepared with goat head pieces and other choice parts, cooked in a pasty broth of the brains, and all enlivened with invigorating herbs and spices. He washed it down with his Star beer, cleaned his mouth, and leaned forward.

"Gentlemen, all we've said so far and more show that current global lifestyles are forcing us to unsettle nature irrationally. Isn't development the application of ideas and knowledge for improved overall conditions? Why leave out nature? Humanity cannot afford this trend. It's like a foetus trying to kill its mother; the first probable result is that it gets aborted. It's not good enough to say, 'I'll be dead and gone before any reactions by nature.' Once we are born, we never truly die. We remain links in the unimaginably large bundles of chains that record human evolution through all yesterdays, today, and all tomorrows, whether history places us among the unforgettable or not. We all have responsibility."

"Yes, indeed," some of us agreed.

Chiamalu said, "The 'NEW AND IMPROVED' labelling still creates and enlarges markets in all manufacturing, while efficient designs for retrofitting are increasingly ignored—more natural resources consumed. Well, the agonies of living, especially in our parts, leave many of us with disabled minds, as the bogey Gumut mentioned. Space. Some thoughts come to mind. First, there's no other Earth within migration-reach now. Unless some people know what the rest of us don't, intergalactic travels with payloads for migration exist only in dreams. Now, suppose Mars was once like our Earth before some events vaporised the fluids and killed all earth-like life there. It's possible that the water on Earth might have come from Mars, a spin-off from the events. Then, just decades into space age, we've covered Earth with space-junk litter."

Osagie said, "Hey, hey, Chiamalu, there shouldn't be too much disruption. We can as well roll with some punches, I think. There're too many strong interests in maintaining the *status quo*."

Chimamlu replied, "All these activities in space certainly result in increased radiation additionally bathing the earth. Since most of our body functions result from tiny electro-chemical reactions, how will the additional uneven radiation from space activities affect those reactions? Who's more at risk?"

Olu cleared his throat. "Some years back, the UN flagged the industrialised world for relocating 'dirty' industries to the Third World. Typical, heh? 'Let's get those their parts fouled up too.'"

Gumut agreed. "Yeah. During the last Tsunami in the Indian Ocean, drums of toxic wastes, traced to a European country, were washed ashore in Somalia or some place in that region of Africa. Remember that here in Nigeria we had toxic wastes from abroad poorly buried in Koko. The authorities have not properly and publicly accounted for them. That's Africa for you."

Chiamalu said: "Development now means that we must cluster together—big towns, big cities. To service these requires untold extra amounts of natural resources being processed, transported, and distributed to these large settlements, which is more stress on nature. I was in Brasil on business some time back when the 'Big Powers' mounted pressure on Brasil to save the Amazon. Brasil told them to put their monies where their mouths were; silence, change of subject."

Chiamalu paused for a drink of his beer. Each time he either drank or ate something, the rest of us would do the same, the whole scene mimicking, as it were, the responses of an orchestra to its conductor.

Danladi capitalised on the pause. "Life has become more pleasant. Look at the increase in human knowledge, improved longevity, varied leisure, ease of travels and communication, and more satisfaction of human curiosity. Generally, the spreaders of western civilisation have been generous, don't you think so?"

Olu sat back, rubbed his growing belly with both hands (we've all been on him for more exercise). "Yes, Danladi, some of all that is somewhat correct. But the overriding point is sustainability. Should we be enjoying all that now at the *rates* that bankrupt posterity? Danladi, have you truly taken a good look at the generosity you mentioned? Besides, is the continued heightening of human expectation that healthy?"

Some of us nodded.

Nduka, his eyes trailing a voluptuous waitress passing by, said, "It was the immortal Nat King Cole, I believe, that sang, 'Is it better to have loved and lost or never to have loved at all?' I now ask: Is it better to have lived and enjoyed or never to have enjoyed at all?"

We laughed.

Chiamalu said, "Some people say that nature can infinitely adjust. They cite cases such as thinned ozone layers usually restocked by the ultraviolet rays from the sun. The flaw in this thinking is that our rates of destroying nature frequently outstrip nature's self-rebuilding rates. Some quality hardwoods, for instance, require decades or even centuries, to fully mature. Loggers have gutted woodlands into grasslands, savannahs, or prairies, leading to global outcries for reforestation."

Osagie spoke in his deep voice, "Yes, look at our fossil fuels consumption rates and compare those rates with the untold millions or billions of years it took nature to make them."

"The economy, the economy; that's what causes the ravaging," Gumut shouted.

Chiamalu agreed. "Indeed, the mentality behind the economy is very much to blame, because it is through economic activities that we derive our rising wants that turn into needs from the system. The economy evolved from the 'snatchers.' Much, much later, man took enormous strides in science and technology that led to mass production economy, cash-and-carry, unsecured monetary systems, all of which entrenched paper money. Inflation has continued to harass this paper money ever since. In relatively no time at all, greed took over—deficit spending the world over: private credits, corporate borrowing, and uncontrollable government deficits. The results of these debts on nature and humans are monstrous."

Olu said, "Isn't all that human nature? Some people are concerned about the trend, though. Environmentalists, for example, are screaming their lungs out."

"Yes Olu, but look at how powerlessly alone they've been, environmentalists in particular," Gumut snapped.

"If we consider the Tibetan affair during the 2008 Beijing Olympics in China as distraction, then we can better understand the signals from nature. Some sports were seriously threatened by environmental pollution, yet we cheer and not rightly fear the near 10 percent annual surge of the economy in China," Osagie boomed.

I sat up. "Nature, Mother Nature, you can be considered as even minutely dispensable only in the zoo of the uncivilised. The civilised steadily promote the common good into very long-term posterity, which includes synergy with you. The uncivilised are irrational, despite riveting logic."

Chiamalu winked at me and said, "All of us affect nature adversely, some more so than others. We should all do less of all that proportionately. Robbing Peter to pay Paul is not the answer, neither is buck-passing. I don't see why galloping technologies cannot be used to catch offenders red-handed. Furthermore, science and technology can provide us with the means of making real peace with nature."

"Indeed, we all need to wake up everywhere. Each of us is an equal inhabitant of planet Earth in that when life can no longer be sustained on it, we'll all expire. Current development concepts need to be thoroughly X-rayed, so that a more sustainable agenda for humanity can emerge," Osagie agreed.

Chiamalu slowly said, "Nature is 'Oga Okwu[1]'. When nature takes revenge, there's not a single vagueness for an appeal. And the rain falls and the sun shines on the prisoner and his guard, as our wise ancestors said long ago."

"Who bells the cat?" Danladi and Olu asked almost simultaneously.

"Of course, those who devastated nature most to acquire and control information and technology, corner and disproportionately own most of the wealth, and control global socio-econo-political puppet strings ought to initiate and contribute commensurately to sustain positive change in the matter. It is natural justice," Chiamalu concluded.

"C & C Diplomat. We're sending you to the UN," shouted Osagie.

Gumut, frowning, said, "I don't fancy the UN. With all the bashing it often gets, it may be losing importance. The elder's headgear should not diminish his appearance or stature, our ancestors again."

On impulse, I stood up, my half-full palm-wine calabash mug in hand, and, as in western-style toast, I declared: "May Nature, Oga Okwu; the Gods of Afrika; the Spirits of our Ancestors; and the Almighty guide us all towards more respect for and protection of nature."

"Iseh-eh-eh[2]!" The rest responded in unison.

After a brief pause, Olu muttered, "What should worry us most is the combined and unguaranteed total capability to blow the planet to pieces, many times over."

---

[1] Oga Ukwu, Supremely respected one.
[2] Iseh-eh-eh, May our prayers be granted.

Nduka, frowning, said, "I worry more about how and why Afrikans turned into Africans and about the loss of that incredible Afrikan love."

I said, "Gentlemen, next Sunday is at 3:00 p.m. and Code One. Here, these are copies of the material Chiamalu used for a presentation to the local Branch of the Nigerian Society of Engineers on entrepreneurship and job creation in Nigeria. The presentation was years ago, but it's still *very* relevant. We shall discuss it on Sunday." I distributed the paper.

We rose to the Afrikan handshake, complete with the finger snaps and hand over heart to symbolise oneness, and then dispersed deeper into **"LEVEL GROUND"** to soak up other offerings.

Later that night, I was tortured by nightmarish thoughts about a possibly looming face-off between the country and us. For the group, I assembled force of intellectual capacity and consequent cerebral eruptions; discipline from top-flight professional grooming; energies entrapped by frustration, bitterness, and disappointment; the directives from affinity with excellence; towering geysers of patriotic imperatives; priming from exposure; unbending spirit; and so on. Opposing them could most likely be a horrid arsenal of persisting intimidation; accidental discharges from official firearms; contrived homicidal accidents; arrays of lethal substances; ritual killers; armed robbers; fumbling kidnappers; mysterious fires and explosions that defy investigation and prosecution; and a host of well-paid and willing agents and decoys.

"Face-off: consequences. Face-off: consequences," got tucked away in the accessible recesses of my consciousness.

2

ENTREPRENEURSHIP AND JOB CREATION IN NIGERIA

Excellent students, trade apprentices, and practitioners often target entrepreneurship as the panacea. The ill-prepared, copycat interlopers do so too. They all imagine entrepreneurship as the flagpole avenue for self-actualisation, acceptably free of others' quirks.

Some entrepreneurs gain the status through unexpected events. Others are peers sustained through fiercely enforced codes, but whose activities are anti-social. This group calls to mind sabotaging gangs that tunnel under the foundation of society—the underground or the underworld—pricking the conscience of an alert society.

The entrepreneur takes risks, alone or with others, to establish an enterprise to pursue the benefits stated above. Scale, relevance, and longevity provide the differences.

Entrepreneurship is a multi-faceted activity. Each facet is multi-pronged, and each prong, multi-directional. Any lack of full understanding of the characteristics and importance of each facet, prong, or direction makes the entrepreneurial seeding idea stillborn. Records everywhere show that the odds are heavily stacked in favour of eventual failure in this adventure, even when undertaken by the well-prepared. The upbeat side of failure is that it provides helpful learning experiences for the entrepreneur of character.

We assume that entrepreneurial projects of interest to most of us here today will most likely be those with technology content. We shall discuss technology in entrepreneurship later.

Global directions, due to their great influence, is our first port of call in our world in which increasing numbers of events can no longer be isolated. The captains of the world economy accelerated "globalisation," the integration of global economies through free trade and free flows of capital, as an openly declared process in the 1980s and 1990s. The awesome combination of computer, space, and communications technologies handed globalisation the initial acceleration that gave it momentum. We are now a few decades further on with the process. What are the results achieved so far?

Right from its initial, open articulation, many voices shouted out in opposition, but were ignored. They described globalisation as another ruse for further impoverishing the non-industrialised. Indeed, it is a marriage of the unequal or a competition between the world champion and the disabled. The bulldozer careered on.

Mounting evidence exposes the self-serving postures of the promoters of globalisation. They are expending efforts on damage control.

While opponents of globalisation may not have changed the minds of its agents, they have scored a significant point: poverty shall remain the benchmark for both sides.

The globalisation scenario can be simplified as follows: The world is divided into two groups—A and B, say. Group A has over-production capacities; leading-edge technologies; capital; over-powering political muscle; a range of expertise; and some potent, but under-publicised, protectionism. Group B has natural resources; little or crude production capacities; low-level expertise; a large population burdened with hunger, ignorance, disease, corruption, and crushing debts; and a lack of political power. Globalisation straps both groups into a regime of free flows of trade and capital. What a travesty of equity. But, the inside trackers remain on cue to their goals.

To bring globalisation up closer, we can review the recent experiences of a company, Ije Uwa Incorporated (IUI). Three young and well-prepared entrepreneurs, two engineers and a business major, started IUI to manufacture and market a product in Nigeria. I had the sad experience of mentoring this company in terms of advice. Their feasibility studies gave all the needed clearances, including the enticing information that the targeted product had a potentially high demand and was relatively unidentified by the big players within and outside Nigeria. They began operations on a small, improvised scale.

They performed above their dreams in their first year. Before their first Annual General Meeting, they consulted me on their plans for expansion. We agreed that they should execute standard expansion studies. The ensuing report was brilliant and could satisfy the most conservative of financial institutions.

They went shopping for funds at relevant financial institutions in Nigeria, including the government-sponsored ones, supposed to aid this kind of initiative. They were put on what appeared to them inexplicable, long holds. It almost became impossible to contain their frustration, but they were still doing well at their scale of operation in the second year.

With only weeks to their second AGM, there occurred an event that chilled the spine to sub-zero Fahrenheit temperatures. I was furiously enraged by it, even from my distance. With the delays from the financial institutions, the three young entrepreneurs used all their available time, night and day, despite attendant risks, to scout our markets for materials, from which they began piecemeal optimisation of their production line.

One of the engineers, in a state of near pre-seizure convulsions, returned from one of these trips with samples that looked very much like their product. More investigations revealed that the samples were imported, enhanced versions of their planned post-expansion product, imported in large quantities. The projectile driven through the heart of IUI was that the retail unit price of the imports was twenty-two percent below IUI's unit production *cost* in Nigeria.

It is easy to guess what IUI's fate was, and who and what were its facilitators. However, the three young entrepreneurs, made of the right stuff, dusted up their CVs, engaged themselves elsewhere, and continued the repayments of the loans that they had raised to set up IUI. Bruised, but much wiser and tougher, they still meet to fine-tune their next initiatives.

One thing that IUI tells us is that, as globalisation governs us in our current situations in our part of the world, we must pace and brace ourselves to our dreams of entrepreneurship eventually fading into a *fata morgana*. "Our part of the world" means Nigeria. What does the entrepreneur, budding or existing, face in Nigeria?

To fully discuss all that Nigeria offers any entrepreneur will require months of concerted effort from us. We shall not do that. We shall limit ourselves to the one factor we humbly submit as cardinal—the state of the principal ingredient for development, the human resource.

We all cry out about the decaying this and the primitive that, the crude this and the rude that, the negligent this and the obstructionist that, the despotic this and the myopic that, the fake this and the ephemeral that, the ambivalent this and the malevolent that, the eroded this and the corroded that, the perverted this and the disconcerted that, the unresolved homicide here and the savage fratricide there, the forceful miscegenation here and the apparent assassination there, the mega larceny here and the pervading kleptocracy everywhere ... the list goes on.

The reasons for all our cries as Nigerians have their roots, through commission or omission, in the massive dereliction of each of us. The taproot of these conditions traverses our recent history to its fading point. Again, we cannot possibly carry our talks that far today.

Great Britain colonised us for centuries. Colonists have only one motive: to reap maximum benefits from exploiting other peoples and places. They plundered with all the greed in them, while leaving comparatively little behind. Also, they cleverly sowed seeds that would ensure long-term dependence on them by their colonies—continued exploitation robed in evolving gimmickry.

After decades of political independence, we still seek their help to conduct good elections for political offices. What seriously concerns us here, however, is that we inherited from them the mentality of exploitation, far in excess of the provisions of our own true nature. This is a significant factor in making a harsh environment for the entrepreneur and others, because it turns the prime-mover ingredient for sustainable development against itself. The driving force behind much of whatever we do for society today is the desire to unreasonably exploit one another and posterity.

A sober appraisal of our "freedom fighters" at independence, and even now, will show that those who were quite impatient to practise enabling followership left the mainstream to found their own ethnic or regional enclaves through appeals to transient sectional interests, often goaded by external interests. These moves gave them the opportunities of advancing their personal agenda, which, in the final analyses, have not been to the best, long-term interests of those they purported to lead.

The point is that, without missing a beat after political independence, we continued to act in ways that ensured that the spirit of exploitation continued to sink its fangs deeper into our psyche. The series of Commissions and Panels of Inquiries on Fraud and Corruption long before, and soon after, our political independence more than proves the point.

It is difficult for the human resource that is preoccupied with unreasonable exploitation of others to fully accept the covenant that *enduring individual advancement is most assured in the environment of the common well-being.* This environment is profusely fertilised, in today's world, by the presence of a good number of successful entrepreneurs.

The entire field of education serves to condition the mind and body for building and maintaining a progressive society. Professor C. S. Lewis knew this when he implied, long ago, in his hilarious, but profound, satire collection of *The Screwtape Letters* that a modern nation needs a very large class of genuinely educated people and that it is the primary function of schools and universities to supply them. *To lower standards or disguise inequalities is fatal.* (The italics emphasis is ours).

We are aware of how we put the full range of our education systems on steep degradation slides after political independence, partly because we manoeuvred ourselves into embracing the "federal character" malaise. This trend is forcing the prime resource for sustainable development into a cocoon to self-destruct with the ensuing straightjacketing of posterity into severe distress. If not, why have we allowed the human resource in Nigeria to become too asphyxiating to the entrepreneur to be desired and admired?

Pervasive, high-scale corruption symbolises how thick the prime resource has been encrusted. Peter Eigen, former Chair of Transparency International, said that "Corrupt political elites in the developing world, working hand-in-hand with greedy business people and unscrupulous investors, are putting private gain before the welfare of citizens and the economic development of their countries. From illegal logging to blood diamonds, we are seeing the plundering of the earth and its people in an unsustainable way...." (http://thinkexist.com/quotes/peter_eigen/2.html)

We must wonder why corruption is going global with such speed and impact. Is it another section of the cycle required for further impoverishing the already poor and debt-ridden? Corruption flourishes in Nigeria because of our domineering propensity for colossal exploitation of every otherwise normal chance for positive service. Corruption makes preparing feasibility studies for entrepreneurs difficult by introducing backbreaking incidental costs, particularly with global competition just outside the door—thanks to our tastes that far outpace our production and maintenance abilities.

Many factors complement this posture of unjustifiable heavy exploitation to make things more difficult for the entrepreneur. The philosophy that the end justifies the means, no matter how dastardly the means, has become dominant. Poor work ethics have become the norm. Morality, order, integrity, industry, and collective purpose all reside more in tutorials. Then, there is the increasing pleasure we seem to derive from inflicting hardship on fellow citizens, additional to provoking vanity.

While global activists are criticising governments for focusing more on four or five-year spans, and questioning corporations for concentrating more on quarterly or annual intervals instead of effectively looking much further into the future, we restrict ourselves to the next moment. This alone makes it a living hell for any entrepreneur in Nigeria who must use the unavoidable technology to compete on a global scale.

Technology itself can be defined as the comprehension and utilisation of applied science to facilitate tasks in industry and in service to humanity. All sciences are Siamese twins with mathematics, and the word "industry" is used here as all-encompassing.

Technology has two principal parts—the hardware and the software, to use the phrasing in the field. The hardware comprises all the physical structures, equipment, tools, aids, and the like, and the resulting gadgets in the development and harnessing of a technology. The software relates to human mental conditioning vital for making and using a technology. Combined, both hardware and software are known as technostructure.

The usual frontline activists in technology development have evolved as the scientist and the mathematician. They unravel basic principles and laws, and propose provable theories. The engineer, with other supporting colleagues, packages these laws and principles, and postulates to realise a technology. There is the user of the technology for achieving set results. Finally, there is the consumer who utilises the results. Usually, there exists an intricately interwoven pattern of social, economic, political, and environmental feedback loops that makes or mars any new technology.

Observing a complex assembly line dominated by robotics is enough to befuddle and mesmerise one into falsely believing that the challenge of technology lies in the effective production of the hardware components of technostructure. *Not so!* The harder challenge lies in the acquisition or development, and the maintenance, of the software quotient, which deals with the mental, psychological, and physical conditioning of all the people who have anything to do with technology, no matter how remotely. This is more so because of the nature of technology: it is often sensitive to sloppiness and indiscipline of any kind or magnitude, whether mental or physical. This certainly adds another layer of obstacles to the pile the entrepreneur in Nigeria must scale. We can all see that *technology empowers the fundamentally empowered.*

We were emphatic at an international pyro-processing conference in Toronto, Canada, about the lopsidedness of international affairs due to the policies of the industrialised world. A participant from one of these places tried to get even at the closing dinner five days later. He showed me in a newspaper a bright, graphic, colour photograph of fuel lines in Nigeria. The picture must have been taken in one of our most uncomplimentary locations, because a massive, multi-coloured pile of garbage was visible in the background. He asked what our problems were, since it had been estimated that Nigeria had then earned well over US$400 billion, *all told*, from the petro-dollar business.

My first instinct was to challenge his figures, but I quickly realised that, even as a national assignment, it would be quite difficult to do that. I eventually retorted back that the picture was proving our point: their standing, overall policies towards Afrika were creating such situations. However, he had some points of interest.

If we go back to globalisation, it is those developing countries that got into the world market with minimum weak exposures and, at the same time, used much of their earnings for the capital development of their human and other resources, that fared better in the process so far. In our case, we earned rather easily and plentifully, but our endemic exploitative tendencies leave us critically shortchanged. This deficiency seriously hinders the otherwise capable entrepreneur.

We can be tempted to conclude that the magnitude of the hopelessness of reality forces us to abandon all entrepreneurial initiatives in Nigeria. *NO!* Our purpose is to truly sharpen our overall approaches so that success will come our way whenever we decide to take the plunge.

The first critical lesson is that *our adjustment to rubbish surely rubbishes us all.*

The African workforce development challenges, of which Nigeria has her usual fat quota, were clearly pointed out in the conclusions of an online discussion under the aegis of the Africa-America Institute as, "Among the world's regions, the African continent is distinguished by the magnitude of its workforce development challenges. The African labour force is growing at about three percent annually, while wages are declining or stagnating, real wages are decreasing and working and living conditions are deteriorating. It is estimated that by 2010 there will be an average of eight million seven hundred thousand new entrants each year to the African labour markets without a comparable increase in new employment." (https://www.aaionline.org)

The presence of many efficient entrepreneurs will surely provide some solutions in the areas of job creation. This is possible, but it requires unrelenting hard work and excellent management.

Entrepreneurs create jobs. They make the private sector, and are dominant determinants in the growth of an economy. They imbue national character and status. If we do not act to encourage the urgent establishments of the largest possible numbers of various, successful entrepreneurs in Nigeria, then all the sacrifices that we have made so far and all the opportunities that we have been fortunate to deploy in getting to our standings today will become underutilised.

We must challenge our essence. The endowment of Nigeria and Afrika shall not be for nothing. *The ultimate challenge of our time is the massive creation of jobs in all cadres.* We must learn from the experiences of the "dot com" companies that derived their lives from multi-layered marketing without growing *in situ* production. They surged out like the humidity haze only to evaporate in short order with the appearance of sunshine. Also, in the wise words of Gandhi, *"We must become the change we want to see."* If we accept this simple, but self-evident premise, then we must quickly go to work despite the enormity of excuses and obstacles daring and staring us in the face.

The following are unranked areas that can aid our *actions* aimed at creating entrepreneurs.

⚷ Individual Preparedness

We have much control over this area. We must ensure that we acquire a comfortable level of intellectual grooming and practice in our specialisations. As people in technology, we must be amply at home with the working elements of such subjects as economics, marketing, finance, banking and accounting, ethics and morality, communication and management, psychology, sociology, and political science. Infectious and transformational leadership should rightly be our earned key appraisal index. Strategically, we must be sound and enduring, while making uncompromising professionalism the long-term investment.

21

⌗ Effective Team Building

This is a crucial area that requires sustained attention from anyone contemplating entrepreneurship, more so, because of the current discouraging status of the human resource here. For any workforce to turn sufficiently effective, it has to be sanitised through careful selection, training, and support. Ordinarily, this is a difficult task, but in Nigeria, it is the *task* of all tasks.

Our present habit of predominantly using individual practice houses is terribly inefficient. It rarely assures us of professional satisfaction, sustained earnings, and status, but it ensures that we are often dragged into the inglorious pool of the fraudulent and corrupt. We must fully confront our twenty-first century tasks by adequately embracing collaborations, affiliations, mergers, and associations, locally and otherwise.

Building an effective team requires expertise, sensitivity, judgment, and a good working knowledge of the identified basic human types.

⌗ Consultant Services

This is a quick way for our profession to make good contributions to the creation of entrepreneurs from our group. If we use good partnership and team building practices, we can see how giant entities, whose total impact will be far greater than the sum of those of their constituent elements, can emerge.

Such large establishments could contribute meaningfully to projects in the public and private sectors, regardless of size or complexity.

With time and performance, these entities would gain respect and power to become the reference conduits for our development. Easily, the needs of the founders of such entities would be well catered for.

♯ Our Professional Society

The Nigerian Society of Engineers is our common forum for strength. It should, therefore, be a citadel, or if you like, a shrine of discipline, performance, and enduring excellence. These are not of the inanimate. We are, therefore, stressing that we should clean up all our individual acts, select our battlefronts, and, like the pieces of a jigsaw puzzle, slot ourselves in to make the big picture.

We should fully tap the powers of peer control by strengthening our Standards and Ethics Committees to enshrine professionalism in whatever we do.

Our data banks should be awesome, relational data warehouses to improve our general services and to allow for coupling with global systems. *We must all insist on more openness in our environmental, social, economic, and political affairs, to make data capture easier.*

Our awards for excellence, such as the Fellowship, should not go the way of some negating practices of society, which neither knows many of its true heroes nor honours them well. We must go further by identifying and adequately honouring those members of our profession, dead or alive, who truly excelled as models for our profession.

♯ Polity and Complements

It is necessary that as many engineers as possible get involved in the polity: engineers to the rescue! As a country, we must shed our cloaks of superficiality, which only give us temporary relief, to find and execute permanent solutions to our disabilities.

The root causes of such features as fraud, bribery, corruption, and bigotry are to be identified and unforgettably neutralised. *There cannot be a new beginning without permanently killing the power of negative precedent.*

We have to precipitate and participate in a countrywide dialogue to determine the enduring ways forward for Nigeria. We expect that a truly Nigerian constitution, among other things, will emerge from this dialogue. Thereafter, it should become easier to think and behave more like a country than like an incongruent and unmanageable collection of bickering and clamouring ethnic groups.

Engineers should be prominent contributors to the enunciation of a comprehensive, long-term development strategy protected by laws. The frustrating cycles of policy reversals should be broken to foster successful businesses. Consumer advocacy will ensure that our production meets competitive standards. Our industries should be given a good chance by fully checking practices such as "dumping." The privatisation exercise should have resulted in the desirable seeding of entrepreneurs.

Current interest rates on funds and our present brands of costs of loan packaging seriously imperil entrepreneurs, to whom economic viability is a strong motivation. We must wonder if economists will consider our banking practices as the boon or bane to our economy. The system needs sustained, serious attention. Equity banks need to evolve to give more entrepreneurs the opportunities they deserve. The system needs to take a more development facilitating posture by including relevant professionals in their staff, permanent and *ad hoc*, to nurture more entrepreneurs.

♯ The Feasibility Study

As its name implies, it is the primary tool for creating enterprises – the enhancing formalisation of the process we frequently go through intuitively in our lives. In the correct form, it clearly defines all pertinent factors and their viability boundaries, and provides a rational and efficient route to a successful project. Many failures of enterprises are attributable to either poor feasibility studies or the wrong use of good ones. Also, it serves, with proper modifications, as an excellent guide for opportunity identification, mergers, acquisition, facility appraisal, and so on.

We must therefore be proficient in the preparation and use of feasibility studies, while noting that collaboration is often needed with other professionals and specialists in such areas as economics, finance, and general management. The required special studies and investigations inevitably invite these other experts and specialists. A good study has a reasonably projected operating budget for the first few of years of the commissioned project.

This tool is very useful in all project phases. *We must be comfortable with it.*

♯ Directions and Opportunities

Our focus should be on the productive sub-sectors. Ideally, we should search for opportunities that will take entrepreneurs to the world market with the hope that earnings will be better utilised.

Another good effort will be to enlighten people about the long-term benefits of purchasing quality products and professional workmanship and services. We know that considering only first costs can become inefficient and sometimes life-threatening.

Entrepreneurial opportunities in Nigeria are enormous. The trouble must be elsewhere: *the motive force is disoriented.*

Our cavorting before the world in our deluding dance, as if we are great and belong, is not the right way forward. It is nothing but the flight of the imagination. We must honestly review what we have on hand. It will be seen that correct enterprises of all forms and magnitudes must be established, since they create jobs efficiently and constitute the vibrant private sector. Any Nigerian who is employed caters for a number of people. This is a lingering tradition of our true Afrikanness.

The availability of jobs will reduce pressures everywhere. Then, we must reform, redirect, and reassure our human resources to become more reliable and productive. At the same time, we must do whatever else is necessary to transform Nigeria into an attractive environment for entrepreneurs and other professional, development catalysts.

We aim to reactivate our human capital long soaked in variously concentrated brews of materialism trimmed off with arrogance, vanity, and group-destructive individualism; the omni-present, ambivalent propensity for rationalising absurdities into doctrines in the pretence of being clever, diplomatic, or philosophical; and the inordinate, expansionism-driven claim to leadership to the exclusion of others and the common prosperity, while being leveraged by parasitism. This, by all means, is not an easy task. Nevertheless, the success we achieve here will allow us to set our sights on laudable, higher horizons.

The engineer is undoubtedly a vital contributor to these desirable changes.

It is quite possible that, with well-tuned prudence, assiduous executions, and unrelenting vigilance, the industrialised world could become a mature "guinea pig" —a reversal of current roles.

How about that for breaking out and onto the mountaintop?

Think this one over a lot more and then pass on the resulting baton.

We are flattered and humbled by your patience and indulgence.

THANK YOU VERY MUCH.

Chiamalu Ofobuike. 17 October 2002

Parting Quotes:

The ultimate challenge of our time is the massive creation of jobs in all cadres.

Technology empowers the fundamentally empowered.

Our adjustment to rubbish surely rubbishes us all.

There cannot be a new beginning without permanently killing the power of negative precedent.

Enduring individual advancement is most assured in the environment of the common well-being.

"We must become the change we want to see." – Gandhi.

3
ANALYSES

Chiamalu and I arrived at the reception a little before 3:00 p.m. to find the rest seated. I was behind him. Decorum stopped me from overtaking him in the short distance to our seats. *They want to stick either Chiamalu or me with "Code One."*

Nduka said, "Chuks, you're most welcome. My first drink is the Jamaican rum with the heart, liver, and kidney pepper soup."

"Have the famed Jamaican super-proof quadruple, if you like. The cook will use lots of his hottest peppers in your soup. Then, I'll pray you burn out your guts and turn into a vegetable. Osagie will happily plant you in his garden," I replied.

"He's welcome, but only to weed. That's all he *may be* good for," Osagie said.

Code One stated that the last person to be seated within a stipulated arrival time for our sessions bought the first round of drinks. If the last person to arrive was late as well, he also bought the lunch. I, declarer of Code One, was stuck with the bill for the first round of drinks.

Thankfully, though, we all abhorred the notion of "African" or "Nigerian" time, which allowed events to start hours later than advertised, a cancer that reduced overall productivity.

To get Nduka off my back, I paid the bill to separate it from others to follow and said, "What about the entrepreneurship paper? Did you read it, Nduka?"

"Yes, I read it. Chuks, why pick on me, heh? You're on Code One. That's the rule, you declared it. Don't blame me for enjoying the dividends of Code One."

Olu, clapping, said, "That was excellent. Our ambassador-in-waiting, again. Great ideas, still very relevant. For starters, our politicians and their collaborators are the gangs that tunnel under our society."

Chiamalu said, "Thanks for the compliments. But, we've all got to choose our battlefronts and give it everything we've got. And, *please*, much better people—Wole Soyinka, Chinweizu, Chinua Achebe, gutsy columnists, and many, many others had said it all, much better, much earlier. Achebe reads, in his book, *The Trouble with Nigeria*, published in 1983, as if he is talking to us about better times."

Olu asked me, "How did the Society of Engineers receive the presentation?"

"They gave it a standing ovation, the usual; that was it. The constraints are just too many."

"Chuks, constraints? What do you mean?"

"Olu, well, it's actually the whole society; problems of leadership and followers. What happens at some elections for national officers in professional bodies? Vicious fights of no merit, the overriding urge for fair or foul fallouts from controlling common funds in return for mediocrity. NSE, not left out. Since the Ministry of Industries co-sponsored the event, some government people were there. The questions and comments at the end of the presentation would be 'daggers' and 'bullets' in action, right? Wrong! Most of what was said during this period were shallow and some, diversionary. In fact, I doubted that some of them understood all that Chiamalu had said. But, the real action was on the queue for the attendance certificates at the end of the event."

Everyone paused, their heads bowed, foreheads wrinkled, and fingers tapping tabletops.

I added, "Mind you, most of the people there were practising engineers."

Gumut said quietly, "Government is not performing; those who should ask why are not asking."

Danladi said, "Yeah, I attended an international course for production managers in the UK. First day, lead consultant introduced the course. Towards the end, he said, 'I hope that we'll all give it a good effort. We'll work very hard these two weeks. There's an awful lot of materials to cover, and we all need to keep up so that the entire course will mean something at the end. Oh, the shopping can be done after the course or during some free times we've provided. Do stay awake.' As he spoke, he looked at the few African and other Third World participants. And we're the first to cry out, these people monopolise expertise. Give me a break."

"Hmm… well, I made some notes on the paper. Does anyone else have notes or should we just go at it randomly?" Olu asked.

Nduka shouted, "Look here, Olu. Do we have two Ambassadors or Professors here? Chiamalu is enough for goodness sake. By the way, combine both titles and we now have our own 'Professador,'"

To prolong impact, I bowed to Chiamalu, while repeating, "Professador."

Nduka said, "Seriously fellows, that was a fantabulous paper. We should just fire away as points come to mind, and I like the Gandhi stuff, 'you must become the change you want to see.' I *now* want to be surrounded by six cushy Uhuru Hut knocker-outers instead of you hard-boned, serious-minded, pseudo-intellectuals. Seriously fellows, what's an alert society?"

Gumut told him, "Easy enough. An alert society is one that lives by the dictates of the common good, right? Any arguments about that definition? Never look around here for an alert society."

A few of us lazily shrugged our shoulders.

Osagie said, "This globalisation thing we're all forced into. . . Chiamalu— I mean Professador—you said it's been decades from when the global economy captains started sneaking it in. How did that happen?"

Chiamalu exhaled, and said, "First of all, there was never an open discussion on this unification of world economies. Some people came up with the idea and went ahead to implement it. This is the sneaky aspect; doing things that seriously affect others without their input. It cannot be an accident. To sneak implies being subtle. Imagine the roles of the World Bank, IMF, WTO and others in the matter. Think about it deeply. Meetings of some of these organisations and of visible leadership, such as the G-8, faced strong protests, some of which turned violent. One immediate response was the enlargement of the group, without materially changing the driving game plans. Then, think about the overall image the rest of the world holds about Africa in such matters."

"Yeah, sources of labour, raw materials, illegally diverted funds, and markets," I slipped in.

Chiamalu glanced at me and said, "The chief motivation for people behind global corporations is profit; nothing egalitarian about it. You have to weigh whatever they give against the consequences of their takings. Their patented smart lines are effective, but only deceptive cloaking of trick. Human nature, aroused this way, goes for more. Variously, globalisation is the result of their efforts to grease their way into more global feasts."

Nduka said, "Yes, yes, Professador, you were right about the 'snatchers.' Remember them? Imagine, in the first decade of the twenty-first century, the same upgraded 'snatchers' paralysed the capitalist system with their actions. That phenomenon was downplayed as global economic meltdown. Then, the thought has been on to increase the powers of the IMF by making it the manager of global surpluses."

Chiamalu said, "The final collapse of the Soviet Union in 1993 hastened and armoured globalisation. Fierce ideological fences fell with the USSR. Competition reduced. Africa had better bargaining chips in the fifty years of the Soviet Union, but at the cost of losing people like Lumumba, Nkrumah, and Nasser. There was the whittling-down of the pan-Afrikan spirit of our 'Zik of Afrika.' Recall the passive containment of Julius Nyerere and his Afrikan socialism. We must remember the nearly three decades of incarceration and, thus, the severe idling of dear, inimitable Mandela.

"With all such checkpoints vacated, globalisation is our new obligatory shadow and bedfellow, here to stay and play. Mega mergers, still ongoing; each creates a larger, more potent colossus that bestrides more of the globe. Globalisation is the prevailing facilitator of their assaults, as they rationalise more focused protests out of steam. The enablement of globalisation includes proliferation of trade agreements that annexed territories for economic domination. We in Nigeria go along, while leaving all our fronts, rears, and flanks nearly irredeemably undercut. We see through the brokering of democracy in which deregulation, open markets, helpful laws, and easy repatriation of earnings are prerequisites. Often, we also see adjustments to brazen criminal thefts of mandates, while democracy remains the advertised preference.

"By the way, comparatively little direct investment capital available from globalisation has reached Africa. Farm subsidies and quotas of the powerful countries block agriculture, the probable entry vehicle into the alleged free trade for Africa. In these matters, they sell us experts and specialists from those that they put through mind-bending routines, those enshrined with global views from handily mounted windows, regardless of nationality. When eventually these experts and specialists come to us, the wings of enhancing African orientation are clipped off from their thoughts. We just get very smart and much-schooled facilitators. Every attempt to stop these people from controlling our economy is habitually ploughed under with promissory propaganda, unchallenged due to the toil of living. Not all of us are fooled all the time everywhere. As our ancestors said, the ears hear what the jaws chew."

A hush followed Chiamalu's flurry. We turned to our drinks and snacks and worked our minds.

Olu broke the silence with, "Also remember what happened to Sekou Toure of Guinea, Sylvanus Olympio of Togo, Modibo Keita of Mali, David Dacko of Central African Republic, Maurice Yameogo of Burkina Faso, Hubert Maga of the Republic of Benin, and others. They were all shunted and African development still blunted in the furnace of French imperialism."

Nduka said, "Seriously, fellows, this is mind-tasking and sad. Sad, since it appears that reversing these trends is almost impossible. Sad again, because we belong to the exploited. But why? Are we the 'hewers of wood and bearers of water'?"

Gumut said, "Nduka, we have to pray and wait for Divine Intervention. Everyone says that these days, but fail to tell us whether Divine Intervention follows man; or man, Divine Intervention."

Osagie said, "I don't know. Oh, again, Chiamalu, that was a great paper. I enjoyed the poetic part, the 'this here and that there' portion. I focused on our massive dereliction and causes going to the fading point of our recent history. Can we find the whys from our history? For sure, Africans are in the midst of an unconscious and powerful change that is defrocking them of their culture and tradition, their identity and relevance. This has been going on for long. Can we return to being the best keepers of our sisters and brothers, as earlier marauders to the continent had described us?"

"You're right, Osagie," I agreed. "Our history tells the story all right, but are human histories not the same? We keep repeating ourselves, and later, we raise questions and distance ourselves from failure by claiming that history repeats itself. I believe Chiamalu's paper focused sufficiently on the critical issue—inadequate human resource."

Olu said, "The 'bedevilling transition' Osagie just mentioned is a form of education that sets the patterns for human behaviour. It's in two parts: formal and informal education, right? Formal education sets the skeletons and the informal one fleshes them out. So, our day-to-day experiences are important. Our problems have arisen mainly from the actual events in our daily lives. Chiamalu's paper described it as 'all enabling qualities residing more in tutorials.' Yes, the experiences of Afrika with the rest of the world—the Arabs, the Europeans, and their distant cousins especially—have not all been to the best gain of the continent, but some of them left us with good education models. Did we make those models more relevant to our lasting needs? *No.* How did Chiamalu explain it?"

Osagie told him, "We put the full range of our educational systems on steep degradation slides, after political independence."

I added, "With current trends in our formal education, our posterity will be in real trouble soon. It's already here. Some multi-nationals in Nigeria are phasing out Nigerians in their processes of global rationalisation. Given the latitudes they enjoy here, we can all imagine what else happens in these 'performance-enhancing moves.' How can our posterity compete for jobs, even in their own countries, if they cannot have comparable formal education and experience with their global peers?"

Osagie, his arms folded, said, "Yes, by far the worst effects of this bedevilling transition are the rapid erosion and confusion of our cultural heritage and the unsettling dismantling of our social institutions—loss of the social pillars one leans on in troubled times. The results are blurred demarcations between self-interest and group interest; unjustified heavy harvesting from fields on which we did not sow sufficiently; and increasingly, immediate gratification overrides long-term projections. We've had enough time to reflect and change. It's easy to see why our situations – gross negligence."

Olu said, "Anything goes here, Osagie; we're not an alert society. Corruption says much, doesn't it?"

Nduka was eager to answer. "Yes, yes. When Transparency International publishes, we protest. Yet we've done so little to curb corruption. When the real fight against corruption begins, we'll all feel the heat. So, if you're wise, get your playtime now. The clock is ticking, ticking down. Professador wrote, 'We cannot have a new beginning without permanently killing the power of negative precedent.'"

"Eh… hold it. Some of our protests have some merit. TI's ratings don't tell the whole story about countries sampled. They only assess corruption in the public sector in Nigeria. Big global economic activities of the industrialised world's public sector are executed by their private sector. Their private sector believes in and teaches that the end justifies the means. For us, the reverse holds. Our public sector is dominant and therefore the counterpart of their private sector. It takes two to tango, as they say, and in matters of corruption, it's the same. What's in the lizard's house is also in the rat's house, per our ancestors. So, where's their share of the runaway corruption? This thing must be re-examined from broader viewpoints. Professador alluded to it in the paper."

Gumut challenged him, "Olu, whom does corruption hurt most? A World Bank President, James Wolfensohn, once said that 'Corruption is core poverty issue, robbing from the poor the little they have.' He also said the world poor grew by 100 million within a decade. Now, where do you find the poor most, heh? So, who is most trapped by corruption and, therefore, who should fight it more? Forget the greed and fun of the other parties."

Danladi slowly said, "You can't blame the rapist alone; your lady displays her nudity by the window at night, her front door unlocked."

Nduka asked, "Hey, Danladi, is there any place that this happens around here? The nudity by the window?"

"Nduka, are you planning on becoming a rapist? Hey, that's when we surely ostracise," Chiamalu said loudly, putting Nduka, who bowed to allot Chiamalu a hit, on the defensive.

We laughed.

Smiling, Osagie said, "That reminds me. Did any of you read the interview of retired Chief of Army Staff, General Victor Malu, in the *Sunday Sun*? In describing today's Nigerian, the paper quoted him as saying that, 'A Nigerian loves himself more than any other person. No single person is ready to sacrifice his life for another. That explains why armed robbers would come to your house, take your wife and your daughter, assault them on the ground, while you put your hand on your head crying. In another country, it's your responsibility to give your life.' That was a graphic picture of the erosion of Nigerian manhood."

Nduka jumped up, placed his hands on his head, and said, "What? Who is saying that the Nigerian manhood is eroding, heh? Hey, Osagie! I'm the only one drinking the Jamaican stuff, unless you've become so full of it that you are now vulnerable to its smell. Haven't you heard about all the multiple births of quadruplets, quintuplets, and so on? What about some personalities who are taking on new, younger wives each time you blink your eyes? Don't pretend that you don't know that the fast money-makers are the cheap hotels or guesthouses that charge by the hour. What else speaks more for the manhood of Nigerians?"

Everyone laughed.

Olu looked up from his notes. "This 'technology empowering the fundamentally empowered' got to me. My colleagues and I discussed it at work. The software component of technostructure is where it's at—a lifestyle, the total conditioning of society, and a disposition to purposeful inquiry. Why has Africa lagged behind in technology?"

"What conclusions did you and your colleagues arrive at?" Gumut asked.

"Well, first we restated that Africa indeed had a glorious past. Some cited publications that document this fact, and one is, *African Responses*, by Mokwugo Okoye, and the writings of Chinweizu and others. One of my colleagues recounted that in Nkrumah's days, he was at a meeting in Europe in his full Afrikan regalia, Ghana vintage. Trust Nkrumah. One of the European delegates, after due courtesies, felt the material Nkrumah was wearing between his fingers and inquired about how it was made. Finally, full of appreciation and struck by rare honesty, the European delegate said that when we in Afrika made silk, they in Europe still lived in caves and smooched with Neanderthals. An unusual moment of truth. We also agreed that currently circulated history robs Africa of her glorious past, another screaming challenge to Afrika's children. We discussed all the various intrusions into Afrika that wreaked the havoc we inherited. But a nagging question remains, why has Afrika not risen again?"

"Don't worry," I said, "What's in civilisations? They come, they go. It'll soon be Africa's turn. This reminds me of the very short-lived program, 'The Moment of Truth,' anchored by Bony Amalu on NTA, that featured the forthright barrister Andrew Anyamene, SAN[3], a few times before the program was yanked off the air. Expectedly, it aired some home truths for taking us to first base—admitting that we've truly bungled things. The distinguished barrister said something to the effect that with all the turmoil, injustice, and aberrations in the world today, the end of this civilisation was near. He lamented that Africa was not queueing up for a rise."

"He must know when Divine Intervention arrives," Gumut said, his nose flared.

Osagie said, "The backwardness in technology is both a curse and a blessing. The lag comes, in part, from nature giving us too much. If you eat oranges and carelessly throw the seeds around, you'll be faced with landscaping chores the next rainy season – cutting down unplanned growths of oranges. What happens in some colder regions of the world, where, for the most part, the leading edge of technology currently resides? They've got shorter growing seasons, and had to optimise food production, distribution,

---

[3] SAN, Senior Advocate of Nigeria.

and consumption. This started experimentation. Then, one thing led to another. We all know that agriculture aided the development of the software module of technostructure. It was about survival, the first instinct of man. 'Scarcely does one tire, when running from threat to life,' our wise ancestors said. The climate did not challenge us sufficiently. We succumbed so easily to external aggression. Did that indict our earlier societies? Making comfort zones habitats, stimulates little, if any, progress or resilience."

"Osagie, that's true," Olu said. "Business contacts and other activities are increasingly automated in the First World, thereby reducing human understanding in favour of profits. Generally, Africa still has some of the cleaner environments, but clearly threatened by global economic expansion. Who knows? If scientific lessons from Mars so far do not change minds enough, something might happen to make the next rise less driven by greed."

Danladi, leaning forward, said, "There must first be fundamental changes in us. Look, generations of various top-class scientists, engineers, and other professionals; our technology remains stagnated. Today, some of them win global awards for excellence when they work outside the country. Once they come home, they disappear, like into an eroding caustic cesspool. Our experiences since coming home—look at them. Push for excellence, you become public enemy. Exemplary deeds that deliver needed results, often muted. The brain drain rises. How do we explain evident lack of purposeful adventure that brings discoveries? The palm wine we enjoy drinking, still procured in the same archaic ways; no increase in efficiency or even labour-saving innovation. The palm-wine tapper still faces dangers in his multiple daily climbs of the palm tree. Oh, yes. We consume what others have produced; no maintenance mentality. But we first hurl accusations of expertise monopoly at others. The situation must be tackled from all directions, full force."

"Bullseye, Danladi," I interrupted.

"Remember, some years back, the BBC featured us in 'The Squandering of Riches,' I think, not sure. They highlighted wasted opportunities; the disaster the trend would bring to us. Decades now. Did we think and change? *No.* This was part of the same West we often condemn. Now, we've been warned; pending disintegration. Look out for our reactions," Danladi added.

Olu said, "Low spirit of inquiry is not limited to technology. The economy, for example. Our so-called economists only parrot what others had studied or proposed. For doing that, they're rewarded with titles and posts. They introduce themselves as, 'This is Professor so and so' or that, 'I'm Doctor this or that.' They have to remind everyone, including themselves, about those empty titles. We love titles so much, no matter their origins. People are quietly exploiting this. General Babangida, the former military Head of State, I believe it was, once wondered aloud why the economy hadn't collapsed. All the indicators fed to him had projected a failed economy. That was a clear, loud invitation to our economists to investigate the real workings of our economy and to, perhaps, come up with truly prize-winning theories that might have influenced global lifestyles. Anyone who accomplishes such need not remind people about earned titles."

Danladi pointed at him. "Part of the problems of education we talked about—punches from the *Nigerian Question*. Professors and lecturers, woefully unable to do their jobs well. Some sanctioned for intentional plagiarism, some for asking for more in cash or kind from their students. The perennial question, relevance of our brand of education, persists. Those of them who stick out their necks for change are persecuted. Our Ivory Towers, supposed fountains of new knowledge and directions, spew out contaminated and contaminating debris. Then, parents and guardians increasingly substitute materialism for quality time and discipline in homes. Education turned on its head. Football—many believe we can set lasting global standards. But what's here? Shameful scenes of intrigues, betrayals, deception, greed, corruption, and bigotry. We idly watch those charged with developing the game waste our resources. Yeah, low spirit of enquiry; it's everywhere, in everything here."

Nduka, clapping, head bobbing, said, "Hurray, Olu and Danladi. You're both inching up to Professador. You desire the lizard's haircut style; will it fit you as it does the lizard?"

Everyone else laughed out tears, but Nduka kept a grim face.

Osagie said eventually, "Chiamalu earlier talked about agriculture, Africa, and globalisation. But the situation is that much of Africa is still very hungry. How can you export what you don't have or, when you can, there are many emaciated figures around you? In Nigeria, we've had hollow slogans on agriculture, some older than our political independence. Operation Feed the Nation, Operation Back to Land, Green Revolution, and Operation Bread Basket to name but a few. It's still that rural farmer, inadequately supported, who feeds us. Of course, the imbalance in food supply creates the crooked importation jackpots. Agriculture, taken seriously on the fields, can provide some answers. There's a price for most things; we don't have an alert society."

Gumut said, "Okay, okay, Osagie. But should this price include crushing public debts and banks that harpoon all attempts to establish good enterprises into financial anaemia?"

Olu explained, "We may criticise past military regimes, and I'm one on many issues, but we failed to do enough to restrain them. We forget all their civilian collaborators, some of whom did much more than collaborate. The debt issue is always blamed on the military in politics. Where are the facts? What are the numbers and values of fraudulent contracts that sank us deeper into debt that military personnel executed alone? And on and on. Critical analysis, that's what's been overshadowed by cover-up distortion. Retired or serving military people helped found some of the more progressive societies; they received intelligent and alert support from civilians. The Buhari-Idiagbon regime started well with debt verification, the first step to debt management. The next steps are obvious. Did their stance on the debt matter encourage their overthrow, in any way? The institution that thrives on debts, banking, needs its own special attention. The current emphases on muscle without sufficient attention to the dominant psychology of people within and outside the industry are not enduring enough."

The arrival of people who moved towards the auditorium signalled the session's end.

Olu said, "Well, I see that people are coming for the adult show. We better wrap things up, Nduka does not want to miss out on the front row seats. Perhaps, the breaking out and onto the mountaintop part of the paper should do the job. The implications here are that Africa is behind in industrialisation;

Africa therefore has all the advantages of precedent. How do we harness these advantages? That's the question, I believe."

I said, "Before that, Olu, entrepreneurship, the main subject of the paper, did not feature directly in our discussions today. Our individual experiences in trying to bring enterprises into existence have much do with that. Subconsciously, none of us wanted to recount them. The fact of the matter remains the quality of people one has to work with at all levels. This makes it rather obvious where the critical tasks are. The Buhari-Idiagbon interregnum attacked this problem correctly; many of their initial programs were directed at reconditioning us, the human resource. Execution here is always a different kettle of fish, however."

Chiamalu added, "Chuks, you're quite right, and that's why the conditions of our human resource took reasonable space in the presentation. It's highly unlikely that anything positively enduring will result without proper attention to this problem. What are the incentives? Harnessing the bounties of precedent Olu just mentioned. Before oil was tapped here, over five decades ago, many parts of the world were long in the business. This business was always associated with shady deals and resulting negative effects on ordinary people, especially when oil is exploited in the Third World. We could have first studied this history before going too far into the business. Maybe, we could have set industry standards that would have elevated the conditions of our people, in contrast to what we are living with today.

"Facts are now available about the role of cultural norms in economic performance. Those with norms that cherish discipline, self-esteem, hard work, and a sense of community have done well. That calls for our emphasising those aspects of our culture. There is a glut of evidence on the negative results of industrial pollution. So, we have information on how to select and run our industries with less of the havoc. Again, these benefits cannot be realised without sharply turning around our human resource."

Nduka hardly waited for Chiamalu to finish before he stood up, hands raised and waving. "Drumbeats rise from near and distant foothills and are reflected onto the mountaintop in tremolos, vibratos, and staccatos by intervening objects and the dips and strikes of the rolling terrain. Which dance steps should one get into—atilogwu, reggae, salsa, juju, mambo, samba, soul, makossa, or what other such irrepressible, vibrant essence we share with our f-f-f cousins? That's the confusion. Is the mountaintop the prefecture for more settled society? Another question."

"Nduka, *please*, what's the f-f-f? You, again?" Danladi asked, amused.

"Forcefully far-flung," Nduka answered in a low voice.

As we rose to go to the auditorium for the show, Olu said to Nduka, "Drum beats rise from near and distant foothills. A good one to remember. Thank you, Nduka. What time do we assemble at your place for the trip to your village next Saturday?"

"Nine is okay, unless you have other reasons for wanting to get to my village earlier. Do you, Olu? I noticed your winking at my pretty niece, Chigozie, the last time we were there. Answer me, Olu, do you?"

"Please, Nduka, whatever you do during the week, please keep this frame of mind that produced your closing remark until after our visit to your village," Gumut said.

Nduka surreptitiously called our attention to a party of three, a woman and two men, and wondered whether any of us noticed their presence, close to us, every Sunday. We didn't make much of the observation, but as I drove home, that warning kept flashing in my head: *Face-off: consequences! Face-off: consequences!*

4

RURAL ECHOES

"Olu, because I mentioned my beautiful niece last week, you decided to be the last one here, heh?"

Before Olu could react, I said, "Nduka, remember..."

"Keep that frame of mind," Nduka finished for me.

Nduka's wife, the lovely and personable Adaoma, said, "Don't mind him and his jokes. Please leave early; greet everyone there for me. Safe journey."

Nduka's larger community, Umuikpo in Ugboigbo village, invited us to their cassava plantation project launching. Of course, our donations were ready; we knew the routine. However, the major attractions for us remained witnessing the ongoing alterations in rural life. The story is the same everywhere in Nigeria or Africa.

Chiamalu, Gumut, and Danladi rode in Nduka's car, while the rest of us were in Olu's. We drove off to Ugboigbo, about eighty kilometres from Enugu, with Nduka's car leading. Potholes dotted the roads in ever-challenging patterns. It rained earlier, but the sun was out. Bigger potholes held water puddles. Nduka and Olu concentrated on driving, because so many other drivers on the road ignore the driving codes.

Government's ineffectiveness is most evident in the rural areas of the South-East Zone. The roads are a nightmare and amenities are seriously lacking. The schools are very poorly staffed and supplied and, in some cases, the falling walls and roofs constitute imminent disasters. The people in the rural areas feel the heat from the bedevilling transition most, as they are uprooted from tradition without reliable options. As a determined people, they manage to survive, but, daily, the wear and tear become more visible.

As we moved through the last stretch of dirt road, worsened by erosion, we attracted a column of youths from Nduka's community, who ran behind us. They were shouting welcoming greetings; we shouted back our responses.

At a tricky spot with several sizeable pools of water, held in place by slippery clay, Olu missed the track. Our tyres hissed, but there was only rocking and no forward motion. Before we could come out, the youths surrounded our car. They urged us to remain inside. They pushed us out of the bog at the price of getting all wet and muddied. They cheered and didn't mind being all messed up. To the younger ones, it was all great fun.

We met a handful of people waiting for us at Nduka's family compound. Again, the youths surrounded our cars. We shook hands with as many of them as we could, thanked them for pushing us out of the mud, and asked after their well-being. In the process, one could not miss their emaciated figures. Viewed in the light of the symptoms of the HIV/AIDS pandemic that has somehow concentrated itself in Africa, this was unsettling.

Amadi, Nduka's oldest uncle and the elder of his extended family, who retired from the Civil Service, invited us into his house. Most of the youths waited outside. A casual survey of the people seated in the large parlour also revealed the same worn-out look. However, each one exhibited an alert spirit, perhaps because of the activities later in the day.

After introductions, two young women brought out kola nuts and their complements of garden eggs, palm wine, and drinking water. When everyone had settled, Amadi cleared his throat to get our attention.

"Thank you very much for honouring our invitation to the launching. Cassava is the thing now. Our community doesn't want to miss out. May the Almighty bless you all. Please, kola nuts are served," he said.

A young man lifted the traditional wooden bowl containing the kola nuts and handed it to Nduka, symbolising that Nduka and his friends were the primary recipients of the kola nuts. Nduka, with his head bowed, thanked Amadi and then handed the kola nuts to Danladi who was next to him. We knew the custom; so we handed the kola nuts to one another with each one pausing to thank our hosts. The kola nuts finally wound up on the table before Amadi.

An older man thanked Amadi for providing the kola nuts and then said, "The kola nuts are now before the elder. Please bless the kola nuts for us, Amadi."

Amadi picked up a kola nut and fervently implored Igboland, lands of Nigeria, the Spirits of all the famous departed, the Gods, the powerful Deities, and the Almighty to bless the kola nuts and grant partakers good health and prosperity, and that intrigues of evil Spirits and people be nullified. He prayed for all present to receive amplified rewards for their good deeds. He then broke the kola nut open and took a bite of one of the pieces. A young man stepped up to break the rest of the kola nuts into smaller pieces, ready for distribution to all.

Amadi said identical prayers over the first calabash cupful of palm wine, which he finally poured on the ground just outside the entrance to his house, symbolising reverence to the supernatural he had invoked in his prayers and who were thus given the first drink. With prayers over, the kola nuts, garden eggs, and palm wine were distributed among us.

Amadi ordered one of the young men serving the palm wine to dispense our own drinks from a particular container of fresh and undiluted palm wine. It was known in our villages, where palm was available, that the seven of us relished fresh, undiluted palm wine, which is indeed healthy. Any problems with drinking diluted palm wine, outside of prior medical conditions, often came from the quality of the water used to dilute it.

The breaking of kola nuts in gatherings in Igboland is touchy. There are set customs and procedures, which must be observed, and these vary significantly. In most cases, the oldest man does the favour, while in others, the reverse holds. When the lands of a people are invoked in prayers, the implications are that all the good forces of those lands—the good Spirits of the Ancestors buried there, the Deities, and all other favourable supernatural forces there—are called upon to hear and grant the prayers. But, as prayer houses of foreign religions are now everywhere, these traditional prayers are slowly but surely being mixed with or replaced by adapted foreign prayers, resulting in regrettable loss of direct stimulus—that bedevilling transition.

During the eating of the kola nuts, we engaged in random exchanges, catching up on the lives of one another. The kola nuts session breaks down barriers and makes for better understanding in later activities.

Some of the kola nuts and complements were sent to the youths outside. Olu added 500 naira in small denominations. When the gifts got to them, they cheered. A little later, we heard their excited voices as they shared the gifts, and we also heard an adult voice warning them not to fight over them.

When everyone inside had taken about two cups of the palm wine, Amadi said, "The launching is some time away. There's an emergency meeting of Umu-Ajaegbu at Obuekwe's house to discuss the letter we wrote to them about the communal piece of land that the court just awarded us. That letter ruffled some feathers. I saw no reason for that. Your friends can come, Nduka. After all, they are no more strangers here. Also, I think that their presence may be helpful. I better explain more. My family is Umu-Ude and there's another family, Umu-Chidubem, with whom we're closely related. Together, we are Umu-Ajaegbu. Ude and Chidubem were brothers from Ajaegbu, their father. This piece of land was won by Umu-Ajaegbu, and it was to their meeting that our correct Umu-Ude letter was written. But some troublemakers insinuated all kinds of things. There was nearly physical fighting."

"Ichie[4], what did your letter say?" Chiamalu asked.

Amadi, his forehead furrowed, frail frame shaking, said, "Let's go; you'll hear about it all there."

All the adults walked behind him. No doubt, he was Nduka's relation; average height, slightly built, light brown skin, oval face, restless sharp eyes—features he shared with Nduka. *His funny bone must have been whittled down by age.*

It was a short walk through dirt roads, which took four people abreast, smaller ones, and narrow footpaths that forced single file on us. Chiamalu

---

[4] Ichie, respectful label for an elder.

and Nduka walked close to Elder Amadi. Osagie, Danladi, and I were in the middle group, while Olu and Gumut were in the rear cluster. Discussions were going on at these three points defined by our presence.

Osagie said to one of our hosts, "It appears this will not be a good harvest season here; the crops don't look that great."

"My brother," he began, then paused. "This is part of our problems in the village, despite Nduka's tireless effort towards our local government officials paying attention to our village. We heard that a lot of money was spent in the purchase of fertiliser for us, but when it was time to distribute it, there was very little fertiliser. The scramble caused hard feelings that required many meetings to somehow manage. Some people are still unhappy, because of the disrespect they suffered during the scrambles for the fertiliser. This year, we used very little fertiliser: that's why the crops are as they are. I don't know what they want villagers to do. How do we feed ourselves? How do we manage our lives? We only get empty promises from the local government. Nduka cannot leave his work and come here to chase them around every day. Since Elder Amadi returned home, he's been doing his best too, but same results."

"How was last year?" Osagie asked.

"Well, a little better; we had more fertiliser, but not enough. Now we depend on fertiliser. When I was a young boy that wasn't the case. We had large, fertile farmland that required no fertiliser for crops to do well. There was much land; you farm here this year, the next year, at another location. Each person had as much land as he or she needed. You have to trek for at least one day before getting to this communal farmland, and the best areas are farther away. We lived in temporary shelters during the farming season. You didn't come home until your crops were planted. After that, you went back there during the growing season to weed and otherwise tend your crops. These required only short stays. So, the patches of farms in the village were not the whole story of our farming. They only sustained us until we got our crops from those major farms far away. For this reason, the village farms are the first ones planted at the very beginning of the season, as soon as you can work the soil after the first rains. Food was everywhere and affordable. It's different today. We have to depend on these small patches of farms here and there, and everyone is underfed, because children and old people cannot farm in the distant places. The new yam festival that announced the harvest season in grand style, particularly for youngsters, because of the sumptuous feasting on all kinds of food, is now a mockery. Some older ones now ignore the festival. You see, most of the able-bodied young men and women have left the village. Never mind the number of people you'll see today; they're here for the launching. Some of them came home last night, and after the weekend they'll all disappear."

"There must be other problems caused by this exodus?" Danladi asked.

"Not only farming suffers. Other events that made village life enjoyable have been discarded. There's a lot of insecurity, as robbers, armed or not, are not challenged. But for people like Nduka, who try to see that the local government pays some attention to a few of our needs, this place would have turned into the land of evil spirits. Our ancestors lived well. Nothing like that should happen here. One rascal in the local government headquarters insulted Nduka some time ago. He told Nduka that if he, Nduka, was interested in politics, he should come home and join them. Imagine! How can honest and hardworking Nduka come and join them in all the mess they are perpetrating? We wanted to teach the fool some sense, but for Nduka's advice that doing so would create more problems. In the past, that moron would have learnt the lesson of his life. The world is going awry. We only watch Nigeria drift."

He paused to urinate into the bush by the road; we waited for him a short distance away. Osagie, Danladi, and I recalled what excessive use of fertiliser does to the soil and crops.

When he finished urinating, Osagie said, "Do you know that human urine is as good as fertiliser?"

"What? No, that's an abomination. How can we urinate on our crops? No, I, the descendant of our great ancestor, Ude, will not condone or participate in that. May the gods forbid."

Danladi said, "How is your village taking advantage of the present call and likely support for agriculture by the government?"

"Well, that's why the launching. We don't want to fold our hands and watch others go into cassava planting. Who knows when the gods will come to our aid? The prices of cassava products are now rising to the treetops. Hopefully, we shall make some profit after the harvest. You know, things cannot be predicted in Nigeria these days. Planning without some assurances is a wasted effort." He pointed at a big house ahead of us. "That's the place for the meeting."

Elder Amadi, on getting inside, raised his voice with a lot of energy three times. "Umu-Ajaegbu, Kwenu!"

Some of the people responded each time, "Ha-a!"

This is the traditional Igbo way of respectfully greeting an audience, while getting their attention as well. We noted that the responses were not as enthusiastic as to be expected from the number of people present.

We were offered seats, and after Elder Amadi had settled into his seat next to a figure who appeared to be another elder, he cleared his throat and said, "Sorry, we're a little late. These are Nduka's friends who've come for the launching. They've come here for many occasions and they've been generous to us." Then he told us, "Gentlemen, this is Elder Obuekwe. Both of us oversee Umu-Ajaegbu. He's also the elder of Umu-Chidubem, as I'm the elder of Umu-Ude. Umu-Ude and Umu-Chidubem make up Umu-Ajaegbu. Everyone here is a member of Umu-Ajaegbu larger family. This emergency meeting is for Umu-Ajaegbu, but I invited them. They may have some ideas that may help in our discussions, if there is no *strong* objection."

There was silence for about ten seconds, which Elder Obuekwe interpreted as there being no strong objection.

He said, "Amadi, nno nu![5] The subject is not a secret and, even if it was, our guests have indeed identified themselves with us. Their presence may help. As Nduka's friends, they must behave alike. Please, the kola nuts have been accordingly blessed; help yourselves."

Elder Amadi, Nduka, Osagie, and Chiamalu each took a piece, but the rest of us politely declined, because the spicy dip with which the kola nuts are eaten appeared to have much pepper in it. We noticed that our doing so somewhat unsettled some people, so we later ate only the kola nuts.

---

[5] Nno nu, you're all welcome.

Elder Obuekwe said, "We don't have much time before the launching. This emergency meeting is about the letter Nduka wrote to Umu-Ajaegbu on behalf of Umu-Ude about the land the court awarded us. Some of us disliked the letter when it was first read at our last monthly meeting. This emergency meeting is to clear up the matter quickly. We don't want to add to the mountain of challenges we already have. Perhaps the best way to go about it is to have our secretary read the letter, and we can take it from there. Secretary Uche, please read the letter. You can sit down, while doing so."

The secretary went into the body of the letter in Igbo language and then in English. He was not aware that all of us who came with Nduka understood Igbo language.

"We of Umu-Ude hereby congratulate each of us of Umu-Ajaegbu on our well-deserved court victory over the long-disputed piece of land. However, we are all aware of the problems associated with land ownership, particularly those that have been legally contested. We therefore suggest the following:

I. This piece of land should be demarcated into two equal portions by a competent surveyor and allocated to Umu-Ude and Umu-Chidubem respectively. This should be easy to do since we have the surveyed plan, tendered in court.

II. We recommend that each of these families should then find most equitable ways of further allocating their portions to their family members.

III. The two families, Umu-Ude and Umu-Chidubem, should also endeavour to register their own portions with the Land Registry, as soon as possible.

Posterity in Nigeria is continually short-changed: we ought to act in opposition to this terrible tendency by ensuring that this piece of land does not become a subject of future contention.

Furthermore, these actions will go a long way in stopping those with whom we contested the land from encroaching on it, because closer monitoring will become possible, and our legal status as owners will be variously well-established.

Please accept our warmest regards.

Yours fraternally,

Nduka Ude

Secretary, Umu-Ude."

Elder Obuekwe said, "Well, there we have it. I think that those who raised objections the last time should speak first. What do you think, Amadi?"

Elder Amadi nodded in agreement. There was a brief pause, and we easily identified some of those who had objected to the letter, because of their body language.

One of them, an unkempt younger man, raised his hand and said, "Yes, I was one of those that the letter offended. I—"

"Nnayelugo!" Elder Obuekwe interrupted him, "You know our code of conduct at meetings. First, it's bad manners to raise your left hand when getting our attention. Then, you don't address us sitting down. I authorised the secretary to do so, because I didn't want him to be carrying his big file while standing and reading from it. You were named Nnayelugo[6], you should earn that name."

Nnayelugo reluctantly apologised and stood up. "As I was saying, I found the letter offensive. Why should Nduka write about Umu-Ajaegbu dividing a piece of land they jointly own? That's creating division. Nduka better tell us why he wants to be an agent of division in Umu-Ajaegbu."

The next speaker carefully observed protocols, but was more hostile.

"The land matter is not yet over. I don't know how many of you have been there recently. Those people who sought to take our land from us are still farming there. In fact, I saw one of their women making ridges for groundnuts there. I wanted to chase her out by flogging her on her legs with small sticks, but on second thought, I decided to first bring it to your attention. Now that I've told you, the next time I see any of them there, I'll forcibly remove the person. With all that still going on, it's senseless for Nduka to write about dividing the land. He's causing confusion."

Both elders just listened without outward signs of any emotion. It appeared that all the speakers so far were from Umu-Chidubem, but that impression did not last.

---

[6] Nnayelugo, the Almighty bestows glory.

One of the men who had walked with us from Elder Amadi's house said, "I, Ofodile of Umu-Ude, will never condone anything that can divide us. Yes, we briefly discussed the land in our Umu-Ude meeting before Nduka wrote that letter. Our ancestors never divided their land among themselves, and I don't see why we should start doing that now. Since Nduka is here, he should explain to us why he wrote the letter the way he did."

Both elders maintained their postures and blank countenances; some of the people murmured. Nduka crossed his hands over his chest and stared into space. The speaking continued in this trend with some speakers, the secretary among them, coming to Nduka's defence.

Elder Obuekwe adjusted his sitting and said, "Well, we're now repeating ourselves. Unless there're still some people who have things significantly different from all that we've heard, we ought to wind up the meeting. Remember the launching."

As if in a contest, two individuals forcefully thrust their right hands in the air. They had facial contortions and puckered lips. One was sitting about five people from the left of elder Obuekwe and the other, next to Gumut, who gave him a deliberate look from his raised hand to his feet and back up again.

Neither of the elders was in a hurry to pick a speaker from the two, but they glanced at each other and then allowed a few more seconds before Elder Obuekwe slowly said, "Yes, Ofoma, what is different from all we've heard?"

Ofoma, from close to the elders, jumped to his feet and said, "For me, this matter is not being handled well enough unless we are conceding that Umu-Ajaegbu no longer has men. If not, then this is what we must do. We must call a meeting; I mean a more serious meeting of all our people, including women. Why women? Just in case there's no manhood left in our men. Then, we must march to the homes of those people encroaching on our land and seriously warn them to stop doing so. If they continue, we must thoroughly beat up any of them we catch in the act. It's only when we've done that to a few of them, that our attention should be occupied by the little menace of Nduka's letter."

A hush fell on the meeting. The elders only glanced at each other. Elder Obuekwe slowly nodded at the other one seeking to speak, Ozoemene.

With greater abandon, he too jumped to his feet and declared, "I totally agree with Ofoma, but before we do what he's said, we must first reinforce ourselves, to be strong enough to tackle the trespassers. Since the genuine elders of Umu-Ude died off, there's nobody of value left there. All they have are as ignorant as children and weaker than women. If not, how can a letter like that result from their meeting? Amadi did not stop the letter. Amadi is a disgrace as an elder. Nduka thinks going to all those schools and foreign lands gives him the right to insult us. Book learning and travelling do not mean common sense. If we are serious, this meeting should be discussing how to sanction Nduka. Amadi…"

He could not finish that sentence, because a younger man, Udoka, from Umu-Ude, sprang on him like a champion wrestler, delivered a chopping-slapping right hook to the side of his face, followed by a good left-hand uppercut to his belly. As he doubled over from the uppercut, Udoka landed a better right-hand hook to his ribs. He groaned.

With matching speed, Udoka grabbed him by the collar, flung him on the floor, and pinned him there by sitting on him. Someone grabbed Udoka's raised fist, in readiness to pummel him. Pandemonium. Most efforts went to getting Udoka off Ozoemene. Osagie, with his over six feet of height and more than 190 pounds, contributed to the eventual separation of the two.

Surprisingly, the elders calmly watched the episode unfold without a word or a facial-muscle twitch. Some people lamented that the fighting before us discredited them. Ozoemene dusted himself off, cleaned the blood from his cheek, and quietly went back to his seat. Udoka was more difficult to control.

"You people should have let me knock out his remaining, staggered, and rotten teeth. The last time this letter was discussed, Elder Obuekwe warned him to mind his language. Today, he had to say worse things and insult Elder Amadi. He's not ashamed that his wife supports him, his family, and his kind mother, who does not deserve him as a son. I wish we were in the old days we've heard so much about. That nuisance ought to be banished or worse. He's a disgrace to Umu-Ajaegbu. Remember that he was the only one from our village who joined those thugs from Enugu to snatch and destroy our ballot boxes during the last elections. His father did all he could before he died to ensure that the shameless idler became useful, but we all know how he wasted all opportunities his father and uncle created for him. He's the laughing stock of his age grade. After this meeting, I'll truly deal with him; he'll not be at the launching."

"No, no! You're not going to do any of that," Elder Obuekwe ordered. "In fact, you'll remain here with me after this meeting, and then you'll go to the launching in my party. That way, I can keep an eye on you. Do you hear me, Udoka?"

"Yes, Ichie." Udoka said, while trying to calm himself.

Normality gradually returned. The two elders glanced at each other again.

Elder Obuekwe sat up. "First, I apologise to our friends for this ugly event. These things happen; there's no way to predict or control them beyond what you just did. Again, thanks for coming. The launching is still on. Now, matters arising. Disciplinary Committee Chairman, where are you? Yes, I see you. What do your codes say about what just happened, Chairman Ogbuike? I hope you have your books with you. You or your assistant is to make them handy at meetings."

"Yes, Ichie. I have them." Ogbuike said, as he sprang to his feet and turned over the pages of a notebook.

With all the official airs he could muster, he said, "For being the first to strike somebody during any meeting, the fine is 600 naira plus three jars of palm wine, valued at 100 naira each. For using unwarranted foul language at any meeting, the fine is 500 naira plus two jars of palm wine. For insulting an elder at a meeting, the fine is 1,000 naira plus five jars of palm wine. All fines must be paid within four days, or a traditional week, otherwise more harsh actions will result, and those actions are to be recommended by the Disciplinary Committee."

"Thank you, Ogbuike, for being brief and direct to the point. You've analysed the event so well; no wonder you're the Assistant Head Teacher of our primary school. You'll soon make Head Teacher here or elsewhere. Keep up the good work. Well, unless anyone has objections, these fines are imposed. The fines must be paid promptly. All Umu-Ajaegbu will be watching you two closely from now on. You must normalise your relationships quickly. Recall, Ozoemene, the abuse of an elder induces a curse on the perpetrator. The spirits of our ancestors are listening. Since we must end this emergency meeting as soon as possible, I think that it's correct to call on Nduka. Do you agree with me, Amadi?"

Elder Amadi nodded his head without even looking at Elder Obuekwe.

Nduka promptly got up and energetically greeted the meeting three times, "Umu-Ajaegbu Kwenu! Nigeria Kwenu! Umu-Ajaegbu Kwenu!"

Three resulting responses of "Ha-a!" were deafening and surprising in view of some opinions earlier expressed about Nduka. His inclusion of "Nigeria Kwenu" was to acknowledge our party. He spoke slowly, in a calm voice.

"I thought I was having a bad dream. The fighting woke me up. I was pained by some of the things said about Elder Amadi and me. I don't see where Elder Amadi's faults or mine are. We've done whatever we could to improve the lives of our people in the village, no matter the consequences. For our ancestors, the most pressing agenda were territorial gain and protection through physical force. Without those efforts, we probably would not be living here today. We must be grateful to them. However, they were nonetheless humans. Only the Almighty can definitely see into the future with accuracy. Recall that they did away with twins at birth, because they saw twins as aberrations. We now call on doctors, hospitals, and the public to ensure the lives of twins, particularly when they are more than two. Today, the challenges are different. We must use current standards to launch those coming behind us into the twenty-first century and beyond. In Nigeria today, enough attention is not paid to this obligation.

"It's not correct to say that our Ancestors did not share land, because we have inherited ownerships of pieces of land by individuals and families. This, obviously, implies the demarcation of land in one form or another and at one time or the other. If we look back to the long land dispute, the amount of money each side spent on litigations by far exceeds the current value of the piece of land. We persevered for the sake of posterity and our pride. Our letter identified some of the better ways of legally upholding our victory without conflicts. The suggestions in the letter will ensure that we are law-abiding, increase surveillance over the piece of land, and ensure equity at the levels of component nuclear families of Umu-Ajaegbu.

"To beat up people on the legs or elsewhere, or to make provoking visits will portray us as aggressors in victory. Furthermore, some of us know that land disputes all over Nigeria, in Africa, and beyond can be disruptive and costly, if they become physical fights. The problem is with communication. Some of us did not think about the full message of the letter, but only focused wrongly on its parts. Please, the letter was not of my making alone. It was the product of a meeting in which sufficient thought was given to options. I really don't see what Elder Amadi or I have to apologise for. Long live Umu-Ajaegbu!"

A loud applause followed. Many people shook hands with Nduka and implored him to ignore the rascals. The elders just sat back and allowed this to go on.

Olu raised his hand, and when he was recognised, he rose and said, "The elders, Umu-Ajaegbu larger family, greetings to you all. The seven of us, including your great son, Nduka, are indeed close friends and we share many ideals we consider important. One is doing whatever we can, as individuals or collectively, to improve our communities. Please, I want to assure you that there's not a thing that happened here today that reduces the respect we have for you, individually and as a family. If we had the time, I could have recounted worse things that happened in my village. We are all with you through thick and thin. God bless all of you."

More applause followed. People walked up to each of us, shook our hands, and pleaded with us to ignore the incident. Udoka, who was permitted to speak, halted this, but before speaking, he pulled out some money from his pocket, and without counting it, placed it on the table before the elders.

"I apologise for my part in the fighting. We all witnessed the reckless provocations."

"Heh! heh! heh! Well done, Udoka. That's the way to go. Now, this is a man in action," some people shouted.

Elder Obuekwe said, "Thank you, Udoka, for so promptly paying your fines. Don't forget my directives to you. Financial Secretary, count the money and accordingly issue Udoka a receipt."

The Financial Secretary counted the money and announced that it was 900 naira. More applause.

"Unless anyone has objections, the Lands Committee should study the letter and present recommendations at our next monthly meeting."

Elder Obuekwe paused to see if there were any objections. There was none, so he ended the meeting.

The elders stood up and shook hands, but I saw them winking at each other. I still wonder what that was all about.

As our party got outside, on the way back to Nduka's family compound, we heard someone inside saying, "Ozo emene, ozo ne eme. Oke onu, nti anu ife[7]. You better come up with your fines on time or that your beat-up motorbike will be pawned. You know I'm a member of the Disciplinary Committee. We are tired of your degrading antics. You, Ofoma, you better watch your mouth and manners. You called us cowards and ignorant people. That will be visited at our next meeting," the voice concluded.

Back at Nduka's family compound, we went into an inner room for lunch. With that over, we moved to the parlour where we found Elder Amadi dressed up for the launching.

"I hope you found lunch manageable?" he said, "This is the village; you have to accept us as we are. Someone will come from the launching site to let us know when to go there. Have some palm wine. Elder Obuekwe and I have to see that Umu-Ajaegbu exists in the best possible ways these days. We're in the same age grade, but he is a few months older than I am. That makes him the chairman of our meetings and head of our larger family. Nevertheless, we consult closely with each other."

Gumut said, "Ichie, you only have a few troublemakers. It's worse everywhere else, it seems. In my larger family, these meetings are like battles; the sensible people on one side and the permanently unruly and ignorant ones on the other. This last group makes the loudest noise. They all dress and act alike—loud colours, outlandish combinations of clothes, and a most offensive vocabulary. My family elder meets with them separately before any meeting

---

[7] "Ozo emene, ozo ne eme. Oke onu, nti anu ife": "May bad events not repeat, more of them happen. Big mouth, deaf ears."

he suspects will be turbulent. It must be demanding to lead families."

Amadi said, "You're quite right, Gumut. It's more than difficult. Sometimes, I find it more tasking than being in the Civil Service. But this is the final lap for people like me, who retire to the village. You see, during my earlier years in the Civil Service, there was order. People had self-esteem. There also, I witnessed the loss of discipline with time, as emphases shifted from service to self. The professionalism at independence started to fade. I served in the Survey Department of the Federal Ministry of Lands and Surveys and I lived in all the current six geo-political zones. Believe me; some of the changes in Igbo villages are also occurring in other parts of the country. What makes the difference is the concerted effort on the part of the people governing us, since the 'Biafra'-Nigeria civil war, to single out Igboland for degrading treatments. Otherwise, the aimless drifting is everywhere. There's too much confusion, too much greed. Here, we have the influence of elders. Then, we have the Igwe and his cabinet, the Development Union, and finally, the local government. State and federal governments are beyond the villagers' reach; we never see our representatives at these levels after the so-called elections.

"No one has harmonised these levels of influence. The immediate result is that we have many grey areas or vacuums regarding where the villagers go to for assistance. Then, charlatans, misfits, capitalise on the situation. With the ongoing reduction of the village population, our culture as Afrikans is vanishing. It's sad. Look, artisans from here did not build the newer houses you see. Ndukwe brought his builders from far-away Benin City in Edo state, where he works, and likewise Obasi, from Jos in Plateau state. Why? First, if you use people from here, they will steal some of the building materials, after inflating their charges and costs. With all that, they will do a poor-quality job, and later there will be burglaries. All because of envy, poor upbringing, and reducing community control. This is the mentality in the villages, strings of abnormalities. To be often baffled or stifled by change has become the price for growing old. Old age is supposed to be golden."

Chiamalu said, "Ichie, you said it's happening all over Nigeria. How do we tackle the condition?"

"Because it's happening everywhere doesn't make it the best way to live, as Africans. We had a uniquely practical cultural heritage, featuring discipline and caring for each other. People are now turning into lower animals out in the forest and only concerned about individual survival without sufficient reference to the rest. It's wrong. What to do about it? If a threatening upheaval breaks out in the market place, people quickly disperse into their stalls or those of their closest relations or friends. We must begin with ourselves, nuclear families, extended families, communities, Nigeria, and Africa. There's too much materialism, greed. Our original Afrikan culture was different. We should re-examine how our Ancestors lived and copy their ways, while modifying those areas we now know were not that good or will not suit the world today. Obuekwe and I spend time looking for ways of doing this.

"Whenever Nduka and I have the opportunity, we talk about this. He tells me about the foreign countries he's visited and I tell him about our ancestors, as much as I recall. If you compare the information we share, you'll find that the ways of our Ancestors were more dignifying from wider and more lasting views."

We listened to him for about ten minutes more before a young man came to inform us that it was time for the launching. As the site was on our way out, we decided to drive there, with Elder Amadi riding with us in Olu's car. We informed him that we would not be able to stay to the end of the launching, as we would like to drive back in daylight. He promised to ensure that we left in good time.

More people from other parts of the village greeted us on our arrival at the village square. Nduka excused himself to assist in the affairs. Part of the preliminaries included our introduction by the Master of Ceremonies as Nduka's friends and honorary members of the village. After some pledges, Elder Amadi walked to the MC and whispered in his ear, after which he handed him the envelope containing our donations.

Minutes later, the MC said, "Nduka and his friends, now as good as our village citizens, have done it again. This bulky envelope contains their donations. Thanks to paper money; otherwise, I would have needed the help of a few strong men to lift it. As usual, they don't want the contents revealed now. Please give them a big round of applause as they stand to be recognised."

The six of us seated around Elder Amadi stood up and acknowledged the applause by bowing and waving to the people. Elder Obuekwe walked over to us and both he and Elder Amadi thanked and shook hands with us. We carefully showed respect when we shook hands with the elders by holding our right hand just above the wrist with our left hand and bowing our heads.

Later, we gathered around our cars ready to depart. Nduka beckoned to someone to come to where we were. This young and big woman struggled to move her huge body towards us. Her face was roundish, well-structured, and indeed pretty, but the rest of her body was in multiple folds of overhanging flesh in stretched skin. After getting to us, she was panting from the exertion. She stood as tall as Osagie's ears.

Before rushing back to his car, Nduka said, "This is my niece. She has urgent matters at Enugu. I told her she could ride back with us. Since we're already four in my car, she better ride with you fellows."

Osagie entered the back seat from the driver's side and I, from the other side, leaving the front passenger seat for Nduka's niece, who needed the space. The car sank further as she did, but we drove off anyway. We noticed a few of the youths running behind us until we passed the treacherous spots of the dirt road, thanks to the increased traction of our tyres. They wanted to make sure we were not stuck again. We waved to them to appreciate their kindness.

5

RIPPLES OF RURAL ECHOES

After arriving for the following Sunday's Uhuru Hut session, Olu rushed to Nduka, feigned Udoka's combination of punches at him, and grabbed him by his shirt collar. Olu raised his clenched fist in the air and then looked at Gumut, who was sitting next to Nduka. Gumut got it; he quickly grabbed Olu's raised fist in the air. We cheered.

"Oga, sirs, you all okay?" the waitress asked.

"No, he's beating me up. Help me, please." Nduka whined like a child.

"We're okay. Just horsing around," Danladi said.

She shrugged her shoulders, giggled, and left. *Grown men are only larger versions of boys.*

"Forget Chigozie and your allegations; Nduka, you have a bill for the servicing of my car's suspension. You fellows should've let me beat the hell out of him," Olu said.

We laughed and then ordered our first drinks.

"Seriously, fellows, thanks for all the support at the launching and the disgraceful meeting. Elder Amadi sent us some kola nuts, bitter kola, groundnuts, and palm wine this morning. Preliminary reports on the launching indicate some good results. The paid-up pledges amounted to a reasonable sum with which to begin the project. They can start site clearing and perhaps more. Maybe we should stop over at my place from here. I put the palm wine in the freezer. I'll call Adaoma to bring it out so that it will thaw when we get there. Okay?"

"Why not?" Osagie said.

After the call, Nduka said, "Yes, yes, thanks for the village trip. That Ozoemene character is quite a problem. He influences others too. They don't change their behaviour no matter what anyone does. Why?"

"Signs of the times, Nduka, signs of the times," Danladi said. "We know what Nigeria is today—region against region; religion against religion; ethnic groups up in arms; minorities crying out against exclusion; communities against communities; families in drawn-out feuds; business partners knocking off each other; and politics, number one business. But villages, just too much; villagers, more aggressive. Many unnecessary disputes to settle. Meetings often prolonged; no one makes any sacrifice for peace. Results? Common good suffers; already bad situations get worse. However, we can correct our situations. But we always look at someone for help or as the cause of the problems."

Chiamalu, smiling, said, "Nduka, I must commend you on your reply at the meeting: well thought-out, coolly delivered. It knocked out everyone. The Ichies were nodding their heads."

"It depends on how many people actually understood what Nduka said," Gumut said.

"I don't know if I've mentioned this before, but Chuks certainly knows about it. He helped in sorting out a few things. When my family and I returned home, we lived in the village for some months. Our children were from four to nine years old. At those ages, they knew the difference between the UK and the village. We quickly built a small house in the village. As in Elder Amadi's story, people digging in their nearby farms later found buried cement bags, cables, and other items. Some people working on the house, or others, had possibly stolen and buried the items, but never recovered them or they just forgot about them. I had it out with the builder, but you know how these things are settled in the villages. Elders from both sides meet to find solutions. It took so long that I finally had to forget the whole thing."

"Yes, Chiamalu, I remember," I said.

"But that was not the end of my woes. We eventually moved to my company's location. My nephew who was put in charge of the house went to work, steadily vandalising the entire house. All movable items such as table fans, a small refrigerator, small pieces of furniture, plumbing and electrical fittings, and on and on were gone. He didn't stop at that. The small generator I had installed because my village was not connected to the national grid at the time was cannibalised—the starter, battery, AVR unit— all gone. It was a calamity. Going to the village afterwards became a downer. I wanted to shoot the *animal*, but how could I, with my parents pleading for him and people like Chuks intervening? By the way, even from when we hadn't returned home, I did everything I could to see that my nephew went to school, but he wouldn't. Instead, he dodged classes, changed schools on his own, and spent his school fees and other monies for his education on drinking, eating, and entertaining his off-character friends in hotels and such places."

Olu asked, leaning forward, "Hey, hey, Chiamalu, where's your nephew now; what's he doing?"

"I really don't know, to tell the truth. Now that my parents are no more, he better keep his distance from my family and me. Un-Afrikan, but everything has limits."

"Chiamalu, such people should not be treated with kid gloves; you must do something about that chap," Gumut insisted.

"In time, in time… This is how bad things are; even at such close quarters, the poor quality of people can be that crippling."

After a short pause, Danladi said, "I truly feel this thing, not yet out of control. Everywhere else has their own problems; outsiders can't put our situations above theirs. As Africans, the situation is high priority."

Chiamalu said, "The disorientation has been on from various angles for very long. We must remember being punished in primary or secondary school for speaking our native languages instead of English. One of many subtle ways in which we were brainwashed to reject our Afrikanness. Many of us now speak and think in English, French, Portuguese, or whatever. How many parents do we hear proudly declare today that their children do not understand their native languages, as evidence of urbanisation or progress? That reminds me, Olu; the funny, but thought-provoking story you once told

Chuks and me about the lunatic at the garbage site. That gives other perspectives. We still have time to hear it, if you don't mind; unless, you've already told it to the rest."

Olu leaned back. "No, I haven't, but it's a long one. My son was home on holiday. He had a Rasta hairstyle with dread locks just cheek long. I've learned not to interfere in such matters; if I did, the thing might become knee long. The family loves having him home, and I certainly appreciate the extra pair of hands.

"One afternoon, he accompanied me on a garbage run. He did most of the work and I, the driving. Traffic forced us to park about ten metres from the dump bins. A lunatic at the site, possibly aged in his late thirties, was rummaging through the garbage for something to eat and items of attire. A tattered towel covered his loins, the rest of his dirty body, sweat-streaked brown, yellow, and white. His very long Rasta-style hair and beard were equally filthy.

"As my son took the garbage to the dump bins, his short dread locks dangled in the air with each step. The lunatic looked up at him for a few moments and then stood erect and grinned. Still with the frozen grin, he stretched out his hands and slowly moved towards my approaching son. He also had this longing in his eyes, as if he had found a long-lost comrade.

"I didn't have a stopwatch, but I believe that my son set his all-time best for dumping the garbage, scampering back into the car, and slamming the door shut. I obliged him with a fast takeoff. My rib cage was almost exploding with the belly laugh that welled up. As I struggled with suppressing the laugh and driving straight, my son kept a stone face. We drove home without exchanging words. When I recounted the incident at dinner, everyone laughed out tears, but my son still kept his unruffled exterior.

"Days later, I narrated the event to my colleague, Akuko. He laughed himself silly. We then took stock of developments in Africa. Any person about to take leave of his senses in traditional Afrika was always taken care of by family, friends, or community. There were no public psychiatric wards, but traditional healers did the job well enough. Such a person would not be left to roam about and feed from dumped garbage. Our ancestors said that if any embarrassment can be associated with blindness, the embarrassment goes to the family and friends of the blind, and not the blind.

"Akuko asked for more descriptions of the lunatic. He lit up in recollection; the lunatic was from his village. His name was prophetic, Ijenu[8]. He was the fifth of seven children. He adamantly refused to attend any western-style school. His siblings were doing well in current terms. Ijenu preferred apprenticeships with herbalists, spiritual healers, and voodoo protagonists. He ingratiated himself into the companies of many elders in his village and elsewhere to learn as much as he could about culture and nature. For running their errands, his meals often came from the privileged servings for elders. When his parents built a modern family house in their compound, Ijenu, then in his late teens, decided to move out. His village elders easily granted his request for a piece of land from the community land located deep in the forest.

"He built himself a thermally efficient hut. The round mud walls encased small hard wood sticks, tied fence-like, for reinforcement, and there were tiny vent holes at staggered heights. It had an interior diameter of about ten metres, and the narrow entrance was covered with heavy, but movable, wooden slabs. It had a grass-thatched roof, about twenty centimetres thick. He piled the earth that he had dug out from the floor area around the outside of the walls with an outward gradient to channel rainwater away. The interior always maintained a comfortable temperature regardless of the weather outside. However, when he cooked inside during the rains or very late at night, the hut was uncomfortably filled with smoke, but that also served to drive away unwanted visitors—scorpions and mosquitoes. However, he used slow-burning, pungent wood and leaves specifically for this purpose.

"As he moved into the forest, an unprecedented action in family relationships, he became the talk of the village. That didn't bother him. He had always considered the villagers as people who were losing the true meanings of life. As a good farmer, hunter, and fisherman, and with a perennial stream nearby, he ate well. Ijenu unfolded as an extreme naturalist.

---

[8] Ijenu, The Journey of Life.

He spent much time, days and nights, in the forests and deeper into the jungle areas, studying species of animal and plant life, and the dynamics of their existence. He eventually became the collector of roots, barks, leaves, nuts, buds, and flowers for his herbalist healer-teachers and others.

"Ijenu was not a hermit. He attended family and community meetings whenever the agenda interested him. However, he disliked people who purposely set bush fires, because the fires destroyed nature. He would rant and rave about bush burning and the general neglect of culture at these meetings. He often fought losing battles with bush fires, but always managed to save his hut and farms. Game and produce he sold provided for his other few needs. He dated village-rooted women who were not very absorbed in modern lifestyles on occasion. Marriage was not a priority, because he avoided commitments that could threaten his lifestyle.

"By his mid-twenties, Ijenu had become a custodian of local tradition, culture, and nature, and a living encyclopaedia on herbal medicine. His patients grew in number over time, because he hardly charged them much except when he knew the patient as a habitual bush burner. If other herbalists referred patients to him, he would give the treatment in exchange for new formulations. His most popular treatments were the inoculations against snakebites, scorpion, and other insect stings; they were truly effective.

"He eagerly enlightened people on the bounties of nature and shared the same whenever he could. Children were gripped by his true stories about animals and plants and always crowded around him whenever he came to the village. Smoked meat and fish, and some wild fruits, were some delights he had for the children who were ever grateful. He nurtured his popularity with children very carefully.

"Some family members derided him for not charging enough for his services. He ignored them. His strategy was to earn future considerations and to lessen the adverse reactions to his chosen existence. It worked. He earned the nickname of "Ichie Nwata"[9] and was often listened to in matters of his expertise.

---

[9] Ichie Nwata, The Young Elder

"Tragedy struck. The government built a new road that passed close to his abode. Much of the nearby forest and some of his farms went. Typically, the drainage systems were either ignored or not put in place well. The next rainy season featured unprecedented heavy rains with flooding and erosions that washed away his hut and the rest of his farms. The villagers rallied around him in protest, but they were voiceless people in the emerging society. He was heartbroken. An elder from a neighbouring village resettled him in an area similar to the one he lost. Ijenu worked hard to recreate his previous environment and was back in business within months. After four years, heavy torrential rains caused the irrigation dam water nearby to rise and engulf his hut and farms. Disappointment and anger consumed him. Reluctantly, he went back to his village, but was never comfortable there. He spoke very little to anyone and kept to himself. People tried to consult him as usual, but he would simply walk away from them. He even ignored the children who gathered around him in sympathy.

"After months of this dejected existence, one of his herbalist teachers he had known and respected very much from when he was a teenager visited him. This resulted from diplomacy by some elders of his village. The teacher convinced Ijenu to relocate to his town about fifty kilometres away. Ijenu built his hut and farms a third time. He found himself and lived his normal life for a few years before a third disaster occurred. This time, the local government cleared his entire location in order to build a farm settlement. Ijenu cried like a baby for days; no one could console him. He went from one friend to another recounting his ordeals. He gradually enlarged his audience from his friends to whoever would listen. This trend lasted a few months before he began chanting. He took to the village roads with his chants. The shock of being repeatedly torn away from nature was too much for him.

"What about his family, close friends of the herbal practice, clientele, and his community? All of them failed to do enough, in the Afrikan tradition, to restrict, reassure, and treat him. The whole society was adrift on a fluid of unknown and varying density. His mental instability escalated to the point that Ijenu, who had stubbornly shunned western modernity, was rummaging in a city garbage dump.

"A few nights before my son went back to school, the Ijenu episode came up at dinner. After the laughs, he reacted this time. 'Listen, *please*,' he said slowly. 'I'm an 'A' student. You always celebrate my grades. I'll finish school at that ranking. Thereafter, I'll become a much-respected professional. I may even do more than that. I'm making a social statement with my hairstyle: do not judge people by their looks.'

"A few moments of silence followed before his younger sister teased, 'Go tell that to your friend at the garbage dump.' I quickly hushed her up and had her truly apologise to him.

"Oh yes, the lunatic at the garbage dumpsite; he tells more than the story of his life, doesn't he?"

The others were body-and-mind into the story. Chiamalu and I had heard it before, yet we were equally rapt. We were all overwhelmed by its messages, some of which took a while to register.

Gumut said, "Wao! Ijenu portrays more dimensions of the bedevilling transition, doesn't he?"

Danladi said, "Yes, Gumut. The Ijenu case is extreme; lots of that at reduced scales. Foreigners did not build the road and dam poorly. Surely it's not their responsibility, looking after our deranged? Characters like Ijenu exist everywhere."

Osagie said, head raised, "To focus on the levels of indictments from Ijenu should be helpful. Olu, what did your colleague, Akuko, do after identifying Ijenu?"

"I don't know. Since he didn't mention the matter again, it's safe to assume he did nothing. What do you expect him to do?"

Osagie persisted, "Well, Ijenu was from his village. He knew him and his condition. Did you remind him of Ijenu later?"

"I see where you're going, Osagie," Nduka said. "The massive dereliction of us all, heh? True, but does Ijenu want to be taken off the streets? He's probably having a great time. Look, haven't you seen some women in his condition out there who are also carrying babies on their arms as they solicit for alms? How do you think those babies come about, heh?"

The laughter that followed brought this session to an end. We finished our drinks and left for Nduka's place.

Adaoma, the beautiful and pleasant host, radiated welcome. We greeted her warmly and she asked after our families. She already had all the stuff from Elder Amadi, her own additions, and some bottles of Star beer laid out for us. We chatted about the launching and attendant events, mainly for her benefit.

We also talked about global disasters; the havoc wreaked by hurricane Katrina in the United States, the Asian Tsunami, the 9/11 of New York City, and all the man-made conflicts. We wondered if the number of Nigerian casualties in all of them would ever be known. Nigerians are everywhere, and to such extents that our under-performing embassies fail woefully to track them, talk less about providing them protection and services.

After my second glass of palm wine, I decided to switch to Star beer, but before I did, I took a bite of a bitter kola. Drinking beer after bitter kola dramatically changes the taste of beer. Good beer drinkers know this; you should try it.

"Hey, Chuks, this is the kind of night you're proclaiming, heh? You know what mixing palm wine and beer does to people. Nduka, you two planned this?" Danladi asked.

"It's a free world, isn't it? We know the limits. If anyone needs a bed, we have space. Danladi, please don't restrict anybody with your conservatism."

"Nduka, you invite people to your home, then call them names. Your kind of person, heh?" Danladi said.

Osagie and I made the switch.

We ate, drank, and chatted for about an hour more before Chiamalu stood up and said, "Adaoma, thanks for a nice evening. You shouldn't have bothered so much on our behalf. But, Adaoma is Adaoma. Hey, fellows, I've got to leave. I still have lots to do before a presentation that's due in exactly seventeen days. Osagie, you mailed my memorandum to the Political Reform Conference for me, because I had to travel on a project. Well, the director of 'Okwukwe Afrika,' the NGO making waves, asked that I make a presentation based on that memorandum to one of their public meetings. It's difficult to turn her down."

Nduka jumped up, hands akimbo. "Oh yeah. Who is this *she* and why is *she* so difficult to turn down? Adaoma, listen carefully; you know the person to urgently relay his reply to, before he gets home."

We focused on Chiamalu and Nduka.

"Mrs. Akpata. She's irrepressible, irresistible. And that's *professionally* speaking, Nduka."

"Oh yeah. And please, Chiamalu Ofobuike, can you tell us here and now what you truly know all her professions to be?"

We laughed. Adaoma patted Chiamalu on the back and held his hand to lead him towards the door.

Olu joined Nduka and Adaoma in seeing Chiamalu off, while he told Chiamalu, "Look, if you need some help in preparing for the presentation, we're all available. Gumut is our computer guru; he can assist with the slides and so forth. And, Nduka, we know, can supply the jokes."

"Mind your language, Olu. That you're in my home does not give you the right to call me a joker."

Chiamalu acknowledged the offer of help and then left with Nduka, Olu, and Adaoma, who was still holding his hand. After Chiamalu's departure, they returned a short while later.

Osagie took us back to the presentation. "Chiamalu didn't mention that when he gave me the memorandum to mail for him, he told me to make a copy for myself, if I wanted to. After reading it, I made a copy for each of us. I think they are still in my car. Sorry, I just forgot to give them to you before now. Typically, the memorandum was great. It didn't go into specifics, but it more than set the stage for a truly serious national conference, and it even threw challenges at us. Let me get the copies from my car."

With Osagie gone to collect the papers, Olu said, "We should give Chiamalu support. I don't know what that should be until we read the memorandum."

Gumut said, "The minimum is to ensure that as many of our friends as possible attend. It's going to be open to the public and free, I imagine."

Osagie returned with the papers and we started reading. I had seen it before, but as I read it again, I noticed that Chiamalu had edited it. It held our attention; nobody spoke until we had all finished reading.

Danladi, hands folded over chest, said, "Consistent, isn't he? As in the entrepreneurial paper, challenges to Nigeria about harvesting precedent. Now, to support him; how, Olu?"

"I don't know now, something special. Let's see… why don't we form a committee of two or three to make suggestions? We can all add to whatever they have. With all the drinking today, it's hard to be creative. The presentation is two weeks from next Wednesday, isn't it? That gives us a little time."

"If there's no objection, I suggest Nduka, Gumut, and Chuks," Osagie said.

"Yes, 'Elder Obuekwe,' there's no objection," I said. "We'll be in touch. We should call it a day, or is it a night? Nduka, any objection?"

"Chuks, none whatsoever. You should all go home *now*, because you cannot afford our charges for bed and breakfast."

"Who are the *we* in *our* charges? Please speak for yourself only," Adaoma said.

We thanked Adaoma and Nduka for a nice evening and left. Those of us in the committee fixed a meeting for Tuesday evening at Gumut's.

Again, I drove home with that warning, *Face-off: consequences! Face-off: consequences!* ringing a little louder in my head.

6

UPSCALE COUNTRYWIDE DIALOGUE

1.0 PRELUDE:

Great nations or countries are not born at tea or cocktail parties. Deep and pervasive traumas that awaken, sharpen, and sustain patriotism in the citizenry precede their births. Countries that have distinct ethnic heterogeneity additionally require unrelenting, conscious effort towards ensuring that a sense of common destiny remains the norm for patriotism to flourish at the required levels for greatness. For diverse countries, recent history shows that attrition or firefighting tactics only serve to postpone and intensify the effects of pending disasters.

Nigeria, a multi-ethnic and otherwise a pluralistic country, has become a large bundle of enfeebling contradictions. Shoddily tended multi-ethnicity has much to do with that. Multiple epicentres of localised interests have become strong centrifugal forces, which deny the country the true greatness that its potentials promise.

How did it all come about?

The conceptualisation of Nigeria before and at the 1914 amalgamation did not target an enduring, great country. That betrayal has remained very poorly addressed to date. That our freedom fighters spent much of their time and energies in trying to uproot the colonialists politically, if only ceremonially, without sufficiently charting and fully committing themselves to a path of enduring greatness for the country, is a valid argument. If they had done otherwise, they would have identified multi-ethnicity and other pluralisms as likely sources of all the crippling problems that today debilitate Nigeria. Their true commitment to the country would have led to finding and implementing lasting solutions. This corroding baton has, ever since, been handed down, upgraded in potency each time.

Despite their variously expressed pursuits of the doctrine of a "One Nigeria," post-independence governments, including military ones, have not been able to cut the mustard. The reasons for these failures are derived, in part, if not wholly, from their respective mandates being acquired from the unwholesome bartering among exclusively self-serving interest groups. The people, the true masters, have thus been manipulated to the outside to look in as doomed observers. There lies the greater danger, because whenever the people have had enough, they often respond with unpredictable mentality.

The big picture is becoming hazy at best. Human capital development continues slipping. Global worth for Nigeria is defined by nuisance value in increasing ways. Many of what we attempt on global platforms, as a country, are diminished by underachievement.

As an example, we employed the Global System Mobile (GSM) technology for communication to reap more stratification of society. The failure to initially stipulate interconnectivity, general prescriptive and performance standards, and the pooling of resources by operators for the relatively fewer infrastructure elements that the system requires, left us grouped into the land-liners, 0802, 0803, 0804, 0805 . . . faster access intra-group communicators. Communicating across groups also was more expensive and frustrating. The relative cost of the system is still one of the most expensive in the world, even with granting that operators have to put electricity generators on tow. International callers to Nigeria will confirm that our global telephony is poor—a rousing prompter to how dysfunctional globalisation has been to Nigeria.

We proclaim great achievements. The status seekers manage to keep up their images by juggling multiple handsets. Imagine the consternation at simultaneous in-coming calls on all handsets before an "elite" group meant to be impressed. I read somewhere that handsets that will serve more than one operator will soon be out and, of course, at more cost to the poor consumer, the model NS (Nigeria Special). Nigeria has her nationals who are innovative experts in this technology located all over the globe.

In the promised, but grossly missed, uninterrupted electricity supply by December 31st, 2001, we swiftly adopted the approach of some fighters of global narcotics who flex muscles in faraway places rather than beat down, in contrast to showily hallowing, the demands for the substances at home. Falsely grandstanding on the 31st of December, 2001, we blanketed a significant portion of the country with "brownouts" until the system could no longer take it. Shortly thereafter, high-profile political activities and highbrow urban quarters defined electricity supply. We also seek jobs for our growing jobless from industries and international investments without being able to supply reliable, quality electricity, even with having the important labour, energy sources, and, apparently, the money. Something must be amiss—the Nigerian Question.

After half a century of hundreds of billions of petrodollars, there is not a single community in the country, except quarters where expatriates reside in and maintain, which consistently enjoys a reliable supply of honest-to-goodness potable water. Water supply technology is certainly within our reach; it predates even the Roman and Greek civilisations.

A thought trend identifies opportunism as a major cause of our current situations. Exploiters, internal and external, could be accused of unleashing the dynamics of our heterogeneity away from the common prosperity to their selfish ends for centuries. We are confronted by deep-seated spectres of polarisation and are unable to galvanise our common essence towards a collective existence that exemplifies human accomplishments and pride, of which we could otherwise be capable.

Where is the relief valve; when will the turning point come for Nigeria?

2.0 COUNTRYWIDE DIALOGUE:

With the semantics of legal experts, professional politicians (whatever that means), political scientists, and the rest aside, this much-delayed and much-feared countrywide dialogue could well be the curing balm for Nigeria. It could become the unencumbered opportunity for legitimate interest to be adequately heard and understood by all. For this to happen, the mind must be fully enlightened and energised to its limits of creativity. To fully liberate the mind means that the fear of the country breaking up from such a dialogue must be discarded as a prediction not based on justifiable probability. Lining up obstacles against organising and running such a dialogue at the necessary intensity should be regarded as a negative mind-set that offers no challenge. The complexity and capability of the human mind are enormous.

The following unranked points could be relevant.

2.1 Probable Cycles:

Experienced participants in think tanks, group efficiency enhancement, and conflict resolution will readily point out that such undertakings go through identifiable cycles.

Based on the matter at hand and the experience of participants, often, initial contacts are characterised by caution and over-done courtesies. Parties are reluctant to give out their game plans early.

With the ground rules set, the next item is normally the drawing up of and agreeing on the agenda. It is at this point that rancour may surface. Arguments about phraseology, the ordering of items, or speakers may arise.

The first phase of discussions is often clashes of divergence, as participants let loose pent-up emotions to secure early advantage. The battle rages without attention to superiority of reason. Some intimidation may occur. This is normal and must be handled well.

A cooling off period follows, as participants retract into themselves and evaluate what others had said against their own positions. Some requests for clarifications may arise. Clear thinking begins and the willingness to trade-off positions starts to emerge. Each side prioritises its demands, in order not to miss out on items that are crucial to their interests.

Trading skills come to the fore in the following phase. Participants do their best to extract concessions. This is also a critical stage: intransigence could surface to throw everything back to square one. The skills of facilitators are counted upon here to deliver good results.

The final stage is the concretising and the celebration of agreements—handshakes, pats on the back, apologies, and niceties.

Surely, the above is extremely simplified, but they propose a starting model for the much larger and more complex countrywide dialogue.

2.2 Nature of Dialogue:

If this dialogue is to be the true pivot for Nigeria, it has to be many things to the majority of Nigerians. It has to resolve many issues from which all of us have been stepping aside from or over for so long. How brutal the frankness becomes will be a key index for success. It cannot be a kangaroo court, a kitchen cabinet, an approval board, or a fixers' forum. It must be the true awakening. "Bait-and-Switch" is a game politicians often merrily play; it will be the real threat to Nigeria, if tried in this matter.

From the foregoing, the discussions must first traumatise the citizenry. This can be done through sufficient application of intellectual rigour and dexterity in programming proceedings. There must be sufficient interactive opportunities for the public so that, at the end, all those who wish to make inputs would have done so.

The discussions need exceptional facilitators whose feet are firmly on the ground, and the discussions must not be teleguided away from popular needs. It should all be an unrestrained affair; otherwise, the trauma and maximum pressure for enduring positive results will be lost.

2.3 Core Participants:

It is possible to set up discussion zones throughout the country from a good analysis of the marginalisation cries in our news media alone. Thereafter, each zone, guided by a set of well-thought-out and realistic briefs, should truly and freely elect their core representatives. The ability to adequately consult with their respective discussion zones must be an important requirement of core participants.

The number of core participants should be such that enough people are available for committee assignments, and yet be manageable. The targets should include making representatives of the cross sections of the discussion zones and the country at large core participants. It is fair to tilt the composition of core participants in favour of the younger generations, expected to bear the burdens from the past, present, and the future.

2.4 Timing and Duration:

Many think that this dialogue is long overdue. All of us, by commission or omission, folded our hands and allowed a few incorrigible and disoriented ones among us to depreciate our heritage and fritter away our common abundance. Besides, dialogues are not new in our collective experience.

A positive perception of this delay, however, is that it has allowed us the time to collect enough data with which to amplify and sustain the gains from the dialogue.

The duration of the dialogue should be such as to give enough time for the exhaustive and, hopefully, conclusive treatments of all the cardinal issues that have so far impeded the sustainable development of *Nigerians* and Nigeria. There should be enough time for direct or interactive participation, at one level or another, of all those who wish to. The goal is to establish the ways of progressively living together that a greater majority of us will identify with and relentlessly promote for the common prosperity. It is reasonable to make such gains at the expense of time.

Many nations or countries that are major players in global affairs had to undergo societal upheavals, many extremely violent and dehumanising, for periods exceeding decades in some cases, before they found their individual paths to global leadership positions. Months or even years are therefore small expenditures in the life of a country, such as Nigeria, in search of enduring greatness. Whether Nigerians can synthesise from history to chart an expedient, yet efficient and enduring path to the league of the majors in global affairs is a relevant question for this countrywide dialogue.

2.5 Facilitators and Proceedings:

Impartiality in human nature is often very difficult to attain, but because of the significance of this dialogue, every effort, no matter how horrid, should be made to ensure that facilitators are Nigeria's best for the task. Not recommended are the sycophant, the court jester, the malleable, the political jobber, the mediocre, the intellectual quean, and the fixated. This cannot be business as usual; many flash points are overheating.

The facilitators should be allotted meaningful independence and should be reasonably empowered. They must understand the full significance of their task. They must be well-funded from our common purse without extraneous extras. Their job should be to organise and run a dialogue that touches and improves the soul and psyche of the majority of Nigerians, so that sustainable development can flourish everywhere. If the facilitators are well-articulated, they should be able to run the balls to the desired posts.

For their near-sacred work to endure, they should find adequate ways of playing back each significant milestone of their work to the people for affirmation and the go-ahead. This should go a long way in ensuring that they carry the rest of the country along. Since the funds available to them will be efficiently determined, and since each of them is of character, there should be no fear that they will interpret carrying the people along to mean that they are to distribute the contents of "Ghana-must-go" bags as widely as possible for cover fire.

3.0 EXPECTATIONS:

Living, positively or otherwise, is the management of the dynamics of alternatives, choices, and options with the implied degradation slide for tardiness or omission. To properly prepare for this dialogue means the anticipation of outcomes by far in excess of what is contained here, a mere distant whiff of the appetiser before the mountain main course. Comments on outcomes here are therefore limited.

What Nigerians yearn for most are more equitable and regenerative ways of living together, while being globally relevant in positive ways. Flashes of excellence have led them to dreams of upbeat legacies for humankind. They smell these legacies. However, there is the off-chance that, if the dialogue does not relieve the suffocating embrace, they could choose disintegration into more manageable smaller units. If this becomes the final decision, we must be prepared to do so in a civilised manner. This is the serious challenge before the facilitators and each of us.

Without preemptive intents, it may be useful to briefly view some of its possible products.

3.1 Corruption:

The immediate picture that comes to mind on our hearing the word "corruption" is that of officials illegally helping themselves from our common wealth. That is the most publicised definition of corruption in our society today. However, to corrupt can mean to deface, to debase, to make impure, to distort, to degrade, to disorient, to counterfeit, to stigmatise, and to make less acceptable. The aggregated interpretation of corruption makes it the real big, bad monster in our society. It is the principal nullifier of our social, economic, political, and environmental initiatives. It is partly the product of that faulty mind-set, the tragedy of the common, which implies that what belongs to all belongs to no one in particular. It negates the burning desire in each of us to belong to an enviable Nigeria.

The dialogue will define the ways in which this monster can be slain and cremated in a most unforgettable manner. To this end, the resulting cremation ashes should be equitably distributed and time-capsuled in each local government area of the land. This is the only way to properly kill the power of negative precedent, so that following initiatives for enduring overall positive change can quickly take root and flourish.

3.2 The Constitution:

The bewildered by the arbitrary ways in which important matters in our collective living have been approached realise the shortcomings of all versions of our national constitution. They have been products of "cut-and-paste" processes. We have been essentially cutting from other's experiences and pasting to our detriment, further aggravated by the "cutters-and-pasters" being substantially driven by myopic forces.

The adequately conducted countrywide dialogue will provide more than enough fodder for creating a relevant and impelling enough constitution that we can all believe in, revere, and protect at all times and costs—a fast bonding of all.

3.3 Socio-econo-political Systems:

Reinventing the wheel is an assured conduit to under-performance; the copycat is bland, being without originality and therefore boring; and the marathoner whose strategy only calls for stepping into the footprints of the leader, runs not for gold. With these thoughts in mind, and with some understanding of global directions, it is altogether possible that the certified decisions from the dialogue could be used to fashion out extremely potent ways of doing things together to the amazement of all, ourselves included.

The world is currently driven by the democracy syndrome without enough questions. It appears that humanity is also in the midst of a maze of problems with association, and which maze is manifesting itself in confusing and venal global values.

A Ghanaian member of the African Union monitors to the elections in the USA in 2004 made some stimulating comments on the BBC. He said, among other prime statements, that he was in the state of Ohio, which had been billed as the place to watch, to see how it would all go down. To the ribbing he had received from some US citizens as to what he, an African, knew about democracy, and why he was in Ohio, he stated that he was there on behalf of Africa to see things for himself, and to report to the AU. He added that with the backdrop of what had happened the last time in Florida, if things did not happen satisfactorily in the Ohio, in the richest and most powerful country in the world today, people would rightly wonder whether free and fair elections could be held elsewhere. He also stated that the nature of the people's mandates and the manner of their acquisition and maintenance were supposed to be central to democracy. With what is now known about the voting in Ohio, his report will, perhaps, make an interesting read.

The crucial point here is that the dialogue should ask and answer many questions about democracy, particularly our brand, to determine not only what will be most suitable for us, but also to forecast the fate of democracy. The same rigorous inquiry should be extended to social, economic, and environmental affairs. Then, the dialogue should lead us to a series of repositioning that could create the country of the future.

4.0 CONCLUSION:

This countrywide dialogue that we are calling for in various names that have tended to raise unnecessary debates, can be used to go beyond getting Nigeria out of the woods infested with mediocrity and insatiable scavengers. It all depends on how much sincerity, ingenuity, and commitment we apply to it. If there is enough of each, it is sound to expect a better rather than a splintered Nigeria.

The eviscerated high emotions at political independence, all the events of the "Biafra"-Nigeria war, and other significant societal fractures could be adroitly recreated and safely managed towards truly galvanising us into a united and purposeful country. The human mind is truly awesome.

Running this dialogue at the necessary standards is not easy. Sufficient time and other resources must be devoted to it. Nigeria's very best, functioning at their undistracted best, should be its facilitators.

All our undesirable situations have arisen from untamed human nature. Human problems are the most difficult to contain or reverse. An approach that gives a greater, properly sampled majority the sense of participation has the best chance for success.

The evolution of human society dictates a very long-term, visionary posture on digesting the returns from this dialogue. The increasing rifts, or disconnects, or dichotomies, arising from various degrees of inequitable participation and distribution of outcomes between governments and the governed in democracies across the globe should attract more than a passing mention. Can Nigeria generate a more responsive system of governance for humankind? To ignore this possibility is certainly to sell Nigeria short.

Today, there are uncharitable levels of disorientation, disappointment, and bitterness, all accompanied by fear blind with rage. These are daily expressed in increasingly disheartening ways. For this dialogue to bring enriching possibilities, it must be executed with undimmed eyes, unattenuated all other senses, unmuffled conscience, and unhackneyed minds.

History, our heritage, and our potential challenge us.

WANTED: *Founders of a modern and truly progressive Nigeria.*

Chiamalu Ofobuike
16 December 2004

7

THE SPLASH

Since our committee meeting at Gumut's was for 4:00 p.m., I took the day off that Tuesday to attend to the makeshift fishpond from converting the small swimming pool in my place into a fishpond. The pump of the mechanically-drained pool had failed. A standing pool of water from the rains resulted and became a breeding place for mosquitoes, frogs, toads—quite some nuisance, especially at night, when the frogs and toads engage in choir competitions and the mosquitoes are out in numbers on sustenance hunts.

Following Osagie's advice, we stocked the pond with catfish and bought feed for the fingerlings. Later, my family researched fish feed and came up with mixtures that seemed to suit the fish. We all took to the effort, and the rush to feed the fish at the appointed times amazed me.

As the fish grew older, they fascinated us with their habits. We welcomed the drastic reduction in the mosquito population, but we could not explain how all the frogs and toads disappeared to give us quiet nights. This was explained to us as being from the activities of the carnivorous catfish.

Osagie advised we drain all the water before removing the fish. After breakfast, my teenage son and I set out to rent a gasoline-engine-driven pump from Kenyatta Market, the hardware and building materials market in Enugu. The fifth pump dealer we interacted with was more knowledgeable and accommodating, so we rented the pump from him. The pump came with an operator at extra cost. These days, even one's shadow needs close shadowing;

personal standing has lost all meaning to scam and sham in society's strata.

We returned home with the pump and its operator before nine a.m. By eleven o'clock, the pond water was gone. Everywhere at the bottom were fish, jumping and sliding around. Fun time!

School was out, so my family, the pump operator, and I went into the pool to catch the fish with our hands. "Chaka," our Alsatian dog, also jumped in, and was the first to taste the fish, as he firmly pinned one of them with his front paws and picked it up with his teeth.

"No Chaka! Stop Chaka!" froze him. I pulled him out of the pool and leashed him, the fish still flapping its tail in his mouth. His swift actions scared the operator, who had been worried about Chaka trailing him.

Occasionally, somebody fell among the fish and had to quickly scamper back up. What a splashing event, people and fish struggling for dominance in what could be upgraded, with a little imagination, to multiple wrestling matches. My daughter, who was seven, kept searching for the fish she nicknamed "ocho okwu,"[10] because she claimed it always jostled the smaller fish away from the floating pieces of food. For about five minutes, we caught no fish, because they slid out of our hands. We then used baskets with better success. At the end, we collected 158 fish that altogether weighed 297 kilos.

Not too terrible for a first amateurish try in months of growing time. As we didn't have enough freezer space, our friends, relations, and the operator got some live fish. Still, we had to smoke some later, another amateurish effort.

The operator and I finished cleaning up and loaded the pump and hoses back into the car, but we had to wait for my son. After three minutes, he still was not out. I blew the horn of the car and screamed at him to come out.

After two more minutes, I again blew the horn, screamed at him, and muttered, "He's either on the phone with girls or he's perfuming himself."

"Oga, go easy on the boy," the operator said.

I cast a stern look at him. He was about three years older than my son. A half-grin was on the right side of his face, his left hand was rubbing the side

---

[10] ocho okwu, bully.

of his face in slow up-and-down strokes.

"As the young cock grows, Oga, it spreads its wings. Easy on him, Oga."

We laughed. I was glad that he didn't explicitly say that the cock spreads its seeds.

When my son and I came back from returning the pump, the rest of the family was cleaning the fish. We joined them. This was less fun and messier. With that done, the queue for showers formed. My wife later made some fish fries that turned out delicious.

As we ate the fish, everyone felt a sense of accomplishment—being able to grow what you eat. However, I struggled with the thoughts about what had happened to all the toads and frogs.

§ § §

Our committee of three arrived at Gumut's by 4:00 p.m.; we had notes on our thoughts. I was the last one to arrive. Before I sat down, I preempted Nduka, while standing on my toes to give presence to my average frame.

"Nduka Ude, if you make any wisecracks about a fisherman, I'll ram my fist down your throat."

"Hey, Chuks, what's wrong? Why are you so uptight? Swear, the truth and nothing but…"

Nduka looked at my clenched fist and paused.

"You just took the shine off the compliments Gumut and I want to pay you on the fish. You don't smell fishy. Seriously, though, thanks for the fish. Adaoma will treat the kids and me to the specials of the Igbos by the rivers—"ofe nsala"[11] and pounded yam. Chuks, you gave us so much. How much fish did you harvest?"

"About 300 kilos."

With a rare, big smile on his face, Gumut said, "Wao! That's a lot of fish. No wonder you gave us so much. Thanks."

"Yeah, too bad your wife is not from the UK; otherwise, you would've been chained to 'fish 'n' chips for lunch, luv?' for a while. Why don't you and

---

[11] Ofe nsala, Igbo fresh fish soup.

Osagie form a cooperative; he supplies vegetables and you, the fish?"

Nduka stopped at that on seeing my raised, clenched fist. Gumut just shook his head and then invited us to sit around the dining table. We harmonised our lists of suggestions, and called Danladi, Olu, and Osagie for their inputs. Finally, we made a tentative financial budget to which the six of us were to contribute. We informed Chiamalu that the group had decided to be involved in the presentation.

Gumut was to take care of computer preparations, while ensuring great content. Nduka was to work on security matters; Danladi and Olu, on lighting and such matters; and Osagie and I on publicity and entertainment. A "win if you come early" package was adopted to encourage punctuality. "Okwukwe Afrika" agreed to pay for some of the additional costs, including for moving the event to the largest hall at the venue. Uhuru Hut was off until after the presentation.

Okwukwe Afrika, Gumut, Danladi, Olu, and the video people were ready at ten o'clock, half an hour earlier than scheduled. They test ran the entire setup on the generator. Surprisingly, minutes later, about fifty people had arrived. Of course, those who arrived at the venue before eleven o'clock picked up their giveaways, for which we made generous provisions.

Fifteen minutes later, the lights dimmed sufficiently for the coloured lights to become visible. Gumut turned on the slide show for this period—a fifty-minute, segmented documentary of sorts on the bedevilling transition.

The first segment was on pre-colonial Afrika: picturesque shots of the continent's diversity, relative peace, and beauty. There were close-ups of exotic flowers, peaceful village scenes, and battles featuring knives, spears, bows, and arrows. The slides on conflicts ended this segment.

The next one depicted the arrival of disruptive visitors to Afrika, starting with shots of Afrikans curiously watching them as they set foot on the continent. Slides of their receptions followed and included inquisitive, but peaceful, scenes that were less in number than the scenes of resistance battles. The battle shots clearly demonstrated the killing power of guns and lancing from horseback. It ended with shots of deceitful peace meetings.

The third began with shots of trade caravans to the Sahara Desert and to the coasts. Pictures of long lines of shackled Afrikans taken into slavery, journeying north towards the deadly Sahara Desert and south towards the coast, followed. Then, there were shots of the accommodation of the visitors depicted by schools, prayer houses, road and railway construction, and emerging western-style urban areas. Shots of various mines—uranium, gold, diamonds, copper, coal, tin, petroleum rigs, bauxite, cobalt, and others ended this segment.

The series continued the unspoken story with shots of early African achievements in foreign lands. Shots of commercial, political, and social activities in Africa came next. There were sequential shots of Nigerian earlier nationalists. Then, the London pre-independence conferences and Independence Day in Nigeria and the handover ceremony were next. Chronological shots of all Nigerian Heads of State followed. Finally, the shots of protests against fraudulent political elections over the years concluded this segment.

The fifth contained shots of Nigerian news headlines and pictures on corruption and investigating panels, the "Biafra"-Nigeria civil war, and the changes of governments.

The sixth focused on general decay: shots of headlines and pictures of public institutions in steep decline—The Nigeria Airways, Railways, ECN-NEPA-PHCN, P&T-Nitel-Nipost, terribly bad roads with high negative impacts, secondary school classes of over 100 students in a class, tertiary institutions in deprivation, strikes, and closures, and others. Sample fuel lines from across the country featured. Unexplained deaths or murders closed this section.

The seventh and last segment was a fast-paced selection from previous ones and a few additional shots, emphasising rapid summation for a final impression.

The slide show was laced with Afro-based music Gumut had selected. The last segment had various drums and other percussion instruments, which started softly and grew in intensity and complexity to end the slide show in a deafening, big bang.

Lighting effects were unmatched. Shafts and various other shapes of light of changing colours and intensities filled the space in mesmerising formations. Signals controlling the lights came from audience audio responses, the main speaker's microphone, and preprogrammed inputs, all of which sedated the audience. The hall being fully lit complemented the dramatic finish of the loud bang of percussion instruments.

The audience cheered enthusiastically at this conclusion, at minutes after eleven a.m.

Mrs. Akpata, from the podium, said, "Special guests; distinguished ladies and gentlemen. Our guest speaker, his friends, and Okwukwe Afrika welcome you to this occasion. Thank you so much for your punctuality. The topic, led by the inspiring Engineer Chiamalu Ofobuike is Upscale Countrywide Dialogue. We shall begin shortly."

The audience loudly applauded with whistling intermingled—perhaps, the whistling, because Mrs. Akpata looked and acted like a matured model. The lights dimmed and went into the slide show type displays, as she went off the stage to bring in Chiamalu.

The lights slowly brightened into a harmonised blend, anchored on a bright, reddish purple. At this illumination, visibility was such that faces could be clearly identified about a metre away. The security personnel stood by the sides and behind the audience and scanned the audience.

Mrs. Akpata walked to the podium under the spotlight and introduced Chiamalu. Whenever the audience audibly reacted or the speaker's voice was raised, the lights responded by momentarily brightening up and changing colours, but this response was dampened to avoid flickering distractions.

Chiamalu went into the presentation with a lot of control. Some of his emphases followed by pauses were amplified with the introduction of slight echoes to the last words. The combined audio-visual effects conditioned the audience and increased the understanding of Chiamalu's ideas. He was truly great, as he went into the body of the presentation.

"You tore yourselves away from pressing issues of living in our country today to be here to collaborate with others on what our only country, Nigeria, could become. Please, let's recognise those of you who had to drive or ride on public transport for hours on bad roads. We are encouraged by your willingness to get involved. We thank you very much for coming so punctually and in such a large number. I feel greatly honoured by being allowed to lead proceedings. Thank you.

"In topics like ours today, it's not the majority that counts. Often, it's not even the leadership or the celebrated classes of society that count. It's always those few who are strongly driven, even to the unconditional price of death, who make the difference—the positive difference in the lives of many, many other compatriots. We may therefore all wonder about how many of us here today will make it to the extra-distinguished league of such committed changers of a drifting society. There's no way of telling. Such rare characters come in differing outward appearances, but deep down within them, the raging fire for the common prosperity burns irrepressibly, energising and propelling their total being.

"The first thing in whatever they finally accomplish is often the clear identification of ideas. This is what we are all here to begin today. Please, we must first of all clearly understand that none of us, the organisers of this event, has all the answers. However, with some effort and luck, we may, together, effectively start the critical task of adequately defining some ideas and how to actualise them. Our topic, 'Upscale Countrywide Dialogue,' could also be phrased in other ways. One that quickly comes to mind is: 'A Modern and Progressive Nigeria.' This is direct to our aspirations. Most Nigerians strongly crave belonging to a country with a lot of positive relevance. Our not having such a global icon despite our potentials is the major point of concern. This is a big part of why we are here today, isn't it?"

The audience applauded.

"Then, 'Alternatives, Choices, and Options' and its implied decay trend is another topic that identifies why and how we find ourselves in our present circumstances. When we set out in life, we often have alternatives to select from. If, for any reason, we delay decisions, the alternatives regularly turn into fewer choices. Then, continued delay makes sure that those choices dwindle to options. Options mean limited choices.

"'Harvesting Precedent' is another good title, because it actually points to a rational approach to our search for a better Nigeria. It says that we efficiently review all relevant events of human history, then package and faithfully execute our selected programs to swiftly lead us to where we all want to be. We are everywhere in the world; assembling information should not be an insurmountable challenge. Yes, some of the things we shall talk about had earlier been sent as a memorandum to the concluded Political Reform Conference at Abuja, under the same title. That Conference ended so far away from the ideas in the memorandum.

"At least three compelling reasons exist for whatever is necessary to mend Nigeria. History tells us that people of Afrikan blood, scattered and often battered all over the world, need a respite in the existence of an African country with much respect in world affairs. Nigeria should be that country, if only because of all her abundance and flashes of excellence. Africa, the seemingly inexhaustible warehouse for labour and material resources, has supplied a good portion of the fuel that has driven this civilisation. But the continent has become the reference for undesirable human conditions— poverty, hunger, disease, ignorance, and bloodshed. All these came about because of persisting lack of good management of environmental, social, economic, and political affairs. Rightly or wrongly, Nigeria is often mentioned as the potential arrowhead for African affairs. The state of our country today hardly indicates that we have understood this challenge, talk less about confronting it. A majority of Nigerians want our posterity to proudly stand shoulder-to-shoulder or better with their global peers. This is important.

"Some think that the things we shall talk about are idealistic, because they ignore the hopelessness of our present reality. However, history tells us that idealism gives initiatives life, momentum, and durability. Idealism lifts the efficiencies of human endeavours and therefore dignifies us. The hopelessness of reality, on the other hand, is a two-edged proposition. The fully committed are challenged, while the unconvinced are discouraged. At the end of the day, though, we hope that superiority of reason prevails. I believe that we should all give any genuine effort at mending Nigeria all that we've got, be they our last breaths. Kindly be gracious enough to choose any of the titles I just mentioned that you feel most comfortable with, and let's get into the thick of our affairs today."

The applause of the audience caused the lights to react in emphasis. Chiamalu was delighted. He swung into the first sentence of the memorandum about great and progressive nations or countries not born at tea or cocktail parties, full of assurance and passion. He briefly went through the histories of the G-8 countries that are now visible global leaders, pretty much followed the memorandum's outline, and held the audience spellbound.

Guiding slides could not have been better. Major points were clarified by the pictures of the events at the times under reference. The selections comprised events varying from the simple and often ignored to matters of flaming headlines. And, as they were lined up, they formed clear, logical, and compelling arguments, because they complemented one another so well. They touched the consciousness of the audience in its diversity.

The ending statement on the last slide, 'Wanted: Founders of a modern and truly progressive Nigeria,' was instantly treated with reverberations that were amplified on Nigeria. The statement was quickly replayed twice more to end the presentation in a tumultuous standing ovation, which was acknowledged by the hall being fully lit for as long as the ovation lasted. Chiamalu and Mrs. Akpata responded by clapping for and bowing to the audience.

Thereafter, the lights dropped to their previous levels and Mrs. Akpata spoke.

"Thank you, thank you, thank you very much, distinguished guests. Do you think that our inspiring guest speaker, Engineer Chiamalu Ofobuike, deserves another round of applause?"

The shouts of affirmation and another more enthusiastic ovation rented the air.

Mrs. Akpata said, "Well, well, well… How about that for a way forward? Thank you, thank you, thank you very much for coming. We have time for ten comments, questions, and the like. Those of us from farther away need to get home in daylight. You know the challenges to travellers these days. Before we get to the ten speakers, I have some information for you. We have some refreshments in the room just across the hallway from our location. You will find copies of the booklets containing the base paper on this presentation just outside the exit doors. Included in the booklets are some blank pages, additional to wide margins on both sides of each page, for your further notes. Please, you can each take a copy.

"After you've gone over the base paper and have fully digested the entire presentation, kindly contact Okwukwe Afrika with your views and any roles you can play in advancing the whole proposition. We will broadcast this session over the TV and radio soon. Kindly alert others who may like the broadcasts, which will be advertised in advance. Our contact information is in the booklet. We all see the need to follow up on today's program as soon as we can. Distinguished ladies and gentlemen, your feedback will dictate our next actions. We are ready to arrange another get-together in the format that your responses suggest. We look forward to hearing from you soon. Again, thank you very much for taking the time to be here punctually and in such a large number. The arrangement for taking the comments is that we hear from ten speakers and then the guest speaker will respond to all of them in one stretch. This may save time. Now to the speakers."

What the ten speakers said related to the modalities for the national conference.

The hall was thrown into complete darkness to heighten the effect of the spotlight on Chiamalu, as he walked to the podium.

"Thank you very much for the comments, suggestions, and questions. They indicate our concerns about the directions of Nigeria. The time is long overdue for more than concern. Please, let's do ourselves some favours. We should all rise, shake hands with, greet, and introduce ourselves to the person directly to our right, in front of us, to our left, and behind us. We should do these most earnestly—truly listen to and take in the introductions."

The hall was fully lit with clear light for this. Voices rumbled as if from a distant marketplace. Some people sitting at the edges of the audience attempted to get the security people involved, but only met statue-like figures that glared back at them. As the introductions ended, the lights dropped back to their former levels.

Chiamalu said, "Now, we should all feel more comfortable from knowing those seated around us. I noticed that the privately maintained security people around us kept to their jobs. Perhaps, they are telling us, 'Do your job; I'm doing mine.' We stated at the beginning that we do not have all the answers, but that, collectively, we can define some remedial ideas. It is after this has been done that we can then focus on action. By all of us being here, the bubbles of air generated at the bottom of the murky pond have made it to the surface. From all the people who have been groaning about our damning situations, genuine concern has brought us together today. It will be presumptuous of me to begin to respond to your comments now. Please, digest what you've heard today, clearly form your views, evaluate your readiness to commit to your ideas, and then contact Okwukwe Afrika. We shall all take it from there.

"Remember, our first objective is to get us thinking together. These comments and suggestions will also deepen our thoughts. Getting to the next stage will necessarily be a second self-screening that will lead to more screenings before we arrive at the few that are good enough for the job. From all that happened today, the more thoughtful among us will realise that the histories of the interactions of Afrika with the rest of the world, Nigeria with the rest of Africa, and Nigerians with themselves will be helpful. These histories can provide us seemingly insignificant, but potent, pointers for creating and sustaining delightful change in Nigeria and throughout the magnificent, yet maligned, continent. Always keep our final goal in mind."

"Wanted: Founders of a modern and truly progressive Nigeria," was replayed thrice, with all the sound effects louder than before, to neatly end the program.

The audience went wild with excitement, and they again applauded with another standing ovation. The hall was this time thrown into complete darkness while they did so; this encouraged them.

When the cheering died down, the hall was fully lit with clear light. We shut down the venue.

8

THE SPLASH BACKWASH

Chiamalu had declared Sunday at 2:00 p.m. Uhuru Hut 'Code Eight.' Curiosity made us extra-punctual. He was waiting at the reception, his eyes frisking each of us, as we arrived to his bear hugs and firm, oscillated handshakes.

"I have no words for Wednesday. You fellows, just too much."

Nduka said, "Yes, yes, Professador, save all that for later, okay? You declared 'Code Eight'; let's get to it."

As we approached our location, we saw the figure of a woman in our normal seats. We exchanged curious glances. On hearing us, she quickly stood up and turned to face us.

"Mrs. Akpata," we shouted.

She beamed a broad smile, moving towards us to shake our hands. She added hugs to her greetings of Gumut, Danladi, Olu, and Osagie, the people she had worked more closely with on Wednesday. Nduka scratched his head, his lips puckered.

Chiamalu, his face still lit up, said, "This is Danladi, Olu, Osagie, Gumut, Chuks, and Nduka. Gentlemen, Mrs. Akpata. Again, names to faces."

"Oh, Chiamalu, why the formality? I'm Nkem; we should all be on first names, after your terrific Wednesday program."

"Hey, hey, hey! Just a minute there. You were key to the whole thing, Mrs. Akpata."

"*Nkem, Nkem.* Please."

"Okay, Okay, *Nkem.* Without you and Okwukwe Afrika, there would be no presentation. We enjoyed working with you all."

"Chiamalu, this is a *terrific* Code Eight. Right, fellows?" Nduka said.

Nduka, sitting next to Nkem, had leaned towards her to make shoulder contact as he spoke. For a fleeting moment, Nkem raised her eyebrows.

"I hope you were not offended by my shoulder contact, Nkem? I just wanted to make up for the hugs Chuks and I missed when you greeted us a few moments ago."

We laughed, but I thought that she was dealing with the meaning of Code Eight.

"After all your hard work on Wednesday, I should begin to pay back. So, when Mrs. Akpata and I, sorry—Nkem—and I spoke over the phone yesterday, I invited her here today. Unfortunately, she has another engagement at six. She may have to leave early," Chiamalu said.

Olu took control. "Yes, today deserves to be different after the build-up and after what appeared to be a successful outing by Professador. Nkem, you're the foremost expert in such matters here. How did you rate the presentation?"

"Wow, Wednesday's event was unprecedented. Everything perfect: content, packaging, delivery, ambience, conclusion, and absorption, all just right. Fantastic! It ranked very high, if not top, among our successful events. The attendance was matchless in size and punctuality. The slide show put the audience in just the right mood. Audio-visual effects sustained that mood. Chiamalu ended it all with suspense and challenge. We've been getting compliments and promises of feedback. I had to jump on the opportunity of meeting you all in a more relaxed setting. What amazes me is that you're all engineers. One often doesn't expect engineers to be so aware, articulate, and versatile. You've got me. It's going to be difficult to get rid of me."

Impulsively, we applauded her. Waiters focused on us. Nduka waved at them to come for our orders.

"Look, give us your very best today. Don't ask me what that is, because I don't know. First, get the beautiful woman the best of her heart's desires.

Fellows, today's bill is on me."

As Nduka talked, he winked at us. He was managing our contributions for the presentation; the bill would come out of them, but we also knew Nduka.

Osagie said, "On Wednesday, I was more in the back with Nkem's people, attending to the gate, tables and booklets, and the refreshment centre. From those locations, I observed two events worth recalling. About the middle of the slide show, this high-level government functionary arrived with three armed police officers as escorts. Some of the people from Okwukwe Afrika and some guests recognised him and were bowing and genuflecting to him. On their getting to the hall entrance, two of our female security personnel pleasantly, but firmly, stopped them from entering the hall with guns. They told him to leave an officer with their guns outside the hall, while they would go in with him to ensure that the other two officers sat next to him in his preferred arrangement.

"I moved closer to them. Oh, the man was furious at first, but he quickly calmed down, because the most senior police officer nodded at him. They quietly, but reluctantly, obeyed the order and were led into the hall. The most junior officer stayed in the corridor with us, holding the guns of the two that went into the hall with their Oga."

Gumut said, "That served him right. These government people always behave like disoriented gods, full of self-importance. They consistently attend events late to be noticed instead of setting punctuality standards. It felt good seeing him obey someone else's instructions for a change, didn't it, Osagie?"

"Yes, Gumut, it did, but I wasn't praying for conflict. The other incident was at the end. The audience surged almost uncontrollably towards the exits. I couldn't imagine the people rushing to the refreshments; they appeared better disciplined for that. I was so relieved when it became clear that the rush was for the booklets. The Oga came out of the hall grinning. He personally picked up a booklet. I didn't care about whatever he did with it. After all, the material had made it to the Political Reform Conference at Abuja. The most senior police officer winked at the one with us; the fellow picked up three booklets. 'Professador has done it again,' I gloated."

Nkem said, "Yes, my people also reported that rush. I can't stop admiring all the refreshing innovations you brought into it all. The only regret I have now is that my husband is away on business; otherwise, he would have been here with me to meet you all. Oh, I'd love to meet the lucky women who are your wives."

If her husband had accompanied her, Chiamalu would have declared 'Code Nine,' indicating that he was inviting two guests.

Chiamalu sat up. "Nkem, you and your people were just unbelievable. I felt so humbled and encouraged. For once, I was so driven by the opportunity of working with dedicated and efficient compatriots."

Danladi said, "Professador, remember you're the inspiration. We, just 'picking our small battlefronts, giving them the much we could.' The young security women reminded me of Gadhafi. He once visited Nigeria with only female security personnel, who used all their weapons to ward off threats. They could've been pretty sharpshooters from any position, deadly with exotic weapons. I wonder what message he sent to us with that."

"Never mind whatever that message was; didn't his people beat up and chase out Nigerians from Libya later? The implications of those actions are still worth worrying about."

"Right, Gumut," Osagie boomed.

Our orders arrived with surprises. The Uhuru Hut manager and two of his assistants led the waiters.

Chuka, the manager, said, "Hello, Mrs. Akpata. You're here too? Oh, I see... your Wednesday event. Otherwise, these are our special Sunday regulars, never in the company of women. Any way you look at it, you're a woman among women, very special. It's easy to make exceptions for you. That your Okwukwe Afrika is making people think more about the purpose of life. You're all welcome, please."

He shook hands with us as the waiters placed our orders on the table.

"My assistants and I were there on Wednesday and we so enjoyed it that when we learnt that you were here, we thought we should say hello. We didn't know that Mrs. Akpata was here too. 'Ogbuefi'[12] Ofobuike, you were truly great. Everyone identified with all you said. The whole package was wonderful, Mrs. Akpata. Our feedbacks are ready. We look forward to hosting some of your events, Mrs. Akpata. Your bill is on the house; that's the little we can do now. Thanks for coming; please enjoy yourselves."

We thanked him and his assistants before focusing on the deliveries.

"Nice fellow, he works very hard to maintain this place and it shows," Chiamalu said.

"Nkem, are those what you ordered? A small bowl of salad and a little fish pepper soup cannot be the best of your heart's desires. Oh, I see…You know best, it shows," Nduka said.

Our laughter lasted for a while before Nkem gently tapped Nduka on his hand.

Olu said, "Actually, what could our earliest 'freedom fighters' have done to stave off all this mess we are now in? They were dealing with many alien forces, which they did not fully understand, and the rest of our people were not that aware of the world at the time, having been so methodically disorganised by invasion experiences. Communication and travels then were quite problematic too."

"Oh, Olu," Gumut said. "They could have done plenty. First, if the lead cow of a herd stumps up the mud at the bottom of the stream, the rest of the herd have to drink filthy water. A good herder makes the whole herd drink from the stream, while standing on its shores.

"Many of the features we complain about today can be linked to examples some of them set, very many uninspiring activities. We must honestly ask whether some of them actually had enough preparation and faith in themselves and in the overall cause they were after. Professador called attention to it in the entrepreneurship paper: 'impatience, lack of enabling following… fragmentation into ethnic or regional enclaves through appeals to transient sectional interests,' I believe. Now, we face the 'spectre of polarisation.' The Research and Development wings of those earlier movements should have done

---

[12] Ogbuefi, provider of cows for feasting the people.

a lot more on anticipating problems and their enduring solutions after the victory. Normally, the victorious has some control over subsequent events."

Danladi said, "Missed opportunities have remained very costly. Each of them, with some sterling leadership qualities; forget they finally focused on enclaves. As humans, each also had limiting personal flaws. Maybe the effects of all those personal failings could have been somehow reduced by their staying together, focused team. Today would have been better."

"I agree with both of you," Osagie said. "There were many obvious programs that could have been urgently pursued. Breaking down ethnic barriers should have come first. Encouraging inter-ethnic marriages and related Afrikan traditions, for example, could have been a good beginning. Traditional Afrikan marriages get families and communities in positive partnerships. Such pursuits, over time, could have helped."

Danladi, leaning back and grinning, told him, "Recall what Elder Amadi told us about Civil Service? Discipline and service. People lived, worked, in places different from their own. Look at what we've done to all that; balkanisation into states that started just before the civil war; 'federal character' malaise; indigene-outsider or -settler obsession. What happened to the respect for public property our ancestors strictly maintained? We shamelessly outdo the Europeans we often blame for our woes in Africa."

Nduka said, "Something like affordable housing estates could have helped, if mixed settings resulted. The lingering Afrikan community spirit is still evident enough. Whenever a family rejoices or grieves, we find that their co-tenants and other neighbours assist in making the occasion what it should be. Often, the co-tenants and others travel to the affected family's village to do that well. What better way is there for promoting understanding? The fields for other social interactions would have increased at closer quarters."

I asked, "What about what children are taught? We had the freedom to change the syllabuses to correctly emphasise more of our history. We had educationists who could have put such packages together before or soon after independence."

"For global relevance, the true versions of Black History should have been included, the true versions," Olu said.

"My husband always talks about the government secondary schools of his time," Nkem said. We eagerly focused on her. "In those years, such schools catered to the total development of students who enrolled on merit from all over the country and from bordering African countries. He also emphasised inter-school sports and debates that took them to other parts of the country where similar schools were located. That improved the perceptions of young people; promoting awareness, togetherness, I imagine. My husband often bemoans what has become of his dear Government Secondary School."

Olu said, "Nkem, all those schools suffered the same fate, more or less. A good program from exchanges by both sides after the civil war was the National Youth Service Corps. States were vying with one another in giving permanent employment to distinguished Corps members at the end of their services. Graduating higher institution students gleefully anticipated experience."

"Hmm..." Danladi grunted. "Look at what happened to the NYSC. Members refusing to serve in states where their safety is threatened. Backlog of batches. Also, write off employment in states of service."

Olu changed the subject. "Okay, let's leave the NYSC alone. The great strides in the GSM communication. Handsets are now everywhere; we're all talking, talking, talking across society's strata—from the Oga to the labourer and even the minor street hawker. Recall the Nigerian innovation called 'flashing,' where you punch in someone's number and then cut off your phone before the person answers. Most handsets record your number, date, and time of call. You do this when you're supposedly out of airtime and it alerts the receiving party to call you back, if that party wants to. Now, that's just the basic flashing. Some use codes that state number of flashings or rings and the intervals between them to interpret multiple flashings."

"Great points, Olu, but we've got to dig deeper," I said. "The inborn ingenuity of the average Nigerian is not in doubt, but what is terribly worrisome is our inability to put all that together to build that great country. The overriding points about GSM communication in Nigeria are its cost and performance. Yes, a lot of people now carry handsets about, but how many know their comparative costs? Often, it's about a status symbol, which makes things worse, because other results that follow are usually not identified. Picture that labourer who comes home to a hungry family, already with an eviction notice threatening them, with much less than he should, because of talking-talking-talking. Then, the unregulated marketing and operational gimmicks of providers further make it a costlier addiction. The Communications Commission should have been properly enabled to study global trends to come up with the specifics for us before operators were allowed in. The rush for engagement fallouts handed operators the market in our country without sufficient guidelines. The Commission has to play along in a miserable catch-up bid. The rest of us have to endure high tariffs and poor services—the system is easily overloaded, because of over subscription and other issues. Often, you can't get through when you need to most: peak working hours, even in emergencies."

Nduka said, "Yes, yes, the operators cancelled the number-of-rings gimmicks by introducing call music at the expense of the handset owner. Then, they introduced lower rates for post-midnight calls targeted at youths. Health experts have been complaining about this, because it deprives young people of good nightly rest they deserve. Rest for some of them may mean something else though."

I quickly said, "As compatriots, we remain vulnerable on all fronts."

"Well, there are some positives, I think," Nkem said. "Slowly but surely, social media are maturing. That's great. Some alternatives to mainstream media. Activism is gaining more channels. Will that help bring change? Time will tell. I hope so, because communicating this way is useful. The regulators will get better. Social media had a lot to do with the 'Arab Spring,' remember?"

We nodded to agree, as Gumut spoke. "Communications satellites that Russia launched for us during Obasanjo tenure, how are they doing?"

No one had answers.

Nduka said, "I was servicing my car yesterday and others were there too. We talked about electricity supply. This older man with us did not speak initially. He just watched and listened. When he finally spoke, we gathered that he was a retired engineer from ECN[13], our power company at independence. Oh, he was cynical. He was one of the patriotic young engineers who opposed the idea of damming River Niger to build substantial hydroelectricity stations. They even petitioned the authorities. They argued that to dam a river whose source was in another country for this purpose was not to our long-term interests. In its place, they suggested damming internal water sources to build smaller and similar plants tied into a loop grid. They cited the advantages of more national security in power supply, more stable supply, easier operations and maintenance from harmony, and reduced costs and pollution. Myopic political decisions then gave us the hydroelectricity power plants from River Niger. He was unhappy about all the problems that have dogged that execution. Some of them lost their jobs."

Osagie, head tossed back, said in a low voice, "We've all been paying dearly for that decision. In the meantime, ECN became NEPA[14], then the PHCN, and self-letting private holdings, without suitably addressing the persisting challenges."

Olu said, "What I've found debatable over the years are the excuses that they routinely gave for failures: reptiles on the lines, cannibalisation of installations, low water levels, over-flooded power stations, institutional debts, unauthorised connections, condensates in gas lines, and the big teaser – 'system failure.' Rains or mild winds cause blackouts. A lightning flash assures blackouts in many places. Phase outages and brownouts—the famous 'half current'—are normal experiences in these times. Utility companies elsewhere guarantee frequency variation ranges. A lot of misinformation."

Nkem said, "Most people wonder about what motivates those who cannibalise power installations and about who aids unlawful connections and debts."

I said, "I once interacted with the power people, as they did repairs in my neighbourhood, which was riddled with phase outages, brown-outs, frequent pops of the makeshift fuses on the transformer, dangling cables, and rationing. I requested for remedies and subtly inquired about the required inspection of

---

[13] ECN, Electricity Corporation of Nigeria.
[14] NEPA, National Electric Power Authority.

new structures before they were connected to the grid, to ensure good electrical works and load balancing. 'Those things you're talking about have been long forgotten. You're referring to the time white people were in ECN,' they replied."

Nduka, rubbing his palms, said, "Hey, someone cynically told me, 'Don't bother with generating sets. Just reorganise your life. For those occasions you must have electricity, just *see* the power people. You can even have a neighbourhood strategy for that. It'll be more cost-effective.' Seriously, power problems are becoming too embarrassing. Sections of towns, where more people live, can be without electricity for months—voiceless citizens who bear the weights of our top-heavy distribution of benefits. The usual eye service ensures power supplies follow high-profiled dignitaries and events around the country."

Chiamalu, more relaxed, said, "Remember the riveting amazement with which people watched the cable conveyor line deliver coal from Enugu to the thermal power plant at Oji River? There's still an abundance of coal here in Enugu and elsewhere in the country. The USA generates substantial quantities of electricity from coal-fired power plants. The expertise is available for doing so with reduced pollution. Since the malicious stripping of the plant at Oji River during the civil war and the ill-advised automation of the coal mines, both are now deader than dead. The buckets of the rope conveyor now hang up there as rusted homes for birds, lizards, and snakes. There's much local unemployment, and pensioners who spend their last years in degrading agonies."

I said, "It'll be idiotic to blame foreigners. The British left us a viable and upgradeable ECN—to preempt Danladi."

A brief laughter was accompanied by fleeting glances at Danladi, who only smiled back.

Nkem lightened the mood.

"Some family friends and their three young children visited the man's younger brother for the summer holiday overseas. On arrival, the man's brother picked them up from the airport. As they drove home, they ran into traffic. Vehicles were moving all right, but much slower than normal and usually with enough safety spaces in-between vehicles. People were being properly allowed to change lanes. After a while, one of the children shouted to their uncle, 'Uncle, we can go faster. Blow your horn. Don't let all those people jump in front of us.' As soon as they got into their uncle's flat on that hot summer day, the oldest child said, 'Uncle, please turn on all the air-conditioners to cool the rooms before they take light.' When we heard these stories of their holiday abroad, we laughed at first, but later on, wondered about what we are all doing to the minds of young ones here."

"Indeed, the conscious create and alter the subconscious, but often, the subconscious prevails," Olu said.

Osagie said, "The old fellow from ECN reminds me of my experiences at Ajaokuta Steel Mill. That project started in the 1960s and it's still to come into any production with billions in any currency sunk into it. I spent three weeks, on and off, to see if spares could be manufactured there. At the onset, it was decided that 85 percent of spares for the mill proper would be made on-site. A wise approach then, because steel manufacturing was a key performance index for economies. Attempts to establish the industry outside the First World were regularly frustrated through the supplies of spares. The other 15 percent were things like bearings, belts, and motors, because they were easily available from many global sources. Good thinking, right? Yes. We've never lacked good people. The curse is that they are continually undervalued and abused in favour of colourless and malleable people, who muscle themselves to the front of the 'demolition derbies.'

As you get there, more than three quarters of what you will see are these support facilities, which, by the way, includes a gigantic power plant and a long-completed administration block and staff quarters. These facilities were ready decades ago. Some are decaying from lack of use.

"When I was there, they had managed to make and correctly finish some automobile parts and other items from the support facilities, but there were no takers with substantial orders. Their costs were too high, because the work stock used for making them had to be imported instead of being produced by the mill. So, the engineers and others just sat it out while drawing their salaries whenever the subventions were available. I heard of great professionals who, for pitiful reasons—indigenes in opposition to outsiders, uncompromising professionalism, not belonging to the 'annihilation team,' 'federal character' rubbish—had to leave the place. If that mill had taken off on schedule, if the power situation were better, and if the many capable hands were well-utilised, what could the country have looked like today?"

Chiamalu said, "That's the point. What about the time value of all that money sunk in there all this time, more than half a century now? The interest on those alone should be able to sustain quite a few of our present local governments, if not states."

Nkem glanced at Chiamalu and stood up. Seven pairs of eyes massaged her frame—every bit in the right size and place, a light chocolate complexion that highlighted her teeth, and drilling eyes on an oblong face of gentle curves. She dug out a set of complimentary cards from her purse and handed one to each of us.

"Gentlemen, it's been a wonderful afternoon. My appointment at six requires some preps; I must leave against my heart's desire. I'm sure I can reach you all through Chiamalu. I find each of you an inviting challenge; I'll give it all I have."

None of us looked closely at the cards. Some of us inattentively slipped them into our shirt pockets. Chiamalu informed us that he had to drive her back to her place, as he had driven her to Uhuru Hut. We walked her to the parking lot and then waited for Chiamalu to come back.

We ordered refills. Nduka pulled out his card and scrutinised it.

"My card is for Adaoma. What about yours?"

All the cards had been addressed to our wives. Nkem had neatly written at the back, 'Hello, Mrs. (this or that),' using our surnames. We mused over it for a while; Chiamalu could possibly know more about it.

Olu said, "Hey, Gumut, how did you create all those slides? They were so many, far back in time."

"After Professador decided on his outline, we researched the themes. For some of them, I had an artist draw some pictures, which we otherwise treated. We went through many slides before we settled on the final sequences. There was time pressure. You and Danladi did a great job with the lights. I heard the manager of the place ask if you fellows would be interested in helping them out later."

What started as helping Chiamalu with a presentation was turning into a wind with a force and direction we could not predict. We had implicit confidence in ourselves. That was important. One felt the willingness of each of us to float with the winds.

When Chiamalu returned, Nduka asked, "Hey, Professador. What do you know about the complimentary cards your 'Mrs. Irresistible-Irrepressible' gave us? Have you looked at yours? Look at the back."

Chiamalu pulled out his card from his shirt pocket, looked at it closely, and then turned its back to see that it was addressed to his wife. He just raised his eyebrows and shrugged his shoulders.

I suggested, "There's nothing to worry about. She said we were not going to get rid of her easily. As a good organiser, she may want to get closer through our wives."

Chiamalu said, "I truly don't know how to thank you all for Wednesday. You went far beyond expectations. You spent some money along the way; what's my share of the contributions?"

"Hey, Professador, you worry too much. The important thing is that we strongly believe in the ideas. Whatever comes will be in proving them," Osagie said, and concluded the session.

As I drove home, full of thoughts, the *Face–off: consequences! Face–off: consequences!* ringing was trailed by slow-decaying echoes.

9

THE RASH FLASH

My mind ticked all night, as scrolling possibilities sacked sleep. I was tired, on a short fuse in the office on Monday. The usual lunchtime pick-up spluttered. I couldn't leave early; a project's due date threatened. I acted my role until after 7:00 p.m. before leaving.

The strange car parked by my place didn't catch my attention as I pushed open the slightly cracked front door. Three young men in our sitting room startled me when they jumped to their feet. One of them mentioned my name and I nodded. He quickly blocked my path.

"What's going on? Who are you? Where's my family? Who let you in?"

I didn't give them a chance to answer. I tried to shove the fellow out of my way. The tallest of them slightly lifted the side of his jacket for me to see the shiny butt of a handgun nestled in a holster by his side.

"I don't think you should do that."

They flipped out their Security Services identifications.

"Okay, what's on? What's wrong?" I firmly asked; no answer.

The tallest one pointed towards the inner rooms to indicate where my family was and then to the front door. One of the other two took my briefcase from me and they walked me into their car.

In the short drive to their office, my faculties amazingly came alive. 'Face-off: consequences' flashed through my mind. I quickly dismissed it and concentrated on other events, because I couldn't identify anything with the group that would interest the authorities. No clues came up. I next focused on my first request, on arriving at their office. Sure, much depended on the reasons for taking me there.

We entered the narrow, dimly lit hallway from an open reception. I heard some voices from a room at the middle of the hallway and recognised Nduka's voice, then Osagie's.

They led me into a room where I found the rest of the group sitting around a table. I was shown a chair and my briefcase was placed on the table next to me. The only person from the presentation who wasn't there was Mrs. Akpata. The men departed without a word.

"Welcome to the party, Chuks," Chiamalu said as he waved his hands at the rest.

"What are they charging us with?" I fumed.

"They've told us nothing. I was the first one here, then Osagie and Danladi, Chiamalu and Olu, Gumut, and now you. When I arrived, I saw them walking Mrs. Akpata down the hallway. Nobody has said anything to us," Nduka explained "You look tired, Chuks."

"Yeah, I know. I didn't have a great day at the office; last night was horrible. Are you saying that since you've been here, nobody has spoken to you? No reasons given for bringing us here?"

No one spoke; everyone just sat, eyes open. I took that as a hint.

I had been in my clothes all day. In no time at all, I became uncomfortable in them. The surge of energy that kept me going started to fade. I crossed my hands on the table, placed my head on them, and dozed off. I was later informed that I snored loudly.

A jarring bang on the table woke me up at midnight and for a few moments, I struggled to remember where I was. It was a stocky man—say, five-feet-ten-inches tall, in a dark grey suit, and not lacking in neutral manners—that woke me up.

"Good evening, gentlemen." Nothing about him indicated that he meant the greeting sincerely.

"Your families know you are here. They or anyone else will contact you only in emergencies. Switch off your phones and put them in this box. Follow me."

He hated the word 'please.' We rose, obeyed his instructions, and moved towards the door he held open.

He pointed at me and said, "*You*, wait here."

I stiffened up, raised my eyebrows, and looked at him. He nodded his head and grinned. As the others filed out, I saw more operatives in the hallway. I sat down and wondered about what was next.

Thirty minutes later, the door swung open and a short and hefty woman squeezed her broad figure through it. Behind her was one of the fellows who had brought me in. They quickly sat across the table from me.

Her voice rasped, "We've come to inventory your briefcase."

I slowly pushed the briefcase towards them. She motioned to me to open it. I did, and she emptied its contents on the table. They went through them; the fellow entered each item onto a sheet of paper. The woman motioned to me to sign it. I did, and they took my briefcase.

"Follow him."

Nice woman; frugal with words.

The fellow led me to the end of the hallway and we turned into a section with rows of small rooms, judging from the distances between neighbouring doors. He unlocked one of them and pointed into it. I entered the room and he locked the door.

Without charges, we are being held in isolation. The others were mentally ahead of me; even Nduka didn't say much while we were together.

Yes, the rectangular room was small. At the far end from the door, a porcelain shower tray was sunken into the floor and a massive toilet, encased in concrete, stood next to it. There were no external plumbing fittings and the push-button flush valve was recessed into the wall. The bad news was that there was no water.

A foam mattress was on the floor and it just cleared the toilet, and only left enough room to walk by. The ten-foot-high slab over the room held a recessed light bulb that left the room in next to darkness. For ventilation, there was an inch space above and below the door.

I looked at the mattress. From what the partial illumination allowed me to see, I used my outer clothing as bed sheet. It was easy to fall asleep.

At seven the next morning, I was woken by a rap on the door, followed by sounds from it being unlocked. Short on sleep and hungry, I observed someone deliver a plastic bucket of water and my breakfast.

I got up, washed up as much as possible, and waited for the water to dry before putting on some of my clothes. Breakfast time. Fork, knife, or spoon, forget those. I washed my hands again and ate my breakfast of the food in season. I flushed the toilet with the water left in the bucket. Twenty minutes later, someone knocked on my door.

"Get ready. You'll be coming to the front office in five minutes."

The eight of us, including Mrs. Akpata, were assembled at the same office we were in the night before. We were about to greet each other when the door swung open. Three operatives, one female and two males we had not seen before, entered the room and stood with their backs to the door.

The female, voice businesslike, said, "Good morning. We just obey instructions here. We are waiting for orders before we can talk to you. Your families know you are here. They are all well and going about their normal routines. For now, no member of your families or anyone else can meet with you. So far, you have conducted yourselves very well. Thank you."

"Pardon me, Madam," Chiamalu said, as they turned to leave. "Is it your practice to hold people this long without letting them know why they are here?"

"As I said earlier, you've conducted yourselves very well so far. Thank you."

They disappeared. Silence lasted a few minutes, during which we mentally queried what normal routines of our families without us meant.

Nkem, smiling broadly, said, "To make the best possible of the situation, why don't we take turns telling jokes? That should help."

We did that, and throughout the jokes and laughs, we stayed away from the project. In fact, no one mentioned anything about it during our time there.

Our lunch arrived, and two operatives watched us eat it, probably because it came with cutlery. After lunch, we settled into one of our worst times—waiting, not talking, not resting, but with our minds spinning. We experienced extended periods of cyclic restlessness and calm meditation, while assuming all imaginable positions on our seats and the table. Time passed ever so slowly.

Dinner was served at 7:00 p.m. and we were informed that we were to go back to the rooms at ten. The period between dinner and bedtime had the same features as the earlier part of the day. We repeatedly used the toilet attached to office. It had water.

Room service was upgraded a few notches in my room: a toilet roll and a plain cotton robe were supplied. Tuesday set the pattern for the days to follow. Each day, we got variants of promises of exchanges after instructions came in. We became more determined with the days.

At ten on Wednesday night of the following week, the tenth night, we were about to go to our rooms when three men came.

"Professador and team," one of them shouted.

He waited for our reactions. He must have been disappointed, because none of us reacted to those words in any slight way; we just looked at him.

"You posed quite a paradox in a few places. Your ideas are logical to the individual, but be warned. A few of your big-time lawyers came here; access was denied them. Your families are all right. Collect all your things. The bus waiting outside will take you home."

Through the ride in the bus, no one spoke. The atmosphere was charged with hair-raising anger and other emotions. The poor driver was terribly uncomfortable; he had to overcompensate with lavish courtesies. From accounts afterwards, each of our homes received us with ecstasy bordering on hysteria, but the rebellion in each of us muffled all that.

§ § §

All our homes were abuzz by Friday evening, thanks to Nkem, the 'irrepressible' one. She had agreed with our wives that our families would come to her place on Saturday for some outdoors activities. Our wives and children were busy preparing one thing or the other for the occasion.

We arrived at Nkem's place within a period of five minutes and the last family to arrive was Danladi's. Nkem and some of our wives specified where items were to be deposited.

The plot was large, with the modern but modest house recessed at the back to allow for greens, flower and vegetable gardens, and three cookouts adjoined by tables cast in concrete and topped with ceramic tiles. Sit-outs covered with insect screens were scattered around, the largest by the house. We praised Nkem on how functional and yet attractive the place was.

"Please, you are all welcome. The women planned this gathering for us to decompress from recent events. The women will organise things some more. Gentlemen, you can sit over there. We'll get you some drinks," Nkem said, and pointed at the large sit-out by the house.

We settled down and within minutes, drinks and some roasted nuts were before us. Nkem's four children eagerly showed our children their playthings and the areas special to them. They finally settled for a football game, with boys and girls in each team.

"Take a look at this," Nkem said as she gave Chiamalu a bunch of stapled sheets of papers.

Chiamalu glanced over the first sheet and gave each of us a set. They were sample responses to the presentation and read as follows:

1. Those who know more than the rest of us have repeatedly called Nigeria a failed state. I once read that an expatriate made a joke about Nigeria by saying that he intended to apply to the BPE[15] to rent Nigeria for a number of years. He proposed to give every Nigerian, regardless of age, five million naira annually during the life of his contract, if he was allowed to run Nigeria for profit. He also stated that he was prepared to meet all developmental targets reasonably set for him during the contract period. These statements, whether in joke or not, are enough to make a coward turn brave. Don't leave me out of the next gathering.

---

[15] BPE, Bureau for Public Enterprises that privatises public assets.

2. Remember the interview by James Eze of none other than the all-round scholar, Chinweizu—the only African with only one name I know, in *Sunday Sun* of November 20, 2005. There, Chinweizu threw some significant light on portions of Black History and related global trends. At the end, Chinweizu asked whether Black people would still be living in Africa, as landowners, 600 years from now. This should worry us, because of the role the world has assigned to Nigeria in Africa and how Africa is perceived by the world. We must urgently do whatever is needed to get Nigeria on the correct tracks for this responsibility. It's a huge task for everyone. I'd like to contribute my best. Please let me know about the next meeting.

3. I remember what Ogbuefi Ofobuike said about idealism and hopeless reality, but we must be realistic. Even General Gowon, the former military Head of State, was quoted as saying that there was no basis for unity in Nigeria. I agree, but we should first identify and correctly punish the cabal that made Nigeria painful and unworkable from the beginning before dividing the country. It we don't do this, members of the cabal will quickly destroy resulting units from dividing the country. Think about that.

4. The whole country is messed up in many ways. It will take some doing to change things, because our people no longer trust one another. It is good to keep the thoughts alive. Someday, some people may use them.

5. Ogbuefi Chiamalu Ofobuike was quite correct. I thank Okwukwe Afrika for the opportunity of listening to him. It is necessary for Nigerians to truthfully agree on who they are and how they want to live together. Trying to amend the constitution piece by piece does not harmonise solutions to all our problems. The better way is to propose and adjust solutions in one process, everything sorted out. I'm interested in future activities.

6. Every regime here has had its own version of a national conference, but the decay continues. It's about time the people took matters into their hands to run a conference of their choice. The first problem is how to get our people to come together to do so and afterwards, how do they implement their agreements? Things are getting worse by the day; we should try anything that can help everybody.

7. Nigeria can wake up the rest of Africa, but it is a big task. The whole thing will require honest and reliable people who truly love the country and our continent. Such people exist in Nigeria and elsewhere in Africa, but they do not make noise. The authorities will do anything, including murder, to quieten any of them who come out openly for positive change. This makes the whole thing difficult to start and finish. However, I'm still interested in attending future programs.

8. I've attended many of your programs, but this last one with Ogbuefi Ofobuike was great. The issues discussed were timely. I want to be one of those invited to follow-ups.

9. Ogbuefi Ofobuike makes a lot of sense, but how many Nigerians understand people like him? We have been wasting all our opportunities for greatness. For me, I am ready to do whatever is necessary for positive change. However, I must be very, very careful about the people I associate with for this purpose. There are too many traitors among us, because we are very greedy and therefore easy to buy off. I will like to attend the next meetings to see how things develop.

10. Congratulations! The program was very good. I've been waiting for such an occasion for a long time. I am ready to join any trustworthy group that will bring about the change Ogbuefi Ofobuike spoke about. All my contact channels are given below. I want the action.

11. The slide show before the lecture said it all. From day one, Nigeria has been making so much noise without achieving anything, despite her blessings. We are not serious. Ogbuefi Ofobuike is correct in saying that the time for action is now, but the problem, as I see it, is who bells the cat. I don't want to be used.

12. From the slide show and discussions afterwards, many of our problems were caused by people from outside. But, they did not have two heads. We should have been able to stop their designs, after independence. Yes, as life continues, it's never too late. I am a political scientist, although I work for a bank now. I volunteer myself for anything that I can do for positive change in our country. I enjoyed the program. My friends and I look forward to the broadcast. Please invite me for the next screening.

13. Thank you for providing enough security at the event. All the unsolved killings of high-profiled people and many others less known over the years are enough warning. Look at the number of innocent people who died during the events leading to the civil war and the war itself. We've seen wicked destruction of life and property over events the victims had no contributions to, time and again. Thank you for the information your program provided. It is only when the public is alerted that anything positive can result. Please, how can I become a member of Okwukwe Afrika?

14. Kudos to Okwukwe Afrika, Ogbuefi Chiamalu Ofobuike, and others who organised that relevant lecture. I hope that similar events are being organised in other geopolitical zones. The fires must be lit at as many centres as possible, to quickly smoke out all the rats that have been making life miserable for Nigerians and their posterity. Count on me for anything I can do.

15. All fallen heroes left clear challenges. Those still alive don't get the honour they deserve. The superhero, Fajuyi, ought to be more grandly remembered for his final loyalty and bravery, no matter how looked at. This is one of my points. Please let me know about the next meeting. I want to prove myself.

16. We have become tribes who are not ready to accommodate one another. In every tribe, there's infighting. Forget pretences. It is senseless to talk about a country. Okwukwe Afrika and Ogbuefi Ofobuike should concentrate their good talents on how to peacefully split the country. Forget this thing called Nigeria. It's a meaningless, artificial creation. It cannot last. If you don't agree with me, watch out for coming events.

17. Okwukwe Afrika and Ogbuefi Chiamalu Ofobuike, where have you been? I've prayed for the chance of joining some committed people who want to mend our country. I'm very capable in many fields— the very good, the very ugly, and the terribly bad. Trust me. In fighting these kinds of situations, you use every means. You must neutralise the ways of the enemy to beat him. You will need people like me.

18. It is necessary to concentrate on mobilising the people across all the divides our exploiters have created. I have some ideas on how to go about it. Traitors must not infiltrate the movement. How can we do this? I wait for the next event.

19. Every Nigerian needs a complete mental overhaul. A people get the leadership that they deserve and preserve. Look at our leaders. Some of them should be outcasts, going by our true Afrikan heritage. We have had so many conferences without any good results. What they have been doing with those conferences is like making a search party

for missing goods of the robbers who stole the goods. We must free ourselves. Keep me informed on coming events.

20. We must face reality. Nigeria is very complex and contradictory. Events in our history show this. Correcting things will be very difficult. The meeting was held in the South-East geopolitical zone. What are the people in other zones thinking about it all? Maybe, this kind of thinking should first be established throughout the country to convince Nigerians that any positive change will be to their lasting gains.

"Catalysts; don't you think?" Danladi said, after his reading.

Olu said, "The foremost catalyst is Nkem. She held up well in the last two weeks. As if to tell us something, she initiated this gathering. On top of all that, she provided us with this information from our presentation,"

"Her type shows up only once in a while," Nduka said.

Osagie said, "I just want to know, is there anyone here who does not feel like hitting someone or whatever with extreme violence?"

"I know and feel what you mean, Osagie. Satisfaction will go to only the party that retains the initiative. Full understanding is decisive."

"Yes, I understand what you're saying, Gumut," Olu said, "without resurrecting the chicken and the egg riddle from time. In talking about human affairs, we often say political, economic, and social affairs. Does this order assign importance? I ask, because our current situations dictate that we go from social through economic and then to political renewal. Our type of democracy, with politics of self-fulfilment the compulsive bounty hunt, destroys our social heritage and restricts our overall development."

Gumut, shaking his head, said, "Don't mention the word 'democracy'; there's no such thing here. Look at all what our recent 'selections' called elections gave us. Our so-called politicians interpret the cliché 'dividends of democracy' to mean: 'Develop your family, village, town, and possibly, your local government area, depending on what position you clawed out for yourself. The other people will have to wait until their daughters or sons grab political power for their own development.' We wonder why all the ruthless tactics are used in fighting for political offices. In a mixed society such as ours, this mind-set can only cause abuse, or at best, doubt."

Osagie said, "A more telling result of the oddities called elections is that we are slowly shifting some elections out of general elections' periods. People are sworn into offices before election disputes are settled. The Judiciary is overused and abused. Then, there is the unbelievable payment bonanza that the legislators approved for themselves that renders the pay structure in the country meaningless. That singular act destroys all ambitions for proper intellectual development and professional grooming."

Danladi said, nodding, "They blaspheme, 'To God be the glory' as they act 'To God be the mockery.'"

"A statement in the base paper about 'the whole world and the democracy syndrome and bandwagon' didn't get full airing at the presentation. The main issue is the future of democracy. Forget that it's the new front," I said.

Nkem came to the sit-out. "Pardon the interruption. The children have been served; it's time for you to eat."

"This is terrific. You put all this together in such a short time? Thanks a million, beautiful darlings," Nduka complimented our wives.

There was a variety of food with quite a few originating from faraway places. The women insisted on huddling around the service point to eat their own food and to more easily serve children requiring seconds.

We settled back into the sit-out to eat. We noted that the women carried on spirited discussions. My guess was that Nkem was telling them about our days with security.

Danladi said, "Olu, your social, economic, and political order. Yes, man started from being more socially helpful before going into economic and then political arrangements."

"That's correct, Danladi," Olu began. "This time around, we should very thoroughly review, as far back as possible, our interactions with ourselves, the rest of Africa, and the world for lasting lessons."

Chiamalu flipped through his notes, cleared his throat, and said, "In our presentation, we challenged Nigeria to come up with a responsive system of governance. Nigeria can surely do that by drawing from the well that is Africa, the cradle of humanity. There's nowhere on this planet that democracy has been close to what it should be. Purists for democracy stressed, over time, that those driven into politics by selfish motives in a democratic setting destroy democracy. They also pointed out that the worst shortcoming has been in the practices of representation that always led to inequitable participation and distribution of outcomes. This failing often resulted from the way all debates aimed at defining popular opinions are held. The people to whom democracy is supposed to belong are often ignored."

"That's not right," Gumut exclaimed.

Chiamalu continued, "Present stockists of democracy have cleverly mixed democracy with capitalism. If the truth must be told, capitalism derives its fuel from stressing the self-instinct. When dominant, this instinct rarely goes well with common prosperity. Massive capitalistic accumulations, far beyond reasonable comfort, are nothing but bleating animal greed that ruptures society. Humanity is still predatory, trampling on the weak everywhere. The short flare of the former Soviet Union was a glaring example. The people who operated that system mortally crippled it with the savage crudity of their exploitation of the human body and spirit. Self-instinct, as it were, tore that system into the shreds that became the combustibles easily ignited to produce the inferno that finally cremated it.

"Everywhere, the serial, traumatic harpooning of the psyche by all manner of pretenders is increasingly commonplace. Our own failure to follow progressive ways of living together threatens us more than we want to know or correct, because a few of us continue to disorganise the rest of us. Another challenge is whether we can learn from pluralistic countries that imploded recently to demonstrate that a heterogeneous society can truly endure, particularly on our continent. That's the least we must target for Nigeria."

A pause followed. I sensed the feeling of release that Chiamalu had at the end.

"That's a tough one, Chiamalu. We all fully understand the need, but it's going to be quite difficult to achieve."

"It's not easy, Olu. But there's no mountain higher. I clearly imagine the view from the top—so invigorating, instructive, and absolutely commanding. Nigeria could and should be up there," Chiamalu said.

We took a few moments to think about it all.

Nduka said, "Fellows, it's mountain climbing time. Which one of you has done that before? Osagie, you'll have to work hard on getting used to heights and, for your huge mass, we'll need heavy gear and truly strong ropes. Chuks, you'll follow the Professador like his shortened shadow. Danladi and Olu, you'll be right behind the Professador, mimicking him. Gumut, you'll be busy asking why there should be mountains in Africa. For me, I'm game anywhere, anyhow, any time."

Our prolonged laughter interrupted him until he said, "Seriously fellows, I believe that there can be no nobler challenge for anyone in our parts. But, the powerful local and global forces sustaining the *status quo* are numerous. They've been around for so long, their roots so deep into our society as to become self-regenerating. To neutralise them is comparable to the removal of a fully developed, malignant tumour, seated in the most sensitive area of the brain. The neurosurgeon for the task must have the necessary expertise and tools for the procedure. She or he must know all the pertinent facts about the tumour, the most probable results of physically disturbing that part of the brain, and the probability for overall success. This is a mouthful, but that's how I see the whole thing now."

Osagie, his voice slightly raised, said, "Yes, indeed. There can't be room for failure. Whatever is needed must be there."

Involuntarily, we applauded him. Our faces betrayed our inner emotions.

"Uhuru Hut tomorrow is at two. I will get there a little earlier with Nkem to set things up," Chiamalu announced.

We all engaged in a few games that involved everyone, including the children. There was about forty-five minutes of dancing to the music provided through the speakers in each sit-out. It was a free-for-all affair, which the children enjoyed very much. Overall, it was a relaxing time.

On our behalf, Gumut told Nkem, "We thank you very much, Nkem, for the most fitting great time that the children enjoyed. You all did a wonderful job of making the whole affair possible in so short a time. Indeed, we're glad to have met your family. My son told me that one of your children is his schoolmate. We look forward to meeting Mr. Akpata when he returns. We commend you for this beautiful and functional place."

Nkem replied, "All this while, I've been talking about the incredible presentation you fellows put together to elevate Okwukwe Afrika. Thank you so very much for that honour. I did not expect less from meeting your families. Everyone, fantastic. Please, for whatever reason, please feel free to drop by whenever you can, particularly the women; we have quite a bit to share. It's been a great pleasure having all of you here, and I have the women to thank especially."

The final departure formalities followed.

10

COUNTER STRATEGIES

"What's on?" I asked Danladi when we arrived at Uhuru Hut to find our normal location deserted.

Moments later, a waitress showed up and said, "Oga sirs, this way please."

The others, including Nkem, were in a charged discussion in a small conference room.

"You fellows are welcome. We are just going over our imprisonment by security," Nduka said.

The group was odd in some ways. How could we all hold back on discussing that experience and yet harbour so much resentment?

Olu said, "That *Professador-and-team* bit was supposed to shock us, was it? I hope they got our message."

What followed next further educated me on the complexity of humans. Tables slammed, chairs kicked, and the floor stomped; some bodies ultimately vibrated excitedly, as we recounted our experiences with the security people. We learned that lawyers from Okwukwe Afrika, and three others for Chiamalu, Danladi, and Osagie respectively had come and were turned back.

After a while, Nkem said, "Gentlemen, the whole episode could have been a kind of mental stressing designed to indicate their capabilities. I've not sufficiently understood the bit about our constituting some paradox in some quarters. Perhaps, the critical issue *now* is: what's next?"

Olu said, "Since the security people adopted this mind-game route, we should pay them back in kind. As much as we can, let's keep them guessing. What Gumut said yesterday about retaining the initiative is quite important."

As Chiamalu prepared for his note taking, I noticed his raised eyebrows and thinned lips.

Danladi sat back. "First, I believe we should clearly spell out our main objective. A deep-searching national dialogue involving every component ethnic group. Results—full precedent harvest for lasting progress. The world is getting more connected, yes. We therefore determine our needs, express them in relation to this world, and bargain with our relevant assets. Foreigners should have nothing to do with this; what's their stake? Forget the blame game. Look at what we've done to ourselves so far."

Olu said, "Danladi, that was precise. What are the assets? Vibrant, youthfully skewered population; rich, pragmatic, and diversified culture; large and varied real estate laden with values; climate that breathes life into everything, and eyebrows-raising stars scattered over the globe. What a waste. How do we maintain the initiative?"

We discussed at length and came up with some ideas.

We were going to play 'scared-and-disbanded.' Okwukwe Afrika and Nkem were to be seemingly no longer connected with us, but she was to visit her sister and her husband to clarify some issues.

Nobody should say anything about the group on the phone or by email. If a meeting of the group became necessary, a proper location and time would be used. We were to attend such meetings without our handsets or other such gadgets.

No more Uhuru Hut sessions, but we could attend other events there.

Our families were to be moved out of the country within three months. Those of us with foreign wives were to try to provide extra accommodation for the others, if needed and possible.

An organisation, Turn Around Nigeria Now and Associates (TANNA), was to be quickly created to drive the project. Individuals, institutions, and organisations that render selfless help would be the associates. TANNA was to be national in composition and character, without losing efficiency. Security and Intelligence (S&I) and Publicity and Communications (ICT) committees were to be initiated. We were to set up an interim structure for TANNA.

Fundraising would start soonest and vigorously sustained, as a critical need.

A meeting with respondents from our presentation would be held the following week at a carefully selected location to cautiously recruit appropriate hands.

We were to urgently tidy up our personal matters in anticipation of the worst, as if we were going to the frontlines of a raging physical conflict.

Everyone sat back through some moments to review the decisions. Osagie left, and minutes later, returned with two familiar waitresses who brought our usual drinks and snacks, but more of Star beer. It was easy to sense the fusing of ideas and mutual strengthening of resolve.

As a final decision, TANNA, like vigorously sprouting mushrooms, would rise in all parts of the country within nine months, latest.

Tall orders, but they were in agreement with our mood. Nkem then left us.

At a point, Danladi said, "It must be clear. All strategies, their resulting events, are from counterstrategies directed at nature or man."

Olu clapped for him. "Strategies and ensuing events are derived from *counterstrategies*. Again, a good one to remember."

"How's that related to what we're talking about?"

Olu explained, "Very much, Gumut, very much so. Look, the parties that hurt us most now are our internal exploiters. The populace plan and execute for their individual good. To reach and hold their positions, the exploiters do all they can to undo the actions of the people with their own counter strategies. It's that simple, Gumut."

I said, "I see your point. We know that not even the most saintly gives up power and its privileges gladly. These privileges in our country are hardly saintly, to boot."

Olu said, "Examples are numerous in our lives today. Think for a moment. We gained political independence from Britain, but the British slipped in a phantom census that falsely raised the population of the north to go with it. Its results weaken us in many ways today. It's all human nature: exploiters always divert people's attention from what the people truly need by using clever distractions, not easily detected."

Osagie said, "Remember that we once had a proposal to sell petrol at different pump prices to commercial and private cars, some years back, and while the whole country debated how to do that, other things were slipped by us. An otherwise excellent, but later fouled, Structural Adjustment Program was one of them. The ongoing attempts to elongate the life of that junta were also pushed along."

Olu focused on Gumut. "Proposals for creating states or local governments always got us going. Funds for campaigning for states or local government areas that would bring more progress were squeezed out of the people. Some traditional rulers stayed in hotels in the process, against norms. Instead of state or local government creation solving our problems, it added more dimensions to the decay. While the campaigns raged, some unpopular programs were initiated or advanced. The military regimes that did the state and local government creations, starting from just before the civil war, used this particular counterstrategy to their advantage, particularly the extensions of the lives of their juntas. Gumut, it's that plain. Any ploy used to distract the people from their needs is derived from a counterstrategy."

Nduka said, "It will be interesting to emphasise some of the counterstrategies that our exploiters have been using against us. Before that, what's the main problem of the country?"

"That's easy enough," Gumut snapped. "The serious problems of Nigeria are caused by the present mind-sets of Nigerians, the human resource. Corrupted and impotent, we find that mountaintop impossible to reach. Frequent indulgence and indolence, both sustained by gross indiscipline, have given us the culture of impunity. These conditions worsen with time."

"That's right on, Gumut," Danladi said, head shaking, hands slapping the table. "A self-regenerating feature we often don't think of—anyone born in Nigeria within five years after or before 1960, who has lived all or most of her or his life here, has no experience of the promises of Nigeria at independence. They are now around fifty years in age. All they have known are chaos and decay; sham and scam, legitimate avenues for earning a living, stupendous living sometimes. They've learned that politics is not service but unlimited personal wealth creation, criminal thefts of the common wealth. The disaster in the education sector, the decline of discipline and standards in our homes, worsen matters. What can we fairly expect from them?"

Osagie said, "There was a notable case somewhere in Imo state involving the chair of a local government council during one of those 'selections.' The youths picked their candidate and dared all the godfathers and kingmakers to change their choice. They were unyielding against all efforts to bribe, cajole, or intimidate them. They took the offensive by openly declaring that all sorts of bad things would happen if their candidate was rigged out. The youths monitored the voting very closely and quite visibly. In the end, they won, as the true results of the voting were accepted. That gave victory to their candidate."

"That was splendid," I shouted.

Osagie said, "The point is: where are our celebrated and decorated political scientists? They ought to have noticed that, analysed it, and written to publicise it, as a way of pushing for positive change in our so-called democracy. Their inactivity only encouraged the *status quo*, to say the least."

Gumut barked, "Why are you surprised, Osagie? If they spent their time and energies doing that, who would then be jostling for all the hollow titles, contracts, or posts? Who would be holding the clinics on 'guts bashing,' which some of them do without dignity?"

"Correct, Gumut," Osagie said. "Stories confirm this as what some of our professors are professing and our doctors, doctoring in these institutions; then, galloping carryovers. In fairness, that activity is popular national pastime confirmed by Nduka's reactions to General Malu's statements—remember? Professors and doctors in schools, first and foremost, moulders of young minds, bodies, for new directions."

Danladi eagerly said, "Not calling attention to that instance, a powerful self-regenerating feature of our bad political culture."

Our discussions on the counterstrategies of our exploiters led to the identification of the following:

1. Keep the people divided and distracted so that they don't come together to fight for their rights.

2. Ignore all barriers we've set up to divide the people; we have a common interest to defend at all times.

3. Use any available means to cover our tracks; never mind what those turn out to be, as long as they are effective.

4. Don't let age or commitments overwhelm you, sustain a strong presence in the corridors of power.

5. Be one of the first to get to information on developments; don't lose your touch with the media.

6. Whoever dares to challenge the system must realise the unforgettable price involved.

7. If you haven't done so, make friends in faraway places, who will facilitate your welcome by storing enough irresistible 'goodies' in their financial institutions.

8. This is a highly exclusive club that thoroughly screens membership. You're unseen, but you're perfectly in touch with one another. Keep the hotlines open, and there're events that provide good cover for any required meeting. To blow our cover is to court disaster.

9. Infiltrate and frustrate any movement or organisation that's likely to cause problems for us. You must be successful here.

10. Remain socially acceptable, economically buoyant, and politically relevant.

11. Always drag out attempts to uncover our tracks. It's obvious what time does to people's memories.

12. Disagreements among us must be handled tactfully. You never fight to the finish, nor do you do or say anything that will unveil us.

13. General insecurity or terror can be effective, but touchy. Their use must be carefully managed.

14. Censorship of information must be achieved, regardless of global information explosion.

    Gumut qualified this one with, "Look, why is the education sector ignored? The Human Rights Declaration by the UN in 1948, to be widely distributed to schools and everywhere, has not been seen by even some of our university graduates of today. The more ignorant people are about their rights, the better for their purposes."

15. Patrol and control the political power field so that the people do not pick leaders on their own. That should let us select leaders who will protect our interests; no limits on actions taken here.

16. If, in the final analysis, an unmanageable threat occurs, push for dissolution from whatever side you find yourself. The high emotions, confusion, acrimony, and possible bloodletting, which will result, will bury our tracks when the dusts settle in the new arrangements. Make yourself a hero for the side you end up in, to permanently cement the graves of our tracks.

11

THE HORNET'S NEST

The list set off the now loud 'face-off: consequences' routine in my head, but Osagie changed our bearing.

"I was going to Ikoyi, Lagos, from the airport in a taxi during a budget announcement of one of our military juntas. The driver liked that he diverted my attention from the traffic mess with small talk. He said, 'Please, Oga, don't mind my ignorance. I didn't go much school. But, Oga, how many do they say we are in Nigeria today?'

"I replied that we were well over a hundred million and that the exact number was elusive. He repeated the figure to himself and kept quiet for about five minutes. He then recounted his gruelling daily schedules, which allowed him not more than four hours of sleep every night. 'Oga sir, please na billions, abi na trillions dee budget be?' I told him that I was not sure of the exact figure, but that it was a lot of money. He changed the station on his radio to the one playing highlife and other African music.

"Minutes later, he turned his radio volume down and sharply glanced at me. 'Oga, why they no share dee money out to everybodee? My share no go be less dan million. At least, I fit end all this suffer-suffer life. Wetin you think, Oga?' We were close to my destination; I couldn't explain how national budgets work. In some ways, his ideas tie in well with our current challenges. All those billions or trillions, where did they all go? If they had been well utilised, the value of a person-year quality of life in the country ought to be

126

more than a million naira by now."

Nduka said, "If the country's earnings and all loans from October 1st, 1960, to date are added up, we'll have the total amount so far available for our development. If expressed in current values, this amount will shock and make us think seriously about our situations."

Olu said, "I can already imagine the size of that amount. Taking that point further by determining how much of it went to what part of the country and when will reveal differences in allocations. Use will make finger-pointing come closer to home."

Danladi nodded and smiled.

"We did it to ourselves. Pre-independence discipline and service, remember Elder Amadi, all have disappeared. High-level establishments of government, and its agencies, over the same period should reveal more. Cries for power rotation will seem justifiable, but the important thing, need for positive change—equitable policy making, participation, efficient project deliveries. Establishment data will show those who've been piloting the ship of state, their abilities. Tying this to the revenue points will surely upset people everywhere."

I said, "Danladi, federal government's derivation formulae over time is irresistible. 'Resource control'—the red-hot topic. It'll be maddening to show that the preferred derivation formulae are linked with the makeup of the centre, spread of high offices, and mind-sets. The evidence of double standards will surely irritate some rational minds."

Osagie shifted his seat closer to the table: "It's all getting interesting. Now, how do we open the ethnicity and indigene-settler Pandora's Box? From crises of confidence over time, we've turned inwards, closer to home. We look at ethnicity and other labels for comfort. Well, this is normal reaction for any people in similar situations, but I wonder how much of it our oppressors figured into their counter strategies. One of the first things to do is to determine the exact number of ethnic groups in Nigeria. What do you think?"

Olu said, nodding, "That's correct. Each ethnic group must be properly located on the map for obvious reasons. Interesting revelations should be what each group has so far suffered in the hands of the rest. We want to pump them up, don't we? It may be simpler to consider the country at independence: East, West, and North. Who goes first?"

"I will," Gumut said. "The idea of Regions makes things easier. But, even within ethnic groups, we'll find features that should increase anger. Domination is both inter- and intra-ethnic. The good use of this fact will definitely rattle the works. The Igbos constituted the majority in the former Eastern Region, and they suffered repeated, serious losses of lives and property in the hands of their compatriots, even long before independence. We cannot forget the pogrom of 1966 in the North especially, and the events of the "Biafra"-Nigeria civil war. A review of the illogic of that war, the manner of its execution that caused one side to confront a global coalition of unlikely allies, and the tainted methods to winning the peace afterwards will agitate decent minds. The conditions that led to the war are still very much with us, sadly. Mounting evidence indicates that whenever any violent upheaval occurs in any part of the country, the Igbos eventually become the main victims, regardless of their involvement or not in the reasons for the upheaval. They fall prey to this injustice time and again."

"A good start there, Gumut, but there's more to it," Nduka said. "First, I'm happy you used 'Igbo' and not 'Ibo' for the group. There's nothing like 'Ibo.' That word came about because our colonisers could not pronounce 'Igbo.' They don't have the 'gb' sound in their alphabet, and it appears that enough effort is not being made to correct that, even by the Igbos. An Igbo person is associated with the Igbo language. Get the drift, heh? It's true that Eastern minorities suffered the same torments associatively.

"The former Easterners, particularly the Igbos, are the greatest believers in Nigeria from the single fact that they more easily settle, invest, and raise their families in other parts of Nigeria. The backlash is that their staying power often earns them the envy of their hosts rather than their being seen as frontliners for integration, harmony, and progress. This shallow appraisal is a persistent misinterpretation of the Igbo. Look at current situations. Since the civil war, this region has remained the most neglected by the federal government, its people, at the bottom of it all. This situation widely introduced the marginalisation concepts into recent national discourse. A fair review of the current national life will indicate an unspoken, but systematic, exclusion of the Igbo. Yes, there are tokenisms to the contrary, but they don't stand the tests of rigorous assessments."

"It should be easy to get the Igbos huffing and puffing," Olu said. "But to balance things out, we should be reminded of their feared self-assured arrogance, vanity, and materialism. Isn't that the generally held view of them? How about Western Region? The Yorubas were dominant there. Who takes that one?"

"I will," Osagie said. "First, this dominance, dominance we keep talking about, has it ever been established? When have we lived with a credible census? Our major points of contact with Europeans were in the former Western Region and the hotbed of our nationalism has been there as well. Today, we hear some Yorubas claim eminence, because their great-grandparents attended prominent schools in Europe, mainly the United Kingdom and Ireland. In the light of all that, the Yorubas feel that political leadership of the country was denied them until the compensatory second coming of General Obasanjo, as civilian president. They also feel insufficiently rewarded for their roles in the civil war. During the more disturbing times of military rule, many eminent Yoruba personalities were either incarcerated, hunted out of the country, or painfully worse. It's true that Yorubas contributed quite a bit in the fight for a freer society. They ought to have had more shots at leadership. The movement of the federal capital from Lagos to Abuja was right, but the surrounding innuendos and threats of sinking Lagos, if opposition to dictatorial military rule continued to be centred there were revolting to Yorubas and all fair-minded Nigerians."

Nduka said, grinning, "To balance things, as per 'moderator' Olu, what about the general view that the Yorubas slid in to dominate institutional wealth and power, especially during the end of the civil war? Recall the green snake in the green grass or the slippery eel image? What about their vaunted dexterity in the manipulation of accounts books? Many believe they have taken a good share of the booty from the lopsided, fratricidal civil war. Remember how they joined up to create the imbalance rather than a stalemate to possibly avoid the war."

"Before you prompt, Olu, the former Northern Region," Danladi said. "The Hausa-Fulani were dominant; that's the hang-up. Osagie's dominance point taken here, okay? By the good old western standards, the North, relatively less-developed, human and physical capital. They fear being left behind. Many careless comments by prominent southerners made this fear real. Northern power structure is feudalistic, feels threatened by modernisation. Mind-set? Often, I see their point. I'm not excusing the situation, mind you."

Gamut said, "Many feel that the North has had more than a fair share of political leadership and that the country has not benefited enough from that leadership, including the North, and that they have taken more than they have put in. Then, the arrogant demand for leadership in exclusion of others by the Hausa-Fulani has not pleased many fair minds."

With major tribes discussed and Chiamalu busy with his notes, I moved us on.

"Stories of minorities in all former Regions are similar: the exclusion and frustration. Human nature? Perhaps. But the point is how these practices contributed to our situations now. There are, today, all forms of agitation for power rotation from the presidency down to the ward councillorship. That's a telling loss of focus."

"Chuks, you're quite correct. The same story everywhere laid the foundation for our 'winner-takes-all' and the 'me-only' mentality of today," Nduka said. "I regret not being there with them; majorities, that is. Oh, I would have made an exquisite collection in a harem to make prominent kings of history envious. Every night, differentiated ecstasy. Well, many of them didn't do too badly, I must concede."

Our laughter briefly interrupted him, but he continued. "Seriously, fellows. We had three political parties then—the NCNC, which started as The National Council of Nigeria and the Cameroons and then became the National Council of Nigerian Citizens; The Action Group; and The Northern Peoples' Congress. The names spoke bundles. The three practised raw, brutal politics towards minorities that led to some bloody uprisings. There were instances when already laid pipelines for water or cabling for electricity in the minority areas were dismantled and taken elsewhere. Nearly concluded road works were postponed indefinitely, all because the party in power did not get the minorities' votes. These were in addition to the minorities being denied party positions or resources.

"Look at what happened in Obasanjo's time as civilian president. He put some people from the North into high offices. Some group from the North challenged him for neglecting the North in his appointments. The fact was that the appointees were not all from the so-called dominant group of the North. In the process, they emphasised a tag, 'Core North.' Former Eastern Region. The ill will the minorities harbour towards the Igbo majority persists today, long after they got states of their own. We know how this bad blood reared its head during the civil war. This loss of confidence between the Igbos and their neighbouring minorities is being exploited to deny the former Eastern Region. In the former Western Region, the same things happened between the dominant Yorubas and minorities, and helped the later creation of the former Midwestern Region. Everywhere, minorities endured much ill-treatment from the majors. The 'we want your numbers but not you as members' attitude. Again, the idea is to dig up and present the worst of these in such a way that people get angry. That's the first emotion we want to stir. Then, we'll reason with them to seek a lasting solution through common discussions and agreements. That's the idea; isn't it?"

Olu agreed, "Quite correct, Nduka. A good summary there. Now, it was you, Gumut, who mentioned intra-ethnic situations. Can you lead us?"

Gamut nodded. "I want to start with the North. Before I do, it's helpful to identify some common features of these major ethnic groups. They are classified as one group, but they are not monolithic. The Yorubas, for example, are of the Ekiti, Egbado, Ijebu, Egba, and so on. They had long histories of conflicts in the struggle for dominance. One of the offshoots of those conflicts and other events is the existence today of a vibrant Yoruba culture in northern Brasil. Then, from Abia to Imo states in the South-East and beyond, strands of the Igbo exist. Similar situations apply to the larger ethnic groups in the North and elsewhere. Cross-border migration, variously motivated, completes the picture.

"There are linguistic differences that often go beyond the ordinary sense of dialect. We find different traditions amongst them. Within these dominant groups or any other group for that matter, there are exploitative sub-groups that monopolise the gains of the general group through skilful, silent manipulations of these minor differences. In the North, the Hausa-Fulani are the focus in the rhetoric of activists. The group resulted from the Fulani overwhelming the Hausa. Their dominance in the North is not from numerical strength; any halfway decent head count will show this. Within them, the Fulani are more tactical. They subjugated their language to the Hausa language, which they made the language of the North. Today, we know that there are many other distinct languages spoken by the peoples of the North.

"Like other such groups in the country, they scatter and settle in their targeted areas, interbreed, and often become rulers. This particular practice spawned the vicious settler-indigene conflicts of today. This is not peculiar to the North alone, I must strongly stress. In practical terms, the Fulani are the ones who traditionally fill most vacancies going to the North in the schemes of national allowance, which their lopsided occupation of political leadership so far has allowed them to control. Proportionately, they are the ones with the most western style education in the North. Their children are the greater proportional beneficiaries of scholarships and grants for education at home and abroad, particularly Great Britain and increasingly the USA and Canada. Often, their young graduates are shuttled from one high national post to the other in such rapid successions that at the end of the day, their *curriculum vitae* sound like those of the movers and shakers of the country, even when other considerations seriously impugn this image. Back in history, earlier impassioned invaders attacked Afrika from the north, and in the process, some tribes aided slavers. Once you bend your psyche to such hideous activities, the mentality becomes difficult to get rid of and somehow gets expression in available ways. We can take it from here."

Osagie said, "Great job, Gumut. Among the Igbo in the East, the story is the same, but not often mentioned. The Aro people played dominant roles in the enslavement of people in the general area and beyond. Current data emanating from DNA studies tend to show that a significant percentage of the people carted off to the Americas were from Eastern Nigeria. Typically, the Aros built networks of scattered settlements in the area and beyond. They blend into their host communities, without forgetting their common roots and interests. They often take on typical names of their hosts. This settlement scheme, it was said, allowed them to collaborate with external slavers. One could picture their instigating conflicts that yielded able-bodied people for slavers. In the lingering tales, they get mention in despising terms, similar to 'Potokiri' for the Portuguese and other light-skinned slavers, in local lingos.

"Terrifying stories about the much-feared 'Long Juju' of Arochukwu, their ancestral homeland, permeated the area. The canard was about the shrine's infallibility. Thanks to a well-structured and widely spread cant, the shrine would instantly kill the guilty in any dispute it heard—the fast arbiter. Repeated stern warnings about the instant death of the guilty were given to those who wished to take their cases to it. For proper build-up, long lists of costly requirements from all sides had to be taken to the shrine keepers ahead of time. Sure, an Aro from the community or elsewhere close was the contact through whom these items were taken to the shrine keepers to book a hearing date. Indeed, the cases heard by the shrine were screened. On taking the items to the shrine for ostensibly the preliminary ceremonies, the contact would return with the information that the shrine had either agreed or refused to adjudicate the case.

"The contact used the opportunity to brief the shrine keepers on the makeups of disputants. Where litigants were unsuitable, the word was that the shrine rejected hearing the case and that the elders of where the dispute occurred were to settle it or risk a severe general curse. When litigants were suitable, the shrine heard the case and of course, the numbers involved also noted by the shrine keepers. Depending on anticipated haul, the contact returned to the community with instructions on further actions. Invariably, that the shrine would hear the case was given the widest possible publicity to heighten the fear of the shrine and to prepare the community for the eventual loss of members. The contact could further inflame conflicts. It was also said that there were instances when these cells joined in active combat, after carefully picking the side to be on. These scattered cells were also used in running guns and the like, soon after they were introduced by Europeans. The shrine, it was pictured, had the trimmings for instilling total horror. Human skeletons, other terrifying objects, eerie noises, and darkness were so cleverly employed to make even the warriors' nerves of steel buckle in fear. Underneath it all was a maze of water tunnels.

"The final rites, the stories persist, involved leading the disputants through these tunnels. The guilty was identified to the normally required audience from both sides by what appeared like blood flowing out of some of these tunnels. The shrine had killed the guilty, while the unsustainable for their schemes were led out of other tunnels as the innocent. Time strips most machinations naked in the end. Some captives who had managed to escape from the slavers blew the lid off. There were quite a few cases of escapees, the mentally and physically super specimens, and quite often credited with supernatural powers, who returned home to tell their experiences. It was said that some of these remarkable former captives narrated instances of meeting someone among the captives that had been declared killed by shrine. The tunnelling at the shrine had inbuilt, adequately manned traps for capturing desirable people. The red liquid that flowed out of the tunnels to signify the killing of the guilty by the shrine was the result of colouring the water with some dye. The point of interest is the imbibed mentality of the Aros and other such inner groups within ethnic groups. Times have somewhat changed, but how much so has this mentality? Slavery is officially no longer permitted globally; what then is the present attraction?

"In current times, we find such subgroups taking disproportionate shares of what benefits from the dynamics of our common living that should go to the entire group through preferential acts. A possibly revealing exercise could be what the backgrounds of the leadership classes all over the country, over time, could turn out to be. Before political independence, contact with the West and nationalist movements also permeated the Igbo heartland through Onitsha, magnificently perched on River Niger's banks. There were also inflows from the coastal areas, south of the current Igbo enclave. People from Onitsha took up disproportionate quotas of the opportunities for western style development through nepotism. All this helped to develop another fragment that inconsiderately feathered its nest from the common opportunity. There are some practical examples of the backlash from these actions. The seat of government in the former Eastern Nigeria had been in Enugu metropolis. If you travel less than a few kilometres outside the city limits today, you will see some villages without any sign of modern development. Yet, these villagers could have been eavesdropping into discussions of budgets, development plans, and other government activities over time.

"Then, there was the state of affairs at the creation of former Enugu state, which resulted from the division of the earlier Anambra state into Enugu and Anambra states, before Ebonyi state was further carved out from that Enugu state. As soon as that Enugu state—current Enugu and Ebonyi states—was created, all public service centres and institutions suffered terrific shocks, because the new state did not have enough qualified and experienced people to run them. This was a glaring indication of how excluded from participation that Enugu state people had been. Current statistics indicate that property ownership in Enugu metropolis and environs is disproportionately in the hands of people from current Anambra state, a situation that arose from falsely disadvantaging and sometimes cheating the original landowners. When current Anambra state was being created, many from outside Anambra state joined in the lobby to site the state capital at Awka instead of Onitsha. Igbo states and, maybe, Rivers and Delta states have such inner groups that unduly exploit common opportunities. These minority inner groups highjack openings and debates leading to them: the subtle slip."

Olu slowly exhaled and said, "Osagie, that really hit home. For *all* ethnic groups, the cleverly disguised internal imperialists must be dislodged before the group's public opinions and needs can become truly common. Birds of the same feathers from ethnic groups have been flocking together and blocking the full expressions of our common abundance. Well done, Osagie. Who does the Yorubas?"

Danladi took a sip of his drink and said, "For the Yorubas, the Egbas and the Creos, or returnees from the Americas and the Caribbean, stand out.

Weighty 'Owu,' similar networks, also there. The Egbas lead Yoruba prodigious efforts—formal business, institutional wealth, and education. Quite prominent among distinguished professionals recognised in and outside Nigeria. More than the rest, they took greater advantage of Yorubas being among the first, if not the first, to make and sustain contact with the West. Their ancestral homeland, current Ogun state, but they, like other such groups, scattered themselves throughout Western Nigeria and beyond, mopping up western development as possible. Not a bad outing there by the West.

"Returnees from Americas, the Caribbean, and Europe gained awareness outside Africa; more ready to imitate the West. Some returnees, the 'Saro,' came through Sierra Leone. Pockets of returnees in Lagos and other places— Portuguese, Spanish, Italian. Alien surnames identify them. Some are arrogant, patronising. Don't attack me; this awareness is in relation to western standards. We're all judged by them today, like it or not. Okay?"

Osagie said, "'Mr. West,' remember that a major reason for ending slavery was that the activity exhausted its economic viability. Those Afrikans in transit and caught in these places by the abolition had to be returned to Africa. Today, football fans in Italy cry out that a naturalised Black Italian footballer is unnatural. This alone underscores the rooted damage done to Black people by that matchless, evil event."

Danladi flashed a doubting expression and said, "For the Yoruba, two principles are at work. First, to unburden the conscience unchains the mind. In time, these subgroups, having situated themselves, needed to firm up their grips. They made special contributions to main society. Many activists for the general good are from amongst them—countrywide good. Resentment mellows; who dares castigate a national hero. Then, element of preeminent time. Exploitation of others had gone on longer among the Yorubas. The inner groups reduced bad feelings by extending opportunities to others over longer period. Often, one prominent Yoruba calls another prominent Yoruba 'cousin;' same for the Aro and Fulani. The degree of exploitation, for how long, makes the difference. But... but, bottom lines, all the same."

I said, "All that is probably correct, but isn't it all human nature? Our

Ancestors said that the fish that grows big often eats other smaller fish."

Nduka said, "Fellows, here we go again. Fisherman speaks. You say I have a one-track mind. What about Chuks, Professador's short shadow? Fish on his mind. Of all the wise sayings of our Ancestors, he likes only the fish line. Chuks, please don't reduce my quota or think about skipping me at your next harvest, because of what I've just said. Okay? Seriously fellows, if one were the big fish, fewer questions and more relish would go with the eating. We have far too many rings of big fishes, many nondescript, eating far too much for even their own good. If this thing we're talking about is done well, all of them will be stripped naked in the market places.

"Professador stated the point well in the entrepreneur paper: 'It is difficult for the human resource that is preoccupied with exploitation to fully accept the covenant that enduring individual advancement is most assured in the environment of the common well-being.'"

I ignored Nduka. "The final goal is to renew each strand in all ethnic groups such that it becomes a cooperative component of that powerful and resilient entity we want Nigeria to become."

Olu said, "We've covered some ground, but we've not talked much about *corruption*. Perhaps it may be better handled at the conference, during the campaign to get the conference going, or both. I really don't know. Well, maybe we should talk about it, because it's so central to our conditions? Perhaps, Professador should go over some aspects, the 'slaying and cremating the monster, corruption, in a most unforgettable manner, and then equitably distributing and time-capsuling the resulting cremation ashes in each local government area.' How about it, Professador?"

Chiamalu was so occupied with his note taking that he appeared not to have heard what was said.

Gumut grabbed the opportunity. "Listen, you all. We all know that Professador has been our main driving force in these matters. Some of him should at least be rubbing off on some of us. I'll chip in here. Listen, the main targets here are Nigerians, each of us. Corruption has destroyed the essence of our individual and collective living. We just have to recognise it as the prime enemy number one. It's too obvious, everywhere, every time, and every day."

Chiamalu looked up from his notes and softly said, "Eventually, unchecked injustice unpredictably migrates aggressively."

It brought a pensive pause.

12

CREMATING THE BIG BAD MONSTER

I told them all, "Gumut, you're absolutely right. Corruption is it, everywhere for so long. The creation of Nigeria was in itself corrupt. Luggard's concubine, Flora Shaw, I think her name was, named us. We still uphold the prophecies of that side action. The British, in creating Nigeria, laid a variety of land mines set to explode at various times and circumstances. Over a century later, we've not been able to accurately locate, concretely decode, and completely disable those mines. I see Danladi's looks asking, 'Whose fault?'

"Again, the Buhari-Idiagbon junta understood that without discipline, there cannot be character, and that without character, there will not be progress for the individual or country. I was so thrilled that they initially focused on harshly knocking out the demons of indiscipline in us, apparently without fear or favour. Well, the rest is history. Various options exist for altering human behaviour. At one end sits a sudden change attended by harsh penalties to violators, while at the other end, is a gentle push maintained over time and based on appeals to propriety. The former yields results with some traumas as a price, while the latter runs the risk of being diluted or derailed, especially in an environment like ours. Some traumas wear out with time. A good leadership settles on the right point on this scale for its followers. They diagnosed the problems well and started with the correct approaches, thereby confirming the individual as the fundamental building unit of any society. Then, genuine appreciation makes up for the loneliness of good quality leadership. How did the country encourage them? Again, the rest is history, and corruption cripples us."

Nduka applauded me and said, "Hurray! The fisherman jumps out of the shadow of Professador. Well put, Chuks."

I raised my clenched fist, we all laughed.

He went on, "Yes, yes! Seriously speaking, corruption is it. Let's dissect the big bad monster, while stressing how it aided robbing all of us. The last time we talked about corruption we agreed that it hurts those in the Third World most, and our own Third World is the rich one. That alone magnifies the effects of corruption. The slant should be on how a few have been wasting our common abundance. Remember the revenge instincts we want to use."

Olu said, "Nduka, that's a good approach and we also have more options, or is it alternatives? We can examine corruption from independence to date, thereby avoiding Danladi's 'missiles.' We can use the point of view of the average person who has experienced pre- and post-independence Nigeria. We can go by corruption's metamorphosis. We can do it randomly. Which way?"

I said, "Metamorphosis is a direct route and we should indicate who the casualties have been at each stage. Danladi, give me some space. The first significant increase in corruption started with the bedevilling transition, which began the moment the first raiders set foot on the continent. Then came slavers; that activity rubbished the control mechanisms of Afrikan communities. It turned the people against one another and devalued human life and original Afrikan love. They used many methods to execute their heartless agenda for Afrika, with many still ongoing. From then on, corruption increased in its destructive varieties, and like water seeping into sandy soil, it's increasingly affecting all of us. Our colonisers picked up from that setting to disorganise societies across Afrika. They employed new methods, but kept the mentality of the slave traders. There's the need to mention their tinkering with spiritual principles, further confusing the Afrikan consciousness."

"Quite right, Chuks," Gumut exclaimed.

Osagie sighed and said, "The bottom line is that we've lost our earlier core values as a society. Without core values, what can any person, organisation, or society accomplish? Studies show that even in the business world, only those organisations that tirelessly maintained their core values lasted. Communities and families have been unbundled for them to be crippled by selfishness, unreliability, and parasitism. We no longer distinguish group interests from individual interests, the enduring from the fleeting, substance from shadows. Our enviable heritage is being wasted, but our diarrhoea of the mouth leads us to repeatedly claim the foremost positions in all aspects of life in Africa, poor Africa. Today, both the admired and the undesired have become like two peas in a pod, equally acceptable, unlike in the past when worth was derived from use of talent for community and individual to prosper. All these because of corruption."

Olu said, "Wao Osagie! Let's cool off a bit. We should break it all down a little more and gather the pieces around our objectives. Right?"

"Corruption; what did we have at independence, compared to now?" Nduka asked.

Gumut bristled and leaned forward. "First, Nduka, no country or nation has been completely without fraud and corruption. It's about human nature and a matter of degrees. Original Afrikan societies had them too. But they had dreaded methods for keeping fraud and corruption in check. Call them environmental control tools, if you like. By 1960, we had absorbed measures of society-killing doses. The earlier slave traders destroyed the fight, faith, and virtue of Afrikans. Danladi can disapprove all he wants; that's the truth."

Gumut paused, adjusted his sitting, and continued. "The people who took over from our colonisers had learned to skim and rip to the individual's benefit alone. Look at the idle nobility all over Europe and beyond. Their fortunes had been quite often derived from their colonies. Yes, the crown got much of the loot, but a lot went to individuals well placed to line their pockets as well. Today, their brood is the loafing nobility, living off history, striving for relevance at home and abroad. At independence, certain conditions were in place to help the growth of corruption. Our politicians of the time, and even today, totally failed to build our politics on well-entrenched core values that target why we exist. It's easy to see why corruption is in every place and everything here. The entrepreneur paper stated that panels of enquiry into corruption or fraud preceded and launched the so-called independence.

"Major activities at the time were political, but with the backdrop of the bedevilling transition, those activities needed to be enduring, to regain some already lost ground. Instead, the political parties embraced being without ideology and discipline. Both imply the alliance of disciplined people with similar minds. Look at what happened in Ibadan just before independence, when a party won an election and was suddenly turned the loser by the famous overnight 'carpet crossing' of unreliable tribal politicians. That singular event encouraged politics without scruples. The politics of independent Nigeria started corrupt. Naturally, economic and social activities, already infected by doses of corruption from the bedevilling transition, paced up with this faulty political wagon at independence. This completed the sowing of the vigorous seeds of corruption in everything about us; some seeds were at various stages of development on 1st October, 1960."

"Thanks, Gumut; deep strokes there," Olu said. "That returns us to the metamorphosis approach. Corruption gained more wings and fangs at independence. We are yet to conduct an accurate census that provides reliable data for development. Good voter registration and the national ID card agenda both turned unsatisfactory and truly expensive, if not felonious. With our rich and diverse heritage in governance, was western-style democracy suited to us? Were there any strong moves to integrate existing social orders into governance? *No.* Today, we live with counterfeits of democracy; they will remain with us until we wake up and change our politics."

Osagie nodded and said, "The breaking up of that political movement into regional or ethnic camps still intensifies the challenges from our diversity. There is the tendency to only focus on what component groups stand to gain or lose from any given situation. This diminishes the whole. Also, some activities of our earlier leaders set the standards for rifling through public property with stealing in mind."

Olu agreed. "Indeed, Osagie. There were the 5-10 percent government contract inflations for party support and the like, but those quickly turned into illicit individual mega hauls."

With a sly grin on his face, Danladi tapped the table and said, "Burden of actions for our benefits, always ours. As normal humans, we should get rid of bad seeds in our rich, well-tilled, and well-raked garden, thanks to Nature. It really doesn't matter who sowed the bad seeds."

"Okay, Danladi, it's time for comparisons. Where are we today; how do things compare with what they were in 1960?"

"Olu, how can you ask those questions, heh? Aren't you living here with us? Haven't you been listening?" Gumut said. "Well, we're going over the situation for a purpose, aren't we? Our wise Ancestors said that 'to bring home firewood infested with ants is an invitation to lizards to a feast at your home'; and that 'the masquerade is now out at the square for public viewing.' We now represent what corruption can do to a society, when unchecked. The more important thing is what the casualty list looks like, and who've been gaining from corruption."

Osagie sighed. "Quality of life and life expectancy should lead the list of casualties. Remember my conversation with the taxi driver. Then, there are the endless stories about our young people frequently risking their lives in irregular attempts to get out of the country. To escape the odium, many of them pass off themselves as citizens of other countries. These alone say quite a lot—loss of hope by the young. The future of the country is the biggest loser here."

I said, "Osagie, as compatriots, we've stopped thinking and acting together. This is a critical state of affairs for all of us, as victims."

Nduka said with a straight face, "For me, to be a casualty is to die. For anyone to die is to diminish love for somebody, somewhere, sometime. And without love, life loses meaning."

We couldn't hold back the laughter, because we knew his brand of love.

He went on, "Now fellows, seriously speaking, all those who die in our country because of corruption pay the ultimate price. First in line are the pensioners who, after giving the country the best of their production under various circumstances, are treated with so much ingratitude. Some have dropped dead in long queues, while chasing their pension. These deaths are the capping of all the dribbling they receive in matters of collecting their entitlements. To see that ex-service security personnel, who risked their lives, while serving the country, are also treated shabbily in matters of pension is just too much. In many cases, it's not that the money is not there, but that bureaucratic bottlenecks are created to mask the acts of those who play self-serving games with pension funds. If things don't change drastically, the same treatment or worse awaits those active today.

"Childbirth-related deaths for reasons of corruption come to mind. Poorly equipped and run maternities, because of corruption, are examples. Unborn children and their mothers require the best of care, but corruption blinds us to this obligation. Look, all the innocent who die in road accidents, robbery operations, protests, and ethnic or religious upheavals because of corruption should be among the top on the list. I'm interested in the ultimate casualties."

Olu leaned back, hands on the table, and said, "Nduka, I'd add those who died from peacekeeping and other violence-prone actions, because of the corrupt ways of handling their support, in and out of action. There are also the fake-drugs-induced deaths. You're correct about the ultimate price index."

Osagie slightly raised his voice. "All those who had worked diligently, hoping to be of maximum possible help to the country and to themselves, and who sadly discover that their country rejects them, are in a class. Many of them spent years outside the country, purposefully acquiring expertise, while enduring ill treatments, often including racism. They kept on, but on returning home, they confronted resentment from their compatriots. Broadly speaking, they belong to the so much talked about 'wasted generations.' Their responses have varied. Those who could, shipped out again to the welcoming arms of their hosts, because of their worth. These Nigerians often function creditably in the upper echelons of professional services in those countries— ready to produce high-level workers that flee the oppressive conditions in their country. Brain drain worst scenario. Some others hang on and grind themselves down with whatever came their way. Many in this group have died prematurely or have been physically stricken by heartbreak. All these people forced to the sidelines sadly watch as mediocrity bungles all critical affairs of the country. It's a very pitiful way to be and to finally go. What other price of corruption can be higher than when one is tortured to death this way?"

Olu said, "The final word is that we are all victims of corruption. Even the very few driven to extremes by animal greed live with constant apprehension, the fear of being found out. At times, the conscience breaks through to recreate the true self, often dramatically. To the suffering masses everywhere, the impact of corruption is directly threatening. Many don't know where their meals will come from. Many have no shelter from the elements and the predators created by corruption. These are the ones to arouse; they may respond faster. The rest of us may need some prodding, but it's clear that most people will act for positive change. A point needs covering, 'the scattering and time capsuling' of the ashes from cremation of corruption. Professador, lead us."

A short pause followed as we all focused on Chiamalu. He quickly flipped through his notes and smiled.

"Thanks, Olu," he said. "Without you fellows and Nduka's brand of love, life would be boring, boring. Many Nigerians have become shallow, unconcerned, forgetful, selfish, or impatient. Not this group. If all we've said so far are carefully analysed, packaged, and executed, the monster corruption will take leave our parts and no one will lament it. *We* treated corruption and each local government area during *our* presentation at Okwukwe Afrika. There's really little to add, eh, we might as well go over it.

"First, it's appropriate to re-echo that the Nigerian mind is in dire need of de-militarisation and then de-colonisation. Much is said about restructuring the country, without *sufficiently* explaining what that should be. The first restructuring is the identification of a countrywide core ideology that the majority of us believe in. After that, it becomes easier to outline our preferred system of governance. This core ideology will highlight corruption in all its forms, so that it can be amply crushed—properly killing the power of negative precedent, including negative fallouts from our interactions with the rest of the world so far. If we jump into splitting the country in any way, as some mean by restructuring, the practised wreckers they inherit will quickly devour the resulting smaller units. There has to be a lasting, clear break from all the disgraceful mess before any reorganisation does any good."

I eagerly interrupted, "Indeed, indeed, the pieces should go in peace."

He continued, "Whenever corruption is mentioned, the average person first thinks of an official illegally tampering with public wealth. It is appropriate to start the action with fanfare here. The occasional activities of a few brave patriots among us show that it's possible to audit the affairs of government within reasonable periods. The private sector usually makes summaries of their affairs annually. That makes things a little easier there. So, as much as possible, we begin with thorough audits of government and some private sector affairs, starting from now and going back to 1st October, 1960. Any person or group of people fingered in the process will be given adequate opportunities to fully defend themselves. If after that they are found guilty of stealing from the people, they squarely face the music from the peoples' heartstrings. They should be convicted for the offence no matter how long ago committed, and then, made to return all they had stolen. Many may have spent part or all of what they had stolen. In those cases, whatever is recoverable will be recovered and the balance should be accounted for by the confiscation of available assets of the thieves. Their activities caused pain at some time to someone, somewhere. It's all justice.

"The convicted are imprisoned with hard labour, meaning visible public works located in the general areas they live in or come from. Their work sites are rotated to cover rural areas. This puts them on display as serious offenders of society who are working for atonement. That's fair to them and society. All confiscated assets other than money are disposed of as quickly and efficiently as possible. All amounts thus raised are put in a special fund. All these actions are given maximum possible publicity, to effectively serve notice to everyone that the highly visible corruption is being severely dealt with. That will be a proper killing of the power of negative precedent; don't you think so?"

We hesitantly nodded; some heads tilted sideways, eyebrows raised.

Chiamalu said, "The public is periodically informed about the growth of the fund, while plans for its use are being made, including for a critical structure that is self-sustaining in each local government area. This could be a school, a marketplace, a hospital, a community centre, or a badly needed road. Whatever it is, is appropriately named in the local dialect. The erection of these structures could also provide work sites for the convicts from the corruption trials. It's going to be difficult, but the whole exercise, if properly done, will indeed result in the ashes from cremation of corruption being deposited to last in each local government area."

Gamut said, "Great ideas, Professador. You forget that these thieves stole so much that they are so rich and powerful that they can do and undo. Besides, they take the concept of carrying others along to more immoral levels by ensuring that a little of their loot trickles down to even the gateman. The auditing is going to be quite a challenge. How many times have external auditors reported that all is well with their audit subject, only for it to crash in no time afterwards?"

"Yes Gumut, we know all that, but I dare predict that once this activity gets underway properly, there will be more than enough squealers for the job. The power that those thieves have is derived from the cooperation of all of us. That cooperation could also go the other way. People cooperate in order to overcome immediate pressures. They know that the generosity these thieves pretend to be showing is made possible by their theft of what belonged to all of us in the first place. Remember counter strategies. If the exercise is well-planned to involve the best auditors from within and outside the country, a good job should be possible."

"Professador, the amounts these thieves stashed away in foreign financial institutions are enormous, trillions! Information on fund deposits is now more available, but we don't use it expediently. Why? There are many powerful internal and external parties to the disgusting affair. Then, the countries where the stolen funds are kept have much to gain from keeping them. That's why many of them only pay lip service to all the cries about the disastrous results of corruption on Africa. In the very few cases where the funds were traced to some countries, those countries made recovery quite difficult by requiring drawn-out legal procedures that reduce eventual recoveries, if ever. They went from carting away our able-bodied people as slaves to ripping off Afrika's natural resources, and now, to the husbanding of development capital illegally siphoned to their countries. It's all a form of economic warfare dressed up in some fancy cloaking of assumed propriety. With all these factors, it could be difficult to recover the stolen funds."

"Well taken points, Osagie. But remember that the exercise is to be properly planned, publicised, and executed not to be repressive or in any way infringe on the rights of the innocent. It then becomes a challenge to the entire world and, luckily, most countries are on record, as being officially opposed to corruption and its effects on Africa. Those countries have to back up their words with suitable actions."

Nduka said, "Professador, your mention of the innocent reminds me of a crucial point. Whenever embezzlement is mentioned, many of us only target lead politicians. They may be guilty, but by far the guiltier ones are the bureaucrats and technocrats in the system, public or private. They know and work with due processes, but they also find ways to circumvent rules to benefit embezzlers. Of course, they also take care of themselves in the whole scheme and sometimes steal more than the highlighted politicians steal. It's easy to imagine how some of them actually initiate politicians and the like into the game. Politicians come and go, but these people remain in the system as entrenched careerists turned masters of the evil game. It's yet to be reported that a Head of State or any other such high-profiled person shot their way into the Central Bank to cart away the people's money."

Danladi sat up. "Nduka, the innocent. Hey, how many of us are clean enough to expose corruption in this way? How many? We all slept; fraud and corruption rose to rule us. How many of us can cast that first stone? Tell me. How many? No value in asking about what countries keep the loot. You need their help to succeed. Yet, we eagerly blame them *first*. You take your breakfast to someone else to eat, you complain of hunger later in the day. Where's the logic or sense?"

Olu calmly said, "Nduka, the guilty technocrats will be identified in the audit, because the paths and control points of the flow of resources will be carefully examined. This will also highlight the major parties that soiled their hands—all planners, helpers, and initiators. Yes, Danladi, we'll note your expected conclusion there and, yes, a good number of us are stained by corruption, but not all of us, by any means. Many upright and capable Nigerians exist within and outside the country. Many of them were shoved aside by insatiable mediocrity, driven by greed. The looters used from unpleasant to savage tactics to bully their way to our common wealth.

"The good people will be too happy to join the fray, if assured of the sincerity of the undertaking. Nigerians have laboured under the burden of fraud and corruption for too long. Most of us will gladly sign on to the effort to decisively deal with the entire menace. We shouldn't undervalue the power of revenge. Recruits can be raised by first providing the opportunity for those guilty of corruption to voluntarily own up, return their loot, and face reduced penalties and earn the people's pardon. Those forgiven this way could provide good information on the practices of the terribly corrupt. What is sought is a good and lasting rebirth of the country. What other points are there?"

Gumut said, "What about those cases where the thieves have died and left no traceable assets?"

Chiamalu was still occupied, so I volunteered opinion.

"Gumut, it's unrealistic to target 100 percent treatment of corruption. The aim should be to show that corruption of all forms is being undone and tabooed. The number of cases missed will depend on how people judge the exercise. In the cases of the dead without traceable assets, it should be enough to note them for history. Of course, extreme care must be exercised, because it wouldn't be right to falsely accuse the dead."

"What about the cases of the super-slippery dodgers, who fine-tune their escapes to those countries without extradition treaties with Nigeria and who will gladly welcome them?"

"Gumut, those too will be hunted down by the international pressures that will be mounted in support of the exercise. Those countries without expatriation agreements with Nigeria will be pressured through intermediaries. 'If the game eludes the hunter today, tomorrow is another hunt,' our Ancestors again."

"You're quite right Chuks, but what's the big picture now?" Olu asked.

Chiamalu was still writing, Osagie then said, "In fairness, some credit is due all operators of the Nigerian enterprise to date. They had to contend with many complex factors, some inherent and some imposed, and all amidst unawareness of the outside world. It's fortunate that we still have the entity called Nigeria. We've had trying times. But we still have the potential for greatness as a country. It's also true that all operators should have done much better, considering the resources and opportunities they had. We can be likened to a sedated champion, while the competition is on. That sedative is *absolute corruption* sustained by gross indiscipline. Our primary objective is finding effective ways of releasing this dazed championship potential."

Chiamalu looked up and said, "Contorted individuals create distorted societies, which, in turn, produce more individuals, more contorted."

13

HIBERNATION

A meeting took place with ninety-four of the most appealing respondents to our presentation. With help from three trusted behavioural scientists, forty-three of them joined the project as volunteers.

We assigned preliminary work on different areas to ourselves, singly or in pairs, and paid more attention to personal matters.

By the end of the second month, all our families were out of the country. A swift start there: we beat the three-month deadline by a month. But for Danladi, Osagie, and Nduka, who were required to show up occasionally, we arranged that our professional matters should not suffer severe damage from our prolonged absence. We finalised our personal issues in anticipation of the worst.

We targeted all geopolitical zones for possible recruits from growing numbers of contacts. Eleven volunteers had intelligence experience. One of them was a freelance criminology operator. TANNA was registered at Abuja as a Civil Organisation dedicated to general awareness advocacy, but not involving itself in partisan politics or other blatantly divisive issues.

TANNA's registration briefs provided starting points for the work Osagie and I were to do—developing a sketch of TANNA's structure and, most importantly, producing a framework for core values and related matters. Nkem and Chiamalu were to prepare fundraising strategies. Gumut was to work on ICT infrastructure requirements. Nduka and Olu were to anchor the initial work on the S&I wing. Danladi was to focus on creating a model of the publicity apparatus. The whole affair became quite intriguing, as each of us could only imagine what the others were doing.

§ § §

A fortnight later, I came home to find an invitation to a wedding at Uyo in Akwa Ibom state. The names on the invitation were strange. I showed the invitation to Chiamalu the next day, and behold, he too had received the same invitation. We decided to attend only the wedding reception, while arriving separately.

When I came up to the entrance of the reception venue, an attendant asked for my invitation. He glanced at it and smiled. He ushered me through the crowd to the back of the set up. From a few metres away, I sighted Chiamalu sitting with two men, Nkem, and her twin sister. The attendant pointed at the only vacant seat by their table and left. The table was tucked away from the bustle of the reception.

I sat down, and Nkem introduced Ike, her husband; Okey, her twin sister's husband; and Ifem, her twin sister; and me. We were able to hear each other well over all the noise of the celebration, because of an intervening service point that cut us off from the active crowd. Nkem informed me that the wedding was of some family friends of her sister's family; it was handy. As soon as I got the chance, I complimented Ike on their place and asked about his trip.

"Thank you for your interest. There were some hitches here and there, but in all, the trip was successful. A Nigerian travelling abroad these days has to be ready for some inconveniences. You know, the times. I watched the video of your presentation; Nkem filled me in on other details. It was phenomenal. All the issues you raised are much overdue for action. It's cheering that some people here still have their wits around them. Sorry, I missed the live thing."

Ike was in the export/import business, with offices, administered from Enugu, in every zone. He had to be on the road a lot, locally and internationally.

To my question about his business, Ike said, "The greatest headache is how to monitor personnel. You can't shadow everyone and every activity. People are so unreliable, and even if one could afford to import workers, it would be only a matter of time before those imports are degraded. You just become a gambler and hope for good luck."

Ifem and her family lived in Abakaliki and she worked in a government agency and also ran her own NGO on the empowerment of rural women. Her husband was in the business of quarrying raw materials for export. The clincher for me was that she also had the same number of children as Nkem, a set of female twins and two boys, but in her case, the twins were the first born whereas in Nkem's case, the twin sisters came after their first son. That fascinated me.

"Just out of curiosity, Ike, were you friends with Okey before you two married the twins?" I asked.

"No, not at all, but we're very happy to relate the way we do through them. I met Nkem in Enugu. Ifem and Okey met in Lagos. Okey and I have become close. He's bailed me out of naughty business situations quite a few times. And, Nkem is the older."

"Only by seconds," Okey said.

"Nkem is a dynamic go-getter; I imagine that Ifem is that way too. Ike, what's our image like out there?" Chiamalu asked.

Ike shrugged his athletic shoulders, "The usual slant against us in these our parts. You know, the long-held image of us, the sustaining mind-sets. Those who cared a little more talked about our elections. I think about the elections too. Bad examples for younger politicians and the public. The trend is not encouraging either: 1999 was flawed and contested, 2003 was worse and fought up to the Supreme Court, and 2007 turned out the worst of them all. The rigging has become cleverer. We are being pushed down the slope."

Okey said, frowning, "The 2007 elections rubbished all the reforms and fighting-corruption hot air. History will not favour President Obasanjo and his ruling party."

Ike stretched out his long legs. "All those whose duty it is to instil good conduct—elders, parents, teachers, managers, and so on—have lost a lot of authority. Such examples from the highest places in the country make their jobs more difficult."

Ifem, in a familiar-sounding voice, said, "There's also the misuse of goodwill. Some countries donated to our election activities. What will they do the next time we have such a need for assistance?"

Nkem said, "The elections raised broader questions: are Nigerians, and by extension, Africans, capable of sustaining a democracy? What about Nigeria's role in Africa?"

"Ike, bringing it all closer, the situation does make things more difficult for people in your line of business, doesn't it? People will tend to generalise. New or even old business contacts may tend to feel that Nigerians are cheats."

"Yes, you're correct, Chiamalu. The damage done by those elections goes far beyond our borders. It will take generations to repair the fallouts."

Okey said, sneering, "The Freedom of Information Bill never became law in those eight years. Instead, unsettling super pay packages for legislators resulted, while the masses continue to suffer. We'll eventually know why and how the legislators got those windfalls."

"There's a worrying trend," Ifem began, then paused. "The party that outrigs the rest to win gives us a one-party government. All the politicians decamp from their parties to join the winning party. Opposition politics disappears."

I said, "It's the rush for the prize. They have to queue up for their dividends, which diminish to zero with opposition politics."

We briefly discussed the evolution and formats of governance constitutions. We concluded that the law was the critical binder in successful governments. For Nigeria, where many divergent forces have been at play for so long, thereby firmly polarising the people, it was appropriate for the articulation of a constitution to involve as many viewpoints as possible. The driving project was again validated.

Okey, elbows on table, hands supporting his jaw, said, "You know, funding is important. They say money makes things happen. I agree, but I don't agree with the notion that money legitimises everything. You'll need money to move your ideas forward. Our wives, Ike, and I talked things over before this meeting. The four of us are donating this to your cause."

He slid a holdall under the table towards Chiamalu with his foot, and said,

"It contains two million naira for your immediate activities; we'll do more as is possible."

Chiamalu and I froze. Nkem and Ifem beamed identical smiles that excited the soul. Ike nodded repeatedly.

Ifem said, grinning and nodding, "You fellows are now pushing this thing without your families. The least four of us can do is offer support, no matter how small. My sister and I will make contacts from our civic organisations available to you and we will assist in developing new ones."

Chiamalu and I were still unable to speak. I wished that Nduka was present.

Smiling, Nkem said, "Yes, we shall remain in the background, but we shall not be ploughed underground. The *paradox* shall be unravelled."

"All my managers will be alerted whenever you need their help. Their locations in the country may be useful," Ike said.

Chiamalu and I thanked them repeatedly and departed. We travelled back together.

§ § §

A week to the three-month deadline, we assembled at a remote farm in Kogi state at nine a.m. on a Tuesday. The important meeting required the presence of everyone—the twin sisters and volunteers included. Our arrivals in small groups were staggered over an hour. Idoko, Osagie's friend and former schoolmate, owned the expansive farm. A thousand people could easily become unnoticeable in the huge spread of integrated farm that raised many animals and crops, and housed processing and maintenance installations. We were assigned an empty holding warehouse for grains, deep in the planted area.

We departed from the venue in the same manner as we had arrived, but under the cover of early darkness, because we initially took a little time to tour the farm in seemingly unconnected groups. The businesslike meeting lasted four hours and resulted in the following.

All preparatory assignments were submitted.

Groups of five persons were assigned to each geopolitical zone to identify individuals from contacts then available, who would form the core of

TANNA's zonal organisations. The Federal Capital Territory (FCT) had three individuals. Each group had as a member, a volunteer with intelligence skills. These core groups were to execute similar selections for the states in each zone. The tasks were to be concluded within a month. Procedures for due care were emphasised.

The core values assignment was to form the backbone of the manual for screening, training, and retraining processes. The bare statement of our core values was only five words: **'NIGERIANS AND NIGERIA ARE PRICELESS.'**

The urgent work on S&I was emphasised.

Two experienced volunteers were to assist in the ICT and publicity areas.

Funding received lengthy consideration. Since the first presentation in the South-East was well-publicised, fundraising should start and ride the coattails of that event. We were eager to test our fundraising plans.

Based on a volunteer's suggestion, pledges of donations came from nearly everyone present. Some redeemed portions or all of their pledges. The cash received was 167,000 naira, while the pledges came to over 783,500 naira. Chiamalu announced the two million naira we had received, without mentioning the source.

Five banks with the greatest geographical spread and more reliability were selected for our banking. Nkem and Ifem volunteered to assist in opening the accounts and in initially managing our funds from behind the scenes. This area would be revisited to ensure best practice.

All those not assigned to teams were to join the South-East fundraising. Excepting those on S&I, and without any loss in effectiveness, every team was to conclude its work soonest and then join the fundraising. Small amounts were given to all the teams.

We broke up into assignment teams to conclude work schedules, and later, randomly dispersed into various directions, after team meetings.

The next month was extremely busy as people crisscrossed the country in all sorts of ways and bearings. We simulated an aggressive species of termites deep in the woodwork, boring and tunnelling, but leaving the exterior undisturbed to the untrained eyes.

§ § §

Our next meeting was held in one of the interior conference rooms of a busy hotel in the heart of the great city of Kano. We lodged in various locations scattered in the city and its vast environs. The time was 7:30 a.m. on a Friday. Two representatives from every zonal core group and the FCT, one representative from the emerging S&I of each zone and the FCT, and the original seven attended. The meeting was brisk, because we wanted it to end at the height of the busy period of the day when many people would be milling around.

It was decided that thirteen people should comprise the core zonal groups. Each zone was to nominate a leader who would coordinate affairs and attend future meetings.

Lagging local government structures received specifics and deadlines. It became clearer that S&I affairs had to be rushed.

After the meetings, the entire group was to move to the South-East to participate in fundraising. This would enhance the exercise and improve performances in the remaining zones. Subsequently, all members of core groups of the zones swooped down on the South-East, the training ground for fundraising, as it were; the final results were remarkable.

The meeting ended and participants got lost in the crowds of the early Friday afternoon. Similar meetings were later held in Lagos, Kaduna, Ibadan, Jos, and Benin City respectively; larger cities provided useful cover. Chiamalu and a member of the South-East S&I group attended those meetings.

The meetings improved TANNA's structure. National coordination was done by the Central Caucus (CC), made up of permanent and non-permanent members. Initially, the permanent members were the seven leaders of the zones and the FCT, while the nonpermanent ones were those invited to meetings based on agenda only. They were present only during the discussions of the issues related to them.

The CC had no permanent location. It met at the zones randomly. All sorts of groups were linked to one another in intricate ways, sometimes with intertwined memberships. The S&I had equally grown in structure and capability. TANNA became more complex, but managed to leave no lasting tracks of its activities, yet things were done with zeal and efficiency.

§ § §

The concentrated fundraising drive in the South-East lasted five weeks, and covered Enugu, Ebonyi, Abia, Anambra, and Imo states in that order before the extra hands went back to their zones. Mopping up was left for fundraising committees of the zone. The excellent solicitation materials helped matters. There was always one for any class of potential donor. Our unfailing habit of swiftly acknowledging donations and issuing receipts earned us the confidence and later support of donors.

The others left the South-East determined to improve fundraising in their zones. Before they left, a 'loose' meeting of the emerging zonal leaders was held at a rural marketplace located near the border of Imo and Anambra states.

First, it was announced that the total donations collected so far in the South-East amounted to about 387 million naira. The next move would be to focus a campaign at all rural areas. It was also decided that since the first presentation took place in South-East Zone, the rest were to be rotated as follows: North-West at Gummi, South-South at Calabar, North-Central at Mokwa, South-West at Ibadan, North-East at Numan, North-Central at Jos, South-South Benin City, and North-West at Kaduna; all former regional capitals were thus included.

The presentations were to be accordingly adjusted to more directly relate to each location and were to be in as rapid successions as possible. Fundraising in the expansive zones of North-Central and South-South was to be aided by combined efforts such as already used in the South-East. Once started, fundraising was to be continuous at every location. More vigour and caution were to be put into recruitment.

That successful fundraising in the South-East excited us to no end. The correlation between effort and funds raised was extremely motivating. Other reactions varied, and one of them was the brief chat Adamu, Timi, and Akin had.

Timi, hands on hip, said, "Ndigbo are puzzling. What drove them to part with all that money on this project, yet they are said to love money more than anything else? I'm surprised."

Adamu said, in a low voice, "Maybe, the Igbos are grossly misunderstood—their true values and everything."

"Core values and their maintenance define self, while peripheral values decorate personality. It's possible that focus has been on the peripheral values of Igbos. However, I welcome this kind of response from any quarter, provided the project remains true and free," Akin said.

Adamu, slowly nodding, said, "I agree with both of you; let's wait until the end to see how it all goes down."

§ § §

I recall the informative and entertaining visit my solicitation group made to the executive members of a traders' union at Onitsha. On our prompt arrival, the chair and his people were waiting for us at their office, a small space carved out of one of the stalls in the market.

A narrow table was between two rows of chairs, our hosts seated on the row facing the entrance. A ceremonial bowl containing kola nuts and their usual complements was on the middle of the table. We were lucky: the standing fan was on—the area was being supplied electricity. It would have been terribly hot in there. On sighting us, they stood up to welcome us.

After introductions, the chair said, "Chidi, please go and inform the financial secretary that our guests are here. I told you all, from their letter, they are not the usual abusers of time. See, they arrived on the dot. You can always smell out serious people from miles away. You're all welcome. We can talk generally, as we wait for our financial secretary. I'm sure he'll soon be here."

Salisu, our leader, spoke, "Thank you all for giving us your valuable time and attention. How has business been?"

An obvious question, but it had such arousing effects on our hosts that I wondered if Salisu had started badly. All of them shifted on their seats, eyes beaming like automobile headlamps on dark stretches, bodies leaning forward.

The chair said, "That's a good question, but I'll answer it when our financial secretary arrives. Our EXCO discussed your letter and agreed on our actions. We shall therefore speak freely, honestly. Your mission will not be affected. I told our members that you were the kind of people to pay attention to, because your letter touched the relevant issues about Nigeria with uncommon style and honesty. Mention traders' union, people often imagine illiterate hustlers who only know profit, but things have been quietly changing. You will be amazed by the backgrounds of our EXCO members."

With a quivering smile creasing her cheeks, one of the women present said, "Mr. Chairman, some changes are very welcome, some regrettable, and a few, children of opportunity."

Ademola, of our group, asked, "Generally, would you say that the changes are positive?"

"It's all relative and about perception. Much of it has been responses to limited options. It may surprise you that I'm a political science graduate. I've been out of the university seven years. After my NYSC service, for the following thirty months, I pounded the streets in search of employment, but to no avail. Those were very trying months, but it would have been worse if I had given up. I tried all kinds of odd jobs, and believe me, I learned a lot about this country during that period."

"What happened?"

"Mboto, that's your name, right? On a personal level, I truly lived out lots of contradictions. It's one thing to say Nigeria is a bundle of contradictions and another to personally experience them, mostly painfully. I better talk about the good aspects."

Mboto of our team and some others nodded to agree with the positive approach.

He continued, "During one of my wishful visits to the market, a trader requested me to translate a letter he had received from one of his overseas suppliers. Obviously, he could not read well enough, and the letter was in English, but not from an English-speaking country. I gladly did so and also helped him formulate a reply. He was so pleased with me that he gave me some money afterwards. I truly was happy to accept it. That was the beginning of the relationship that resulted in my becoming one of the traders. One thing led to another: the stitching of events to make a story."

"Lucky events for our union," a man exclaimed.

"As I got closer to many of them, I admired their guts. Illiterates and semi-illiterates, as some were, they all had the confidence to do business globally. A few got hurt, but that was not a deterrent. Instead, they always spread the news about how the bad deal was done to them, and the others often chipped in to help the victims overcome the setbacks. Group learning through practical experience, yet they compete fiercely among themselves; qualities that are not easily noticed.

"My first contact here, who is now one of our union patrons, encouraged me to join them. He helped me acquire a stall and loaned me some money. I also raised some funds from family and friends. Now, I've repaid all the loans with some voluntary interests on them. The important thing is that I've continued to handle much of their paperwork. This service grew into other things. I've initiated a few beneficial seminars on export/import business that were tailored to their needs. Things happened naturally and delightfully."

The arrival of the financial secretary interrupted him, then he said, "Just months ago, I was elected the chair, and our EXCO is made up of enlightened men and women. We've gained much from this quality. We've put together a code of ethics, despite initial inertia. We're working on quality standards and pricing. The selling argument has been the advantages of credibility. Honestly speaking, business has continued to improve, especially with more returns that are predictable. Some other unions are copying us. Many of the things we've done were supposed to be done by regulating agencies, but we all know how government agencies perform. You asked about how we were doing: that's the general picture. Maybe, someone has more to add."

Obiajulu, the woman who spoke earlier, said, "Mr. Chairman, I like your modesty. It was he who brought all these changes. Before him, things were in the manner of the stereotypes of traders. After accepting to run for the chair, he first brought sanity into the process of electing the executive committee. People actually campaigned and had to detail what they would bring to the group, if elected. He led the way by carefully listing the challenges before the group and how to tackle them. All of us who were eventually elected followed his examples. We've all experienced great changes for the better. Our members are confident that things will continue to improve, especially with the trust we are gaining from customers. This is in very sharp contrast to what was happening before and, if I may dare say so, also to what is happening in the country, with our leadership voids."

The Publicity Secretary spoke. "Talking about Nigeria, what about our experiences in the Obasanjo tenure? Thank goodness, he was unable to extend his stay. All the noise about reforms and yet no one in his administration asked why all our young people want to get out of the country. They risk their lives and endure severe hardships elsewhere in Africa and beyond. To me, that's our biggest problem—the exit of our youths."

As the Publicity Secretary was speaking, the other woman present was flipping through a pile of newspapers on a table at the corner of the office.

She found what she was looking for and said, "Talking about Obasanjo and his party in their eight years' *reign*, this is one of the things Louis Odion wrote about them way back on the 9th of November, 2003, in his column, "Bottom-line," of *Sun* newspaper. You just have to hear the relevant portion. 'Obasanjo is the de facto petroleum minister, (Funso) Kupolokun heads the NNPC, Rasheed Gbadamosi fixes the pump price at the Petroleum Products Pricing Regulatory Agency (PPPRA), while General Oluleye's son serves as Secretary of PPPRA. Come to think of it, the seaport serves as the gateway for oil haulage. Again, thank God, Adebayo Sarumi is the new Managing Director of the Nigerian Ports Authority (NPA). What happens to the proceeds from oil sales? It is banked with Joseph Sanusi as the Central Bank Governor and when the account books are to be examined, of course, we are obliged to turn to Joseph Ajiboye, the nation's Auditor-General. What more, the nation's Accountant General, Kayode Naiyeju, is also a Yoruba man. Mind you, anyone who challenges this order risks being arrested by Tafa Balogun, the Inspector General of Police . . . Surely, never in history has the Yoruba conquest been this total.'

"The piece says it all about the reforms by Obasanjo and his party. Surrounded by his Yoruba kinsmen, they managed the country's biggest generator of revenues. Not too much can be further off from the reform of the old ways than that, knowing what could go wrong with that arrangement.

So, this EXCO is pushing our group away from such practices. I know that it's a limited, very small application, but it's truly the right beginning. Our chairman brought many of the changes."

Things were getting really stirred up, typical of discussions on Nigeria. Perhaps, out of politeness or the new habits, the men tactically yielded to the women.

Obiajulu said, "Things get juicier when you examine the other circles of cronies. The wealth creation of that administration targeted only a few. Recall that the el Rufai's BPE was at one time promoting some form of legislation similar to the US anti-trust laws to protect us from monopolies. Remember? That initiative was quietly dropped, no reasons given. Now look at what we have in some sectors, from sugar, cement, spaghetti, flour, textiles, communication, food, power, defence, to oil and gas, and others. Yes, reforms indeed. Yes, we're all being reformed into poverty and general insecurity. How more badly off can a people be?"

The treasurer said, "I've been following many discussions about our situations on TV and radio, mainly on Sundays. Most of them allow audience participation. You'd be surprised what you hear sometimes. I came to the conclusion long ago that our problems came from our loss of values. One thing for sure though: I trust the vitality and resilience of Nigerians. We shall bounce back."

Obiajulu said, "Oh yeah? But you aided the enslavement of your sisters and brothers. That's not a thing of the past. Today you are forcing your women into prostitution, causing child labour and other abuses, kidnapping children, causing economic enslavement, you are setting fire to public buildings and records, and on and on. The trend continues from one administration to the next. What vitality, what resilience are those? My brother, often, your optimism is too much."

Their auditor spoke in a low voice after a brief silence.

"Events naturally vent the advent of wisdom. Let's wait for a while, for history to settle. Obasanjo may have scored some good points for this country."

"Oh yeah?" Obiajulu said. "Our patient and meticulous auditor has vented his wisdom, after auditing their books and behaviours."

To calm things down, the chair cleared his throat, shrugged his shoulders, while raising his eyebrows.

He said, "Well, ladies and gentlemen, again you're welcome. We thank you for giving us the opportunity of being part of your commendable project. It's more than obvious that our country needs a severe cleaning up—you know what I mean. Before we go on, please let us have some kola nuts. We were waiting for the financial secretary and got carried away by the discussions. Now, he's here."

That changed the mood instantly. After the kola nuts traditions, the chair called on the Financial Secretary to present their donation to us. The cheque for 150,000 naira we received surprised my team. We very excitedly thanked them and, of course, we came back with the official acknowledgement and receipt a few hours later.

14

THE SURGE

Akpan, Musa, Adesina, Mfarga, Omatseye, Ahmed, and I were the fundraising team that called on a Traditional Ruler in the North-East Zone. He spoke to us from his elevated majestic chair, a little distant from us.

"Thank you very much for considering Traditional Rulers daily belittled by change. Results? Things are neither here nor there, but everywhere; every place, suffering and insecurity every day. Your letter pleased me. People of your age normally come here with personal problems. I very much endorse your project.

"You know that many Traditional Stools in this country date back to centuries, some, thousands of years. Before people with different skin colour came here, Traditional Rulers had firm control of society. Things were different. We had discipline, purpose, and direction. We had firm and set ways of dealing with all issues that faced the individual, family, community. By the time the British left, they had totally disorganised the roles of Traditional Rulers. These were the people who led resistance against them. However, the most painful development is that after they left, our politicians continued to devalue Traditional Rulers and our culture. It never occurred to them that we are Africans with good governance records. It never occurred to them that some constitutional roles should be assigned to us, in order to continue some of what we inherited from our Ancestors, which make more sense to more of our people everywhere in the country. Results? Confusion everywhere. However, when these politicians mess things up, they run to the Traditional Rulers for help. That does not make sense. Think about it.

"For instance, some decades back, a large sum of money then, around 100 million naira, was made available for nomadic education by the federal government. We could have played a good role in the project, but we didn't see any of that money. What was done in the nomadic education program, and where are the traces of infrastructure and results? Over time, matters concerning Traditional Rulers have been made government concerns, including the selection and, quite distastefully, the dethroning of Traditional Rulers. We now depend on government subventions instead of being able to raise our own support through the old systems of taxation of our subjects in return for keeping things under proper control. All these have been taken over by government, and how well are these politicians running the country today? That's the *Nigerian Question*. This situation must be corrected soonest, if we are to develop as Africans—unique, progressive, and yet, relevant and respected.

"My colleagues and I wish you every success. There's no better way to tackle our present circumstances than to pause, remember who we are, where we are and why, and where we want to go and how. You know, starting from home base and then growing and reaching out to the rest of the world in no subservient manner. This makes more sense than blindly plunging into unfamiliar systems. Thank you, again, for remembering us. My secretary will give you our small donation. You need help for taking the matter all over the country. Right? Good idea. Good luck."

To interrupt him would be rude, but it would have been fair to mention that from politicisation, a few unwanted characters had been wangling their way onto Stools, thereby causing more problems for the institution. We very politely thanked him for being so caring.

His secretary followed us out of the reception and handed us a cheque for N75, 000. The next day, we turned in the receipt for the donation to the secretary, with more appreciation. He told us that since receiving our letter, the Traditional Ruler had not stopped talking about our initiative to all his important visitors.

§ § §

Weeks on, TOMORROW, a social organisation devoted to youth matters, fired the imagination unforgettably in Ibadan. My fundraising team was then made up of Omoregie, Titilola, Helima, Ifeoma, Utange, Bunmi, Kolapo, Shehu, and me. On receiving our letter, they invited us to their EXCO meeting.

To our amazement, our hosts were punctual to the last person. The meeting started without fanfare.

Soon afterwards, their chair shouted, "TANNA! TANNA! TANNA-A-A!"

The rest heightened our surprise with their instant response. "TOMORROW for TANNA! TANNA for TOMORROW! TOMORROW for TANNA-A-A-A!"

A short pause did not clear our surprise; the chair spoke again.

"TANNA, you're welcome. We know of your activities, and if we maintain our motivations, we are both concerned about the same thing—tomorrow. We're only dealing with local issues, but symbolically, we represent the youth of this country. We are a small, focused group that believes that the results we finally achieve will be widely infectious, pace setting. Hopefully, our organisations will merge somehow, sometime."

They spoke with much passion to define their objectives. We listened.

Young people were increasingly and alarmingly being turned into functional illiterates educationally and otherwise, thereby exposing them to all the dangers of incomplete knowledge. Following that, they were idled by lack of noble opportunities to participate in nation building. Hence, they were being diverted into objectionable activities, which only led to troubled dead-ends. Their past was being obliterated, their Afrikan culture disregarded, while being persistently bombarded with elements of alien cultures that often do not sit that well. Uprooted and neglected, they remained alienated, as they watch our common abundance frittered away and transformed into liabilities to them and future generations. Worse still, they said, opportunities outside the country were made more difficult by the stench from the ongoing disgrace in Nigeria. Not even thought was given to recognising how the negative mind-set the rest of the world holds towards Africa, and Nigeria particularly, came about, talk less about acting to reverse the situation. They strongly emphasised that the situation would continue to handicap them in global affairs—what uphill tasks.

The rapid battery of fiery, yet flowery eruptions, a vibrating activist register, numbed us with the harsh brutality of their truth.

Our leader, Titilola, managed to respond.

"Indeed, if we both stay on course, we are about the same things. Yesterday, today, and tomorrow are intricately connected; we must treat them as such. Thank you very much for allowing us to share your time. We look forward to TOMORROW becoming a valued associate of TANNA."

Soon after, we received a donation of 5,000 naira from TOMORROW. We sincerely thanked them, as if they had donated five million naira, and left.

We remained awed for quite a while by that brief and intense encounter. We were in the South-West; where else in the country could such a young group exist?

§ § §

About a month from the last meeting of the zonal coordinators in Benin City, TANNA's structures became reasonably in place at the zones and states. Temporary groups executed activities with the exception of fundraising.

Each office in the zones was selected mainly from the points of single occupancy, availability of some residential spaces, and reasonable access to transportation. Critical communication went via hand deliveries, except in emergencies, when the Internet, under automatic, random codes, was used.

We acquired a few small boats and a fleet of vehicles, some fitted with electricity generators, loudspeakers, projectors, and enlarged first aid kits. A few were off-road types. Publicity materials had been prepared and edited. TANNA felt that a groundswell in the demand for the conference from the rural areas would be significant.

Chiamalu had prepared an operating manual in two parts, physical and mental. The mental dealt with possible negative reactions to the project and called for proactive intellectual sharpness. The physical stressed personal dangers and called for more vigilance and due process. Typically, he included with two energising statements: 'A high-end sensation is the relished enjoyment of the fruits of one's hard labour. To break through barriers to sufficiently influence people is to purposefully communicate.'

A concise statement that included TANNA's core values was taken from the manual and recited at the beginning and conclusion of meetings. On a personal level, the 'face-off: consequences' inner ringing in my head often shunted my mental processes.

§ § §

Seven months after our detention by security, teams from every zone surged out into their rural areas with blaring speakers attracting attention. Market days, Fridays, Saturdays, Sundays, and others with activities that assembled people in large numbers were first stressed.

Quite delightfully, Traditional Rulers in some parts of the country were supportive. We noticed further concerns about our activities by politicians and others. This propelled S&I into more development.

The people were sceptical at the outset. Many wanted to know whether TANNA was a political party. After answering these initial questions, the teams went into the business of their visits. People were finally told that all those who wished to be involved should submit their names and contact information. Many did so.

The publicity committee kicked off a national campaign in the media at the same time. Grades of newspapers were used periodically to introduce the mission of TANNA: an uninhibited countrywide conference that suitably heals, organises, and better focuses Nigeria. Many social media chattered too. This message was in English language.

The presentation had received some attention and was ready for the North-West Zone at Gummi. A presentation team, reshuffled for each zone, was in place and had done its work for Gummi. Ike's manager in Sokoto was helpful in this regard.

A lead speaker, a professor of history at the University of Abuja and an indigene of southern Sokoto state, was selected. He was very agreeable to our terms, which included what the general people from the area suffered in the hands of the rest of the country and intra-ethnic imperialists. He also supplied us cultural music and a list of all distinct ethnic groups that co-inhabit the zone. He bluntly refused the honorarium we were offering lead speakers.

Being from a minority group in Sokoto state, he must have been motivated by the experiences of his group. His output set an excellent template for the rest of the presentations.

The rural blitz and media campaign started on a Monday and the presentation at Gummi was on the Saturday of that week. Chiamalu led the presentation, and an eloquent TANNA member from the zone was the moderator. The presentation turned out better than the first one at Enugu. The contact details on the booklets were those of TANNA's zonal office. There was also the rush for them. A pleasing differentiation was that over three-million-naira donation was instantly realised.

Our funds were growing from fundraising activities all over the country and the efficient management of our funds that included staggered investments in reliable short-term instruments. On the Monday after the Gummi presentation, a concentrated fundraising force worked the North-West zone. The boost lasted through the two weeks between Gummi and Calabar in the South-South. This arrangement was maintained.

From Gummi onwards, things picked up beyond our dreams. The Professador got better, the package continued to improve, fundraising got better, and volunteers grew in number and quality over more expertise fields. After the presentation at Kaduna, we decided to do an extra one, the tenth, at Abuja, the seat of Government, as a finale.

With this progress, we certainly felt the not-so-minor irritations we were causing in many quarters, as indicated by more surveillance from arms of the superfluous authority. We reacted accordingly.

The Abuja presentation was indeed a very good end to the series. Many government functionaries attended. The presence of security personnel was unmistakable from the persistent questions asked in various styles and formats about sponsorships, and the modalities for the conference. Of course, Professador and the moderator expertly parried the misleading ones. We also picked up a number of civil society groups.

§ § §

The presentations and the surge into the rural areas ended the same week. To sustain the momentum, we fortified each zone. S&I became increasingly awesome. Occasionally, they ferreted out suspicious infiltrators who were disgraced and booted out. Their activities introduced quite a few rituals everywhere—the constant drumming in of our core values and some clandestine activities, for instance. They eventually became elitist.

The real action had begun, and TANNA, so far, proved equal to the task.

The names of those who wished to be involved at the rural levels led to flexible structures in all local government areas. We picked a coordinator in each local government area and organisers for the wards. Individuals, ordinarily considered opinion-makers, made the lists. S&I in each zone later amended those choices.

Selected rural individuals were invited to meetings at the state capitals for further grounding in the project. We planned the meetings so that they had to spend two nights in high-end hotels at the state capitals, a first-time experience for many of them. Each one got a little allowance for incidentals. After the meetings that ended on a Thursday, they went back to their communities as ardent promoters of the project.

On Saturday night of that week, we were stunned in every zone, excepting the FCT. The residences of some moderators and speakers of our presentations were methodically set ablaze. Chiamalu's house was one of them, and it received special attention. The worst damages occurred in the South-South, North-Central, and South-West, where the targets lived in complexes. Fifteen people died and forty-seven others received severe burns, but no moderator or speaker died.

The original Uhuru Hut seven were scattered throughout the country, but my Yenagoa in Bayelsa state location made me the closest to Enugu. I got to Chiamalu's house around 2:00 p.m. on Sunday to see only charred walls and everything else in either ashes or still smouldering. The strong smell of combustible fluids still filled the air.

When I relayed the news to Chiamalu over the phone, he paused, heaved a laboured, long sigh, and muttered in a fading voice, "Everything has a price, don't they?"

I heard his pain.

TANNA promptly paid for the medical costs of the injured, burial costs, and general reliefs as appropriate.

S&I, feeling humiliated, sprang into comprehensive responses. Tuesday morning, their preliminary report also indicated that some members of the so-called political class, in keeping with their perverted portrayal, which tips the scale in favour of harlotry, of the run-down cliché that 'in politics there are no permanent friends or enemies, but permanent interests,' highlighted TANNA as a group to watch. We tightened slacks in our programs. Our funds were growing and, in the words of the same politicians, our 'war chest' was in fair shape.

The gathering of intelligence on these people was not extremely demanding, thanks to overbearing and misguided confidence, leading to loose, showy lifestyles. S&I developed groups primed to match their antics; we were not oblivious to the saying that it took a thief to catch a thief.

Again, the attempts by arsonists to torch our four zonal offices, the night after the S&I report, rattled us on Wednesday morning. It was surmised that every zonal office was targeted for simultaneous action. S&I was brilliant. The misfits were videotaped and stopped just before they lit up.

S&I thoroughly debriefed them before handing them over to the authorities. Later reports revealed that after S&I had effectively explained what the project meant to the arsonists personally, they revealed their sponsors. S&I followed up to give us some potent tools.

They developed what they called Damning Dossiers (DDs) on each of the sponsors. A fully developed DD read like a far-reaching story of the subject on the wrong side of everything—him/herself and humanity. After reading many DDs, one would be tempted to again ask whether philanthropy was most times inspired by guilt. S&I very strongly directed that the DDs be used very sparingly, to allow for proper containment of reactions. The events directed more attention and sympathy our way.

Speakers and moderators at our presentations became fanatical extremists to be 'leashed' or 'stalked;' who could blame them? Most members of TANNA became more dedicated as well. The loss of lives and Chiamalu's house struck painful chords in my consciousness. The 'face-off: consequences' routine was also in the background. But, I kept faith.

Our publicity committee squeezed out every ounce of publicity and sympathy from the events. They placed spot announcements and participated in live discussion shows, while reeling out strings of arguments favouring the project. The more permanent arguments were carefully produced to be properly argued.

We started new campaigns in the rural areas based on the message that: "Life for every individual will improve now and in future, with less deception and theft of our abundance. All other places have enough problems of their own and will only intervene in our conditions if their interests are unduly served. Our future is truly in our hands. To secure that future is to get involved in correcting the affairs of the country. If you are in favour of the national conference TANNA has recommended, sign up now."

The professionally expressed message was supported with events and conditions that people were concerned about. We had sheets of paper ready for capturing converts. The campaigns took time, effort, and other resources, but they provided us with the overriding voices of the people.

Our offerings were receiving feedback. Countrywide, we were getting 57 percent approval, 13 percent outright rejection, 17 percent qualified approval, 8 percent unsure, and a striking 5 percent attack on TANNA. What pleased us most were the results from signing up supporters from rural areas. We then projected that we were ready for the apparently more elusive and self-styled sophisticates of the urban centres.

§ § §

The national adverts in print media in English continued, but the electronic media ones were translated into local languages. For urban areas, we used "Pidgin English."

Neither Labour nor student organisations at all levels openly pledged their support, but we felt that we could get backing from them. We shifted to secondary schools and tertiary institutions, where we organised lectures and debates. Soon after becoming familiar with those environments, we initiated the collection of signatures. We wanted more.

The long vacations were weeks away, so we started recruiting and training students who would help with the urban campaigns. Many were glad to support us and earn some money.

S&I initially kicked against it, but still, it was decided to initiate the urban campaigns with rallies held concurrently at all state capitals on a Saturday morning. Popular speakers were recruited to speak, but their speech outlines were edited to avoid extreme provocations. We then ensured that every venue was properly booked, and obtained formal promises that the police would cover all locations.

On Wednesday before the rallies, many state offices received warnings from S&I that it was likely that our rallies would be disrupted by bands of thugs. It was then too late to cancel the rallies that had been widely advertised. S&I promised to do their best.

At about 9:15 a.m., people started gathering for the rallies billed for ten o'clock. The performers we had engaged entertained them. The little booklets we had printed, outlining our proposal for the conference, were distributed to the people as they arrived. Things generally took off as planned at all locations and went well for about an hour, on the average, before the thugs struck. They came with whips, sticks, and a few handguns, which they first fired in the air, before charging at speakers' positions. What happened next credited S&I.

In response to the provocations everywhere, a group of young men and women who could only be identified by their disciplined carriage and fast actions took on the thugs, blow for blow, and tried to control the crowds. These latter actions minimised injuries and, in all cases, the advances of the thugs towards the speakers' stands were halted.

Not surprisingly, when the thugs could be generally identified, many of the people present joined in paying back the thugs at some locations. Normality or something close to it eventually returned at most venues for the rallies to run to programmed ends. The rallies were terminated only in three states—not bad at all.

The police were present, but only in such small numbers that they could not have been able to successfully deal with the situation. They finally arrested many of the thugs, but it later became evident that most of thugs' ringleaders were not immediately handed over to the police. S&I spirited them away in the confusion and interrogated them before taking them to the police.

The police generally had a permissive attitude to all that S&I did. This raised the question about how far our arguments had penetrated the system. However, all the arrested thugs were quietly released later. From their own interrogations of the thugs, S&I significantly enlarged their DDs' lists.

TANNA contributed greatly to the medical bills of the injured, and thank goodness, no one died. All relevant committees used the opportunity to reap more publicity and support, while promoting the drives for signatures. The incidents were very beautifully covered in the media in impressive ways that kept them relatively long in the headlines, thanks to some associates.

The urban campaigns began throughout the country. The students and others from the bloated, unemployed legion, trained for the drive, took to the streets, handing out the booklets and collecting signatures. Most people contacted were aware of TANNA, its project, the earlier fires, the arson attempts, and the disruptions of the rallies. S&I still provided some subtle cover for our workers, whenever they were in areas highlighted as probable trouble spots. Many of the people who signed up sent their reactions to the booklets to us.

All committees and subgroups worked long hours to keep to schedules. Signatures collected were being processed into wards in the format supplied by ICT; materials were being produced for later campaigns; responses to our booklet were analysed; budgets for projected events were being prepared, and fundraising was on.

Within five weeks, the first phase of the urban campaigns was finished and was hugely successful. Most workers were paid off, but those still on were carefully selected for the follow through for some time.

Relevant committees edited the booklet to add some suggestions from the public. We took the resulting draft to some members of the Judiciary, some trusted activists, selected members of the traditional institutions, some members of the media, a few university deans, organised labour, national students' executives, selected leaders of the private sector, and some individuals for their comments. Nearly all of them responded and their meriting contributions were included in the draft.

Quite a few thought it would be difficult to pull off the conference for reasons ranging from the reactions of the government to the problems associated with keeping the process reflective of the wishes of the people. TANNA pushed on.

Signatures collected were organised, crossed-referenced into wards, local government areas, and states, and centrally data banked according to zones by ICT. This was tedious, but they did it right and on time. The originals were taken outside the country.

§ § §

From options available, TANNA selected pushing for the passage of laws that would provide the authority for the conference to be held in our advocated form. Our relevant committees spent some time producing a draft of the required bill, edited several times before being sent to the legislature, and copying the Executive and Judiciary.

Surprisingly, all three promptly acknowledged the receipts of the drafts. They were short and polite, but we waited for S&I reports. Without an official agreement, they had possibly decided to frustrate the project with tactical silence they hoped would diffuse the pressure. Off the record, the legislature lined up excuses for putting off our proposed bill. If we made things difficult, some controversies would be contrived to postpone action on our bill.

TANNA, seemingly, was waiting to hear from the legislature, but we quietly used the time well. The urban and rural campaigns for more signatures, for example, were reviewed and reinforced. The effort gave us handsome returns—a few notches added to our percentages in numerous wards. All additional signatures were quickly included in the databanks shipped out. It was uplifting to find that we had hit 78 percent of people eligible to vote in the country.

We called our draft bill The Affirmation Confab Bill; it quickly acquired the acronym, 'ACB' that cluttered the airways and print media.

For a start, ACB stipulated that each ward should nominate five electoral officers. These would select local government electoral officers from among themselves. The local government officers would similarly select state electoral officers, and that the state officers would also select national electoral officers. The minimum qualification for ward and local government officers would be WAEC or equivalent, and university first degree for state and national officers. ACB also stated that replacements at all levels would be made for all those picked for higher level duties, and that the people should be able to successfully conduct these exercises, if adequately informed and supported.

All the selected officers were to be seconded to existing staff of the Electoral Commission to make them familiar with operations and for identifying needs. As soon as these were completed, the current staff of the Electoral Commission would temporarily vacate their seats for the new team, until the end of the conference. The suggested time limit for these activities was three months.

For the creation of a potent voters' register, the draft ACB specified as follows. Each head or proxy of the nuclear family would complete a full range demographic form, including the family's lineage to a minimum of five generations. The head of the extended family, where such existed, would then check and countersign the form. Otherwise, the community leader or Traditional Ruler would serve the same purpose. The local language spoken in the area, where appropriate, should be stated, along with other locations that share the language.

The ward nominees earlier selected would collect the completed forms from extended family heads and community leaders or Traditional Rulers, and check that all families in the ward had completed the forms correctly before forwarding them to their local government electoral coordinator. The forms would be checked at the local government for completeness of coverage before being transmitted to the state electoral coordinator.

In urban and other areas with mixed residences, the property owner or his alternate would function as head of extended family, but with less responsibility. Employers of labour would be required to confirm that all their employees of voting age were registered.

The information on the forms would be checked for complete coverage, entered into databanks, and cross-referenced at the state levels before being sent to the national headquarters. A list of eligible voters would then be provided for each ward from the national headquarters. Verification would be ongoing. Some other recommendations were noteworthy.

Any head or equivalent of a nuclear family, who wilfully falsified information, would be liable to three years hard-labour imprisonment without option of fines. Any extended family head, community leader, or Traditional Ruler found to have colluded in committing such offence would be liable to similar two years imprisonment. All the electoral nominees at all levels found guilty of collusion to commit such offence would face a similar three-year imprisonment. Of course, our draft ACB provided for just and expeditious hearings by Special Courts prior to the impositions of the prison terms.

All the electoral nominees were to be paid according to the existing terms of service of the Electoral Commission, but with liberal bonuses to all outstanding performers.

For the delegates to the conference, we proposed that each resulting dialectical group was to meet as often as necessary, within a period of one month, to harmonise their visions for the country and to prepare to elect delegates to the conference. Each group was to send three delegates to the conference as follows. A delegate each from the age brackets of eighteen to thirty, thirty-one to fifty, and fifty-one years and above, with each delegate possessing a minimum educational qualification of WAEC or equivalent, but the higher the better. The election for selecting delegates was to be simplified and conducted by the new Electoral Commission.

Each dialectical group was to present two candidates in each of the age categories, making six potential delegates. The election in each ward was to consist of a cheap, but functional, booth assembled from locally available materials, such as palm fronds in the rural areas. Simple ballot boxes behind which large, colour-coded photographs of the candidates would be placed, and wooden or plastic chips for casting votes were to be used.

As voters lined up, they would each be given three chips, colour coded as the photographs, with which to cast their individual votes for one candidate in each age category. Voters were to wait after voting to witness and certify the vote count before the results were forwarded to the local government collation centres, then to the state headquarters, and finally to the national headquarters.

The Electoral Commission would confirm the elected delegates through its final announcement of the results from its national headquarters. Errors detected at this point would be quickly corrected, as results of elections would also be available at all levels subordinate to the national headquarters.

Elected delegates would sequentially assemble at local governments, states, and zones to formulate stands on probable issues for the conference. One of the items to be agreed upon at each zone would be the people to be presented for election into the Conference Steering Committee (CSC).

ACB recommended the election of CSC as follows. The CSC would be made up of the Chair and the Vice, the Secretary and his Assistant, the Financial Secretary and his Assistant, the Treasurer and his Deputy, the Auditor and his Deputy, Protocol and Logistics Officer and his two Deputies, making a total of thirteen members. The age schedules were: the Chair - forty-six years and above and the Vice - thirty-one to forty-five; the Secretary - forty-six and above and his Assistant - thirty-one to forty-five; the Financial Secretary - thirty-one to forty-five and his Assistant - eighteen to thirty; the Treasurer - thirty-one to forty-five and his Deputy eighteen to thirty; Auditor - thirty-one to forty-five and his Deputy - eighteen to thirty; Protocol and Logistics Officer - forty-six and above and his Deputies thirty-one to forty-five and eighteen to thirty respectively. All CSC members were to participate in all meetings relating to their ethnic groups.

All elected delegates would assemble to elect these members, starting from the chair. The results of the election to each position would be announced before the election of the next member was done, to place the burden of equitable spread of CSC membership on the delegates, without compromising quality, of course.

We suggested that two members should come from each geopolitical zone and one from the FCT. Every zone and the FCT were required to present a candidate for election to each position in the CSC, and the voting would be simplified, but secret.

The election of the CSC was to take place three months before the start of the conference and would be facilitated by the new-face Electoral Commission. It became the responsibility of the CSC to organise and run the conference. Remember that the informed and motivated people selected them at all levels.

Our draft ACB tackled the often-raised matter of the possibility of having parallel governments in place, if the conference was to have sufficient authority, by carefully stipulating duties based on the fine argument that both the government in place and the conference were serving the same masters, THE PEOPLE. It therefore placed the functions of ongoing governance exclusively in the hands of the government, but made the conference a heeded adviser.

Since the conference was for the long-lasting good of all, the funding strategy ought to make everyone contribute. Our draft ACB then stated that everyone eighteen years and above should pay a flat levy, the total of which would amount to one-quarter of the estimated cost of the conference, while the private sector on one hand and the federal and state governments on the other should each come up with three-eighths. We estimated the starting budget as ten billion naira.

The delegates were to be properly maintained and paid additional, nominal allowances. The monies contributed for the conference were to be deposited at the Central Bank, and the CSC, the Accountant General, and the Auditor-General were to operate the account, while publishing monthly reports. There was the provision that the central government would come up with any advances required to keep the conference going, pending the collection of the levies.

From three months before and throughout the conference, no new capital project would be allowed.

The timing, the beginning and duration of the conference, was left open in the case of duration, but the activities leading to the conference were to start no later than a month from the signing of the bill. Six consecutive weeks of sitting were to be followed by a two-week recess to enable delegates interact with their various constituencies.

Every decision of the conference was to be based on consensus, failing which, voting took place. For any issue to be approved by voting, it must receive 74 percent total yes votes, but must also receive no less than 40 percent yes votes from every state and the FCT. Every delegate was to vote at all times. Any rejected matter was to be rescheduled for more discussion and another vote. If after three attempts and the matter still failed to pass, it would be listed for discussion towards the end of the conference. If it failed again then, it would be put to the people. Any such matter put to the people was to be expressed for simple yes or no vote. For such a matter to be approved, it must receive an aggregate of 70 percent and no less than 35 percent yes votes from every state and the FCT respectively. If the matter was vital to the final goals of the conference, and if it failed to be approved by the people, the delegates would be granted a two-week recess for consulting their constituencies and acceptably representing the matter before the conference, to begin another cycle of similar voting. We envisaged this situation as extreme.

15

FAST FORWARD

Mansur and Irabor of the Publicity Committee were travelling from Yola to Port Harcourt in our station wagon when they had a mishap close to Obollo Afor, in Nsukka. At a long bend, two north-bound heavy vehicles, one a tanker full of petrol and the other a semitruck carrying a mixed cargo of construction materials and a few people sitting on top of all that, suddenly loomed before them. The semitruck was overtaking the tanker at the bend. This left very little reaction time. Mansur and Irabor shouted warnings to Amobi, the driver—Mansur from the back seat and Irabor from the passenger's front seat.

The road did not have much shoulder room and whatever was left after the pothole-strewn tarred area was filled with erosion washouts. However, the terrain gently dropped off from both sides before the side they were on rose sharply into a hill about seventy-five metres away.

Amobi swiftly steered the car between two trees and into the gentle drop. He worked fast against off-road challenges in steering the car away from direct impacts with trees that dotted the area. On one occasion, the steering wheel spun out of his grip. Like an endangered, but striking cobra, Amobi pounced back on it. The car banked violently from side to side a few times and then flipped over on its side, rolled down the slope, first slowly then faster, and came to rest on a tree at the base of the hill.

Mansur was trapped inside. Irabor and Amobi were thrown out of the car, still strapped to their seats. They suffered bumps and bruises and were conscious. Amobi quickly freed himself and rushed to the car. Mansur was pinned inside, unconscious and bleeding heavily. Irabor joined Amobi a few moments later. Blood trickled down their faces, but they ignored that. Shock overrode pain.

Often on all fours, they scampered back onto the road; the trucks were long gone. They frantically flagged down vehicles. Passengers in three commercial minibuses and two private cars that stopped followed them to where the car was and, with makeshift tools and raw muscle power, they pried out Mansur and carried him to the roadside.

A nurse or someone in that category was among the people who helped. She gave instructions on how Mansur was to be carried up the slope and placed by the roadside. An empty ambulance travelling to Enugu stopped. As Mansur was being carried into the ambulance, Amobi borrowed a handset and contacted our South-East S&I.

Some people from the village nearby heard the noise and came to the scene. Amobi commissioned them to watch over the car, while he travelled with Mansur and Irabor to Enugu in the ambulance. The car had been low on fuel and was to be refuelled at Obollo Afor. This sufficiently reduced the chances of an explosion or fire, but Amobi sternly warned the villagers not to get close to the vehicle because of the possibility of an explosion. His instructions might have saved the items in the car, which were all accounted for later.

S&I had no trouble in having them admitted into one of the better-run private hospitals in Enugu, but S&I was fully stretched. Danladi and I were then summoned to Enugu to take care of the situation. I was in Lagos, and Danladi in Calabar. Mansur's younger brother, Jibril, joined us from Katsina three days later.

Mansur was unconscious in intensive care, but the doctor assured us that his situation was not as hopeless as it seemed. His room had a small antechamber that could hold no more than three people. One could view the inside of the room through a connecting, small, clear glass window, if the curtain behind it was not drawn. The curtain was not drawn.

On arrival, Irabor and Amobi were examined, their wounds treated, and were kept on daily checkups. Eventually, they became part of the team of Danladi, Adesina, Ikpeme, Akachi, Jibril, and me that had the responsibility for Mansur and related hospital issues.

Next day, the doctor spoke to us after being with Mansur. She said, "All three gentlemen took some banging around and they lost some blood. The other two were luckier; that's not to say that Mansur is in terribly bad shape. He lost some blood all right, but he's stable. We've not detected any internal injuries to be concerned about. He's scheduled for more scans and tests later. He'll come around."

Jibril had to ask, "Doctor, thank you very much. Why are his eyeballs, Adam's apple, toes, and, at times, feet moving and he's not fully awake?"

"Those are good signs," the doctor said as she departed.

When Mansur was discharged from the hospital, he was in fair shape, but not good enough for him to travel back to Katsina. His rib hurt a little from a healing, hairline fracture. We took him to the house of a volunteer whose wife was a nurse and worked out a schedule for being with him on a 24/7 basis. On his third evening from the hospital, and at his request, he addressed ten of us, including his direct hosts, about his accident-related experiences.

"I can't call you all friends; you're like family. First, thanks so much for caring so well for Amobi, Irabor, and me. Mr. and Mrs. Ochiagha so easily made Jibril and me members of their family. Mrs. Ochiagha even feeds me some of my Katsina choice meals. I feel much better now. Thanks. I want to share my experiences from the accident. Because we are all TANNA, you will not ridicule me. Those bloody trucks so thoughtlessly blocked the bend. Abreast with each other, they kept coming at us, and, for some moments there, we were terrified. I screamed something to Amobi. His reactions were excellent. Perhaps, we should sponsor him for race driving after the conference. He battled to keep us off the trees. We were thrown from side to side so quickly and violently until we finally tumbled onto a tree. On that crushing impact, I blanked out, but I slowly regained what now seems like partial consciousness. That may not be the right description.

"First, details of my life quickly flashed through my mind; from events in my early childhood. It all happened rapidly and vividly, but I understood it all. When it got to the accident, I blanked out again, and there was this deep void of darkness. Later, the state of partial consciousness, or whatever it was, gradually returned. I was lifted out of my body and I floated in the air. I could watch all the activities connected with taking me, my body that is, out of the car and carrying me to the road. It was bizarre; the double existence of my body and another conscious me elsewhere. I observed all the people shouting, pointing, and rushing up and down the slope. I tried to tell them as loudly as I could that I was all right, but no one heard me. I just gave up and watched proceedings, close to me and farther away.

"The dark-complexioned woman who was directing affairs was good and self-assured. She acted like a field commander, confidently telling people how to covey my body up the slope and finally into the ambulance. Everyone obeyed her without question. You know, purpose and focus constitute an efficient filter. I don't know whether the next events make up an omen or were the products of our general focus on our project. At the end though, we got the country of our dreams—I've jumped a lot there; I'll back up for a better flow.

"After a while, I saw a pinpoint light that grew bigger as it moved towards me. When it got close enough, it changed into a most colourful display of illumination, gorgeous and calming. The space was filled with cloudlike formations of substances that continuously glowed and changed colours. Everything blended so well. Then, after a while, I saw some images in the shapes of women appear far away, and like the tiny light, they grew in size and definition—something like a zooming-in action. They finally stopped a few metres from me and were seven in number. The one who was their leader was the most dazzling. She moved to the front of the group and came a little closer to me. Oh, she had that attractive smile and enticing mannerisms; you know, the 'come on' types. She beckoned at me and with a voice that sounded like some romantic music, she said, 'Mansur, you've been wanting to get out of the darkness, haven't you? Come with us, we have a lot to show you. Lots of fun. You'll love it.'

"Naturally, I was willing to obey her, and just by thinking that I wanted to go with them, and particularly her, I was instantly floated towards them. I felt awkward at first, but soon got used to being able to alter my speed and direction by mere thought. All the women were more able to do the same things; that was why all my effort to catch up with the leader failed. Whenever I got close to her, she would look back at me, wink, smile, and then swiftly glide away. This cycle of events repeated itself, but I found myself unwilling to give up the chase. The more times the cycle occurred, the more determined I was. On one occasion, she said, 'Mansur, just follow us. You have Naija to visit; Naija of your dreams. Or, are you not aware that your old Nigeria has changed to Naija? Come on, you'll love it there.' I responded with the thought that it was her I wanted. She immediately looked back and smiled. Her voice also had a fading tremolo to it; that made it all more appealing. As all this was going on, I was unaware of speed and distance. All that mattered was that my thoughts were immediately translated into actions.

"Suddenly, the colourful clouds cleared like some floating dust swept away by a strong gale. What looked like a modern farm appeared. The woman looked back at me and pointed towards it. Next, I found myself on a road there, and all the women disappeared. I did not feel anything like a landing. I just found myself on the road. From then on, more amazing things, produced by my thoughts, happened. My first thought was: when did Nigeria become Naija? Sadly, I didn't add the how.

"Instantly, I was at this ultramodern parade ground and by its looks, a derivative from Okpara Square here at Enugu, the ones in Lagos and Abuja, because it had some features taken from all of them, but more harmonised, beautified, and spacious than any of them. It was packed with people, and I could locate myself to any point in it that I desired to be at. The public address system worked very well, without the dominance of upper frequencies. The sounds were amplified, more natural, and clear. The events very quickly played out. The march past by schoolchildren, older students of higher institutions, workers, and some others came first. Cultural dances followed, and acrobatic displays were next. The Armed Forces ended the parade with a flurry of thrills. People who appeared to be leaders spoke about the name of Nigeria being changed to Naija, without saying why. The final event was the lowering of the familiar green and white flag of Nigeria and the raising of another flag with 'Naija' inscribed at its centre. As soon as this happened, there was a barrage of gun salutes, a loud roll of assorted drums, and the whole place erupted with applause. It all echoed like a very powerful, distant volcano.

"I then asked whether this Naija occupied the same space as Nigeria. I found myself sufficiently elevated into space, as to see that it indeed was the same area as Nigeria. The national boundaries were in brilliant orange. Many super highways crisscrossed the country and linked major cities and towns. There were the rail lines for super-fast and slower trains. I saw them all in use. When I thought about how people lived, I was immediately seated before a large screen in what looked like a big cinema hall. The major cities and some rural areas flashed by. It all happened so fast, but I was able to understand whatever aspects interested me. I saw that some names of cities, towns, and streets had changed. Many new roads traversed the rural areas, which contained carefully laid out farms. The people I saw in most of the scenes appeared happy.

"I thought about all the unemployment, hunger, poverty, ignorance, and disease. The relevant scenes appeared before me: first, a workers' parade. Workstations were displayed according to the nature of activities, starting from agriculture to manufacturing, construction works, public and private offices, an impressive lineup of markets for various commodities and merchandise, down to small enterprises in rural and urban areas. Most of the people conducted themselves politely. I saw that the roads, communication systems, and general sanitation were in decent shapes. Sample activities in the formal education system, starting from pre-kindergarten to universities, scrolled by. The public healthcare sector showed service and infrastructure at high standards, even for the few relatively indigent. Through it all, it was clear that the ever-elusive power supply challenges had been conquered. Perhaps, because of the unemployment part of my thoughts, the typical hangouts of the idle in Nigeria were shown without anyone loitering. Instead, there were many productive activities at those locations.

"Just by wishing to see and interact with some people, I was whisked onto a street that was busy at about midday. I was more curious about the people than they were about me. I had become a little cautious about what I thought about, so I just let my mind float. That was a little difficult to do. Occasionally, some people glanced, smiled, or nodded at me. I found myself responding in kind. A curious thing always happened whenever I was interested in a woman: the subject would briefly turn into the lead woman. I didn't know what to make of that. At one point, I was sitting among a group of people, male and female, old and young, who were watching a very large screen for what eventually turned out as different reasons. The reactions of each person to what was on the screen varied noticeably—at the same times, some smiled, some appeared totally absorbed, some sad, some angry, some rejoicing, and some clowning. For me, what was on the screen was a long procession of enchanting cultural displays. They included those for weddings, childbirths, celebrations of maturity, achievements, funerals, and festivals.

"My thoughts returned to why the reactions of all the others were different from mine, because whenever I involuntarily clapped for the performers, nobody else would. Instantly, the screen broke up into tiny thumbnails, equal in number to all present. Amazing! In other words, what one saw on the screen was what one's mind called for. Hey, that was way out; a mind-controlled monitor or something. My scenes returned shortly afterwards. Some got up and left, while some more people trickled in for their own sessions. The entire setup was quite familiar to all of them, it seemed. I then queried the relevance of Naija to the rest of the world. Zap! I was transported into an extensive underground location beneath a big mountain. Here was a large complex of mainly scientific workshops, laboratories, and observatories. The place was secured mechanically and by guards, but I was able to get through without questions. All my encounters with people were cordial, as if I had been expected. However, none of them stopped or even slowed down in whatever they were doing. They all ignored me in a permissive way, and I could look at and touch whatever I wanted to. Everything I touched felt so real. I was so happy to explore the place.

"If you stood before a large mirror in one of the laboratories, you saw your entire anatomy, as all your organs and systems performed their functions.

Blood flow was in dark to bright red, nerve signals in grey, electrical signals in blinking bright silver, chemical reactions in assorted colours, depending on what the reactions were, airflow was in off cream, but quite visible, and water was in blue. The incredibly large number of activities in the brain and the working of the heart and its circuits were so amazing. How I now miss all that expertise, environment, and independence.

"The most captivating place was the space control room. It was the size of three football fields and was filled with screens of all sizes and shapes, control knobs, scopes, varied sizes of computers all linked to hundreds of huge servers working in tandem. It was easy to identify all the leads to the collection of antennas mounted on the mountaintop. The crackling noises from distant space filled the room from the very efficient speakers. On the largest and most central screen were the images of five spacecrafts, launched some time earlier and on an intergalactic mission towards a planet spotted in another galaxy, and which was found appealing in the search for intelligent life, as usually understood. Now I wonder, understood by whom and by what standards? This screen was the hub of activities. Quite a few people had their desks clustered before it and they were frequently looking up at it, down on the much smaller screens on their desks, and then entering information into computers. The images of the five vehicles had occasional zooming-in actions on them, to keep them in view on the screen: they were travelling at such high speeds. Their images were brought together on that screen, but actually, they were very far apart from one another, on extensively separate trajectories and at varying distances from target. These were the incredible outer space distances.

"Each of the five vehicles was equipped with MFACS[16] and CAMS[17]. The MFACS took care of flight parameters for all of them, and were layered five times in each vehicle and could work well in options narrowed down to one. Any one lagging behind, in relation to their distances from Earth, gathered all the information, amplified, and relayed it back to Earth. The combined actions of the MFACS and CAMS were responsible for the disappearances,

---

[16] MFACS, Multiple Flight Automations System.
[17] CAMS, Collision Avoidance Manoeuvring System.

on occasions, of the images of the vehicles.

"A most incredible technology, MRM[18], was on each of them and captured all exhaust materials, upgraded and reused them, in addition to radiation conversion, other traditional sources of energy, and interstellar gravity. Because this was possible, their speeds continually increased. If all went well, the lead vehicle was to go into orbit around the target planet to make preliminary surveys, and then communicate findings to the other four behind, so that they could make needed adjustments for their individual missions. This automation of their flights was necessary, because the turnaround time for signals to them from Earth was then getting to fifty earth days. Incredible speeds, incomprehensible distances, and amazing feats, all competently handled. Of course, the whole world watched.

"I recalled the hot issues of 'resource control,' violence in the Niger Delta and other places, and the threats to planet Earth by all forms of pollution. Boom! I was taken back to the big screen in the large hall to see that all the spillages had been cleared off from Niger Delta areas and that lush vegetation surrounded all developments. No more acid rains; the flaring had stopped. Aquatic life was back and the residents were again enjoying some of them in tasty and healthy aquatic cuisines. For these to happen, no new oil exploration was allowed for some time and all other operations were raised to high best-practice standards. Attitudinal adjustments towards more equitable living resulted.

"I next went to a research centre engaged in energy issues—solar, wind, fusion, and harnessing the power in lightning. A good focus was on making absorbers and storage. It was clear from what I saw here that Naija was genuinely preparing for when fossil fuels would be prohibited.

"*Medicine, what's up there?* I visited the international airports in Enugu, Port Harcourt, Lagos, Kano, and Abuja respectively. I observed many people of Afrikan ancestry, among others, proudly vacationing. *What has medicine got to do with tourists?* I had to witness the streams of patients who visit Naija for the treatment and management of many of the long-standing health

---

[18] MRM, Matter Recouping Module.

challenges and the occasional unknown illnesses. *Now, wait a minute; how did all this come about?* I sequentially reviewed twelve imposing medical research centres scattered over the country. Each of them had a number of laboratories and the staffs were conventional medical scientists and traditional herbal experts. They were highly motivated and cooperated with one another, resulting in novel medicines and procedures.

"The traditional healers came from Asia, South America, Australia, the Caribbean, and African countries. They brought their established formulations and procedures. Their inputs were regularly reviewed. This blend aided the discoveries in Naija. *Okay, where are the patients treated?* Zoom-zoom, I was the inspector of healthcare centres in Badagry, Brass, Nsukka, Jos, Sokoto, and up the Mambillas, all constructed to bring out the best of their local climates. Each one was vast, picturesque, and equipped with facilities for properly taking care of many categories of patients. Because physiotherapy was a significant element in the services, recreation received much attention. Each centre was a dream treatment and convalescence place for the old, young, and many cultures. Good export business thrived on the discoveries. Often, discharged patients and some tourists were reluctant to leave.

"*Hey, what about sports, especially football?* In a twinkle, I was before the big screen in the large hall. I watched the final matches of the Super Eagles and the Falcons, when they won their respective World Cups. From the matches in the national leagues, I saw that the game had gained much respect. The stadiums were world class and, apparently, the management of the game had improved tremendously, because I saw a number of foreign players in those games.

"After the number one sport, I toured sports development centres across the country. Adequate attention had been paid to other sports, as evidenced by scenes of sportsmen and women from these centres winning global laurels. *Oh well, everything has been upbeat; what about the overall impressions the world has about Nigeria?* Highlighted print materials, edited TV, and radio commentaries scrolled by on that screen. The world was awed by the turn of events. Global organisations became respectful. People with roots to Afrika regained esteem everywhere. In summary, Naija was also nicknamed 'The Ebony Star.'

"How did all these changes come about? There was a quick flashback to familiar Nigeria and her many challenges and, towards the end, a large conference was ending. All participants were congratulating one another, smiling, and raising their hands, as if they had achieved some great victory. Next were scenes of court hearings with convicts heckled as they went to prison; series of meetings everywhere; feverishly heightened activities on everything; and finally, the launching of an Earth satellite for a deep survey of Naija.

"Later analyses of the satellite reports led to extensive archaeological excavations in nine sites. The most challenging, but equally rewarding, ones were in Plateau, Anambra, and Akwa Ibom states. The one at Akwa Ibom was flooded by groundwater and a battery of huge pumps had to work continuously. In Anambra, all workers had to wear masks or spacesuit types of garments to avoid the noxious gases oozing out from cracks and crevices in the formations. In Plateau, the challenge was the movement of enormous amounts of materials removed. From all three sites, still legible, but much-worn records, including the remains of what appeared to be a space vehicle, were unearthed. A few people, more eccentric than normal, assembled to decode them. They uncovered some ancient and forgotten knowledge, which formed the backbone of the driving force in the emergence of Naija. All operations and related issues were extra top secret, with very severe penalties awaiting anyone who violated the secrecy codes.

"Suddenly, I wanted to see that elusive woman. Bingo! There they were before me, she was near me and seemed willing to oblige me. With all the effort I could muster, I sprang at her. Just as I was about to touch her, they all disappeared and my hands met each other in emptiness. I felt angry and humiliated, but since I had become airborne, I continued a fall through everything—the floor, the ground underneath, and the core below. At first, I was startled, but soon resigned myself to whatever came next. I didn't think nice things about her. My fall continued until I was again in the luminous, cloudlike material. My rate of fall was accelerating, but, being in this environment, I eventually attained terminal velocity. I was quite aware. In fact, I started enjoying the fall. I flipped around like the daredevil, acrobatic skydivers. Suddenly, I hit darkness and lost consciousness or whatever.

"Later, the face of that woman kept flashing through the darkness. I totally ignored her. I turned off and focused my attention on tying things together, because I gradually became aware of the hospital, the people there, and reality. That's about it. There were other diversions, here and there, but not relevant, I think. That's it, and what do you all make of all that? Hey, I'm so glad to be back. It all felt strange."

A long pause followed.

Mr. Ochiagha ultimately said, "You know, Mansur, what you experienced is not new. My wife and I have heard such stories. No human can claim the full understanding of our world. It was like a dream, a good vision for us. I pray it comes true. Just rest up; it will all clear up in time. You need rest."

Jibril, his palms facing upwards and head bowed, said, "Did you eat anything there?"

"No, or yes. You see, whenever I felt hungry, I would immediately feel like I had eaten something."

"Did you speak to anyone besides the women, and what did the language, 'Naijan,' I guess, sound like?" I asked.

"The only person whose voice I heard and understood what she was saying was that woman. All the people were speaking to one another, but I never heard a sound of what they were saying. At the same time, I had full understanding; they all read me correctly. Now that you ask, it was kind of weird. But, since I understood what was going on, I didn't think about it; maybe I should have."

We spent more time with him during which we made him focus on his full recovery, so that he could go back to his family in Katsina at the earliest possible time.

16

BACK ON TRACK

After a month, TANNA sent polite reminders to the legislature, executive, and judiciary, while reaffirming that ACB reflected the yearnings of the majority of Nigerians, and that confirmation was coming.

A fortnight later, our zonal offices sent a few people from their zones to Abuja. Daily, they flocked into the public galleries of the legislature in their native attires to reflect every part of the country. Members of S&I were carefully included. The legislators took notice, but showed no discernible reactions. A week later, we received a polite reply from the legislature that because of the complexity of our submission, the principal officers were studying it before assigning it to their relevant committees.

From the encounter, the DD list grew longer, the more influential speakers in the legislature were identified, and we became more familiar with the workings of the legislature and government in general. We gained the regular email addresses and telephone numbers of the legislators and of some key government functionaries.

Surprisingly, the legislature took a break for the upcoming public holidays, which were a week away. Thanks to ICT, S&I, and others, we followed them home. Whenever anyone turned on a radio or television set in the country, they heard variants of the following message first.

"Your representative in the legislature is now on recess. Engage him or her on passing ACB quickly. YOU and *everyone else* will be involved in the national conference this time around. Thank you. TANNA."

For these broadcasts, ICT produced hand-held gadgets they called Mobile Mini-Broadcasters (MMBs) that functioned like radio stations. They were so small and light that a small child could move them around easily. Recordings on them were sent to and stored in the antenna sections of all radio and television sets within a certain radius. The sound packages lasted for sixty cycles of playback. They were heard first and uninterrupted once the set was turned on. TANNA fought gallantly for temporary permission to broadcast from relevant authorities.

Many were astounded the first time this happened. People started turning their TVs and radios on and off. Some even changed stations, while doing so; still, they heard the message. It took several cycles before many got over the novelty to sufficiently focus on the message.

Halfway through the recess, ICT reloaded the broadcasts in the local dialects; this truly took the heat to many legislators.

Many people confronted their representatives with strong arguments in favour of the conference. Some representatives finally realised that they were the servants of the people, after being reminded of recall options and their post-elections unavailability. About 60 percent of the legislators were contacted by their constituencies—many had travelled out of the country.

ACB and TANNA were hot topics during the recess. S&I reported that a significant number of representatives wanted to fight on, instead of doing the work on ACB. The hard-core among them felt that TANNA should be stopped.

The legislators were classified into friendly, hostile, and uncertain camps. TANNA mounted grassroots campaigns for more legislators. Within days, those hostile legislators could not use their phones or cope with incoming mail. A few of the undecided joined the friendly camp. Nevertheless, some of the infuriated ones felt that TANNA had really overstepped its bounds.

ACB was sent to committees of the upper and lower houses, and both committees opted for public hearings in the hope of causing more delay. It took nearly three weeks for both committees to finish reading ACB before calling for memoranda from the public. Meanwhile, all members of both committees were again categorised by S&I. When the committee hearings finally ended, they adjourned to write their reports. Of course, that meant another wait without any visible action.

Because of the implications of ACB, it became more obvious that, in the final analysis, the hostile legislators were not alone. Many others, serving or retired from government or the private sector and from the public, felt the same way about ACB, because of self-interest. TANNA then conferred extensively with all its relevant associates to prepare for massive showdowns.

Our first focus was on the release of the reports of the committees to their respective general houses. Two-week-long support marches were programmed for the state capitals. These were to lead to the biggest one at the legislature in Abuja, a week later.

Participation in all the marches was to be restricted to only those who had been screened and instructed on how to behave. The sympathising public were to be kept at bay without antagonising them. The marches at the state capitals were trial runs before the big one at Abuja. Daily, the marchers were to assemble at the state legislatures, from there move to the state secretariats and back to the legislatures. Variants of signs with only the simple message— 'ACB NOW!'—were approved for all marches.

Marchers, selected from state marches, were to come from all zones and were to always wear their native attires for the Abuja march. All signs were to carry identical messages, only differentiated by their states of origin: 'ENUGU STATE WANTS ACB NOW,' for example. Entertainers from the zones would be brought in for pageantry and range.

We explicitly obtained all permits for the marches. S&I had their work cut out in order to minimise disruptions. Our PR people put out instructions, and repeated them during the matches, that it would be in the interest of the project if only certified marchers joined the lines, and that the marches were peaceful and purposeful. All Police Commands promised to cover the marches. Acting in collaboration with appropriate associates, we lined up national and global news outlets.

We energised all our structures. Improved systems of initiating call-ins and write-ins from all wards to any target resulted. We encouraged more discussions on the project in order to have as many as possible mentally ready to take on opposition arguments. ICT produced bound copies of the signatures we had collected, arranged by the constituencies of legislators. They came to some big truckloads.

The state marches began the following Monday. S&I wore blue tops that had 'March Guides' boldly printed on them in white, front and back. They had no serious problem in keeping things under control all over the country.

We didn't expect any direct actions on ACB from state governments. Those who came out to cheer the marchers grew in their numbers daily; this was our goal. We used the marches to announce that people should contact their representatives in Abuja to urge quick passage of ACB. We projected that the state marches would send more signals to the national legislators.

Two days after the state marches, the committees of the legislature released their reports on ACB to their respective houses. That was not all: the leadership of both houses convened a joint press conference at which they announced the receipt of the reports. They pleaded with the public that, based on the size of ACB, its far-reaching implications, and its conflicts with existing laws, especially the constitution, the need for caution could not be overemphasised. They projected the possibility of splitting ACB into more bills. They acknowledged that a 'significant' number of the citizenry, as they put it, were in favour of ACB, and thanked them for their inputs. They promised to study ACB and the reports of the committees carefully before slating it for debate, and that when that happened, the debates would be open to the public. Reeling out a long list of items still on their table, they sought the understanding of the people, as regards to pressure of work. Finally, they made some passionate pleas for enough time for a good job on ACB, without suggested time lines.

Politicians always had their way with words and, as they spoke, they were holding copies of ACB, which they conveniently shoved before the cameras. They sounded convincing and, without saying so, they were able to put forward that they were already marked out for victimisation, even as they were not directly responsible for all the country's ills. They didn't mention the write-ins and call-ins that had occurred. Not that we craved publicity, but that they didn't mention TANNA sent some signals to us. Of course, we recorded the entire press conference. Our response was unmistakable.

First, we produced short rejoinders that were immediately sent to the field, starting from the constituencies of all legislators at the press conference.

The Abuja march started days later. Recall that it didn't have any set duration. The first week of the march passed without any grave problems. The police was atypically helpful, maybe because things were then happening at one location in full view of the world. After the second week, the call-ins and write-ins trickled in to the identified hard-core hostile legislators. S&I closely monitored reactions.

The leaderships of both houses started closed-doors meetings alone and later, jointly. Some regretted letting TANNA have all the free hand it had enjoyed. The critical issue, they grudgingly agreed this time, was the *overwhelming* proportion of the citizenry in favour of ACB. A suggestion that a law should be made to stop the push for a national conference in favour of amendments to the constitution was abandoned because of the strong arguments against that approach, which TANNA already had in wide circulation. The option of going to court was also debated, but, in the end, their lawyers convinced them that the chances for success with that route were rather slim and that failure would amount to an undeniable evidence of stalling. Eventually, they met with the executive to sound them out.

The president and his select ministers and advisers were more of listeners. It was finally agreed that the judiciary should be informally consulted, while the legislature should dig into ACB for options. TANNA, most agreed, had been able to get so far only because the people wanted it to and because TANNA's tactics were peaceful. Many had dismissed TANNA as just another NGO striving for relevance.

You could depend on our people. S&I had done enough work to cover most bases—the police, the armed forces, executive, judiciary, politicians, and the shakers and movers of society. They had enough DDs to instigate vicious class wars; human instincts have always stayed the same, only expressed in evolving ways.

Two important press conferences took place in the first week of the Abuja marches. Labour and the National Students Body proclaimed that they were watching developments around ACB. If things did not go as desired, they would join the marches. The participation of the two in the marches could lead to unpredictable consequences. We liked the increased pressure; we added the call-ins and write-ins.

All hostile legislators had their phones ringing continually. Whenever they changed any of their numbers, it would be minutes before the new ones became cluttered. That frustrated them. The alternative of switching off their phones served them less. The more vindictive ones talked about getting even with TANNA. S&I kept close tabs on those thoughts. The media helped with editorials and commentaries, talk shows, and the whole affair sufficiently filtered into the international arena.

The Abuja marches were restricted to the premises of the legislature. The idea of the conference had potential gains for all; that might have been a reason for the peaceful ways of the marches. Our people were prepared for eventualities, however. The entertainment segments took place near the end of the day, when the legislators had left and workers were on their way home. Every day was a different show from a different part of the country. Short announcements were interspersed about the need for ACB's quick passage.

The very comprehensive ACB even had appendices that suggested steps for eliminating disruptions of the system that could arise from existing laws it ran parallel, concurrent, or to the contrary to. The way the legislature was acting could be explained by human nature: very few in their positions would like to be told how to do things.

When the debates on ACB finally started in the general houses weeks later, the marches were temporarily suspended, but we were in the public galleries. Just before the open debates, the executive invited TANNA for a meeting. We sent a representative from each zone, ostensibly led by the FCT representative. Small numbers of leaders of the legislature as well as the judiciary attended. Our team was intelligent, articulate, and proactive.

TANNA was first commended for its peaceful methods. Questions were asked about the originators of the ideas, the funding, the final goals of the recommended conference, and the possible consequences of its failure. From some winding sentences, our people gathered that the meeting wanted to know what we thought would happen, if ACB and the proposed conference were stopped for being redundant. There were no threats; just simple, polite exchanges. At a point, pleas were made for the continued maintenance of peace and less pressure on the overwhelmed system. The representatives of the judiciary hardly spoke after introductions.

Our people noted the disguised questions on whether TANNA would turn political. The response of our people, wrapped up in many superfluous expressions as well, indicated that the entire issue belonged to the people and that it was up to the people to direct affairs.

Because ACB did not have direct sponsors in the legislature, one way of blocking attempts to tamper with it was to pressure speakers who sought to do so. To this end, we sent secret notes on the relevant parts of ACB to such speakers. The notes reached targets at unexpected moments, not too long after they had spoken disparagingly about ACB. Such agents as house ushers, bartenders, waiters in restaurants, barbers, wives, girlfriends or mistresses, door attendants, their drivers, airline hosts, vendors, and relations, all delivered the notes. A psychological effect was that such speakers felt that they were watched. To some, this was unsettling, but a few who did not care much remained steadfast in their opposition—deluding arrogance.

We called in the carts and wheeled in the bound copies of the signatures, arranged by the constituencies of the legislators, into both houses of the legislature. On the day this happened, debates were cut short and most of the legislators gathered by the signatures, which had been laid out accordingly. Of course, our people were also around to pick up earful of comments.

From unmentionable invectives to high commendations for thoroughness for TANNA, they heard it all. A legislator, whose retired parents signed, expressed concern about his next trip home. Another, whose wife-to-be in weeks signed, worried about his next conversation with her. All the grown children of a third had signed and upon seeing their signatures, she shouted that it had become a family affair. A fourth, whose political godfather had signed, wondered aloud about the change of heart of his political benefactor. The wealthy parents of the fifth signed, and on her seeing their signatures, she proclaimed that her parents wanted to upset things, including the family's position in society, out of boredom. Overall, the displayed signatures had sobering effects on most legislators. This made things better for ACB, which had become one of the leading news items. However, the debates crawled on ever so slowly over the repeated ambushes of rules, regulations, standing orders, and procedures.

TANNA hung on doggedly. With the gates to the international arena pried open, wider and wider with time, the inflows of funds from donations by mainly Nigerians and their friends all over the world was empowering. The ploy to split ACB into more bills, a scheme for more delay, was defeated. The amendments to all existing laws that shared infractions with ACB took much time, even though the appendices carefully indicated the ways out. The legislators spoke as if those appendices did not exist.

Finally, all debates on ACB and related issues ended after two weeks. Both houses raised a joint committee to harmonise results, but the sitting of the committee was restricted. Still, we were able to stay connected to their activities. They took only two weeks to conclude and submit the final draft to the legislature. The reviewed final draft was sent to the executive for the ultimate signature that would make ACB law. Good progress, but the battle was yet to be won. TANNA, more than anyone else, knew that.

The DDs became the super instruments of persuasion. They were detailed and deadly accurate. Both features struck fear in their targets. Each DD was packaged in grades that started with matters in the grey areas of right and wrong. These were the warning ones. The subsequent ones got more embarrassing or incriminating. Again, S&I very strongly directed that the DDs be used only in critical situations, as last resorts.

When debates became favourable, we directed more attention to the executive. The first information we picked up was that the offices of the Justice Ministry and the judiciary were engaged in frequent informal consultations on ACB. That notwithstanding, we relocated the signatures from the legislature to Aso Rock, the seat of the executive.

This was harder because of stiff resistance we met from security at Aso Rock. Eventually, somebody intervened in our favour. Our first day was planned to coincide with a Federal Executive Council meeting. Nearly all those who attended the FEC meeting spent time viewing the signatures despite their severe schedules. We gathered that TANNA and ACB were informally discussed at the meeting with most people expressing mixtures of admiration and awe. Of course, being who they were, they also wondered about the future political relevance of TANNA, a faceless, but effective, mobiliser of the people.

Anticipating massive grassroots campaigns for keeping ACB on track, we reinforced our structures. We let a few call-ins filter to a few elective office holders in the executive, including the president, to the effect that ACB should not be crippled at any stage in its evolution into law. For those calls, we used the confidential telephone numbers of the targets. We then maintained an informed watch on the executive, after their receipt of ACB and related bills. Should there be any undesirable vetoes, we were prepared for far-reaching confrontation. Nevertheless, we allowed the executive reasonable time to consider and possibly include amendments before signing the bills. S&I indicated that the executive did not waste time in swinging into action on their receipt of the ACB package.

On Thursday of the third week from the transfer of ACB, a milestone event occurred. The president called a press conference at which his key cabinet members and advisers, top leaders of the legislature and the judiciary, some former heads of state, six Traditional Rulers—one each from the geopolitical zones, some state governors, and a few other personalities were present. That press conference took TANNA by surprise, because S&I knew about it only a few hours earlier. No harm was done; the press conference was an unexpected facilitator.

The president did not take questions afterwards.

"Today is a fundamental turning point in the history of our country, Nigeria, The Almighty willing. Today, we acknowledge that there are no breakers strong enough to stop the energised tidal waves of the needs uppermost in the minds of the people. Today, we must remember that clashes of rights inspire differences, sometimes most violently. It's a fact of recent global history that even the mightiest of the mighty powers cannot permanently kill the will of a determined people, regardless of the people's apparent weakness. Flashpoints of suffering are increasingly dotting the globe. This is happening contrary to the promises of increasing knowledge and easier communication.

"Our sworn responsibility is to safeguard our country, as is possible. Perhaps, the answers are in the collective will of the people. Perhaps, the people's will is therefore supreme. Yes, we admired the evolution of the Affirmation Confab Bill as it took roots among our people. Any administration standing in its way breaches the peoples' confidence. In this regard, then, action or lack of it is the ultimate communicator.

"In a little while from now, the Affirmation Confab Bill will become the Affirmation Conference Law. Before that happens, there are a few things to emphasise. First, the whole matter truly belongs to the people and it has been entirely people driven. It is therefore the responsibility of the people, each of us, to ensure that the spirit behind the proposal lives to the end, so that we can all reap the enduring, glorious fruits of the undertaking. Every so often, it is not the system that is faulty, but implementations arising from the mind-sets of implementers. We must all constantly remember that whenever we point an accusing forefinger at someone else, the three other fingers are usually pointing back at us, while the thumb, in its imposing dominance, points to the heavens, in a symbolic reference to the All-Knowing, Ultimate Arbiter.

"I assure our international friends the continuity of our relationships through and after the conference. At the same time, we all realise that the worthiness of continuity often depends on the value of what is continued. Finally, TANNA, the amorphous organisation or whatever it is, has done an exemplary job in facilitating the articulation of the peoples' needs in connection with the advocated conference. They have gone about it meticulously, relentlessly, and above all, peacefully. We should commend them, in all ways possible, by acting as expected throughout the exercise. Two of the better ways of doing so are to keep strictly to the time lines, as will be laid out in the upcoming ACL[19] and by maintaining peace.

---

[19] ACL, Affirmation Conference Law.

"This administration will not be prompted to do what the people truly need. Copies of the law will be made available to the public soonest. Reports of all relevant previous conferences, panels, commissions, and committees have been assembled, ready to be transferred to the conference, as soon as it convenes. We have also directed all security services to ensure that they adequately maintain the public peace in a friendly and fair, but firm, manner throughout the exercise. As we watched ACB evolve, we concluded that the most worrisome points will arrive after ACB becomes ACL and the whole process is again turned over to the people. It is at these times that disruptive elements, however and by whomever influenced, are most likely to act."

He then proceeded, in the full view of the world, to sign ACB into law, and at the end of which he further said, "History and posterity anticipate us all. It's now all up to each of us. May the Spirits of our Ancestors, the Gods of Afrika, and The Almighty Guardian guide, protect, and bless us all. Long live affirmed Nigeria!"

From rural farms and hamlets, slums and highbrow areas, motor parks and airports, markets and schools, and everywhere, the whole country exploded in jubilation. TANNA was greatly relieved; ecstatic! We then took down our arsenal aimed at the executive and related others and went back to our structures, down to the wards. We still had much to do during the preconference activities, the conference itself, and after it. In fact, we also worried about the disruption points the president mentioned.

We quickly held series of meetings to decide our next actions. Soon after those meetings, copies of ACL became available. We obtained enough of them to be able to allocate five copies to each ward. The next series of meetings of our people from the wards took place at the state capitals as before. It was at those meetings that copies of the ACL were distributed. We carefully highlighted all the crucial areas of ACL to be drummed into the people. The most important suggestion to the people was that the best-qualified individuals should accordingly be nominated for electoral duties and elected as conference delegates. Another crucial point was the transition from ward activities to those of ethnic groups. We then hit the field afterwards to spread our suggestions to the people who placed some trust in us. The president's news conference also improved our standing.

Not to be outdone, ICT rolled out another of their specials. They offered what they called the Targeted Messaging System (TMS) that functioned thus.

Each time either a radio or television set was turned on in the country, the following was heard: "Congratulations! The Affirmation Conference Law is here, thanks to *your* invaluable support. Make your voice heard. Understand ACL, get involved accordingly, and keep the peace. If you personally don't make it as a representative of your neighbours, make sure that the person who does is of character and can truly do a good job of projecting your voice credibly. Everything has a price, but the country of our dreams in priceless. Thank you, TANNA."

There were other trimmings. If a radio or television set was connected to a power source, and no matter the position of the power switch, this message played at pre-selected times. The set turned itself on for the message to play and then turned itself off afterwards. A feat was that they also translated the message into the various languages we had identified and that those translations were accurately targeted at the localities where each of them was normally spoken. In these cases, the translations and the English versions of the message alternated. For all urban areas, they alternated the English and "Pidgin English" versions.

We monitored people's reactions. We were relieved that majority of the people were captivated by the way the message was heard. And, true to the implications of the president's speech, all state-owned radio and television stations added jingles similar to our message. They also featured ACL in their programs. The correct focus was on mobilising the people. Incidentally, the extension of our temporary permits to broadcast became mere formalities.

We paid special attention to the rural areas until things started happening. All the nominees for electoral duties came on board well enough; the super potent voters' register was well generated and centralised at state and national levels, but vetting remained ongoing; and harmonisation of views and projections for the country and familiarisation meetings took place among all ethnic groups as scheduled. Then, the people acted excellently by electing credible delegates to the conference. Many of them could have led the conference as chair. S&I confirmed this, as none of them qualified as an alluring DD subject. A very small number of them had negligible, incidental, or collateral light blemishes.

Many things aided that string of exceptional events: the president's speech; the presence of an off-character police—they comported themselves so well; the sights of security forces, as they hovered at the fringes of activities; sustained bombardment of the people with information and directives from many sources, including TANNA; and the awakened consciousness of the people. This consciousness was truly overriding, because the entire country somehow returned to the old days and ways of Afrika by acting in group-motivated and focused concert, aimed at seeing that the people's countrywide conference happened successfully. TANNA deliriously basked in the entrancing emotions of achievements, but remained focused with more impetus.

17

PRICELESS CONFERENCE

Right on schedule, the conference assembled and elected the CSC as follows—Chair and Assistant Secretary: South-South geopolitical Zone; Vice Chairman and Deputy Auditor: North-West; Secretary and Deputy Treasurer: North-East; Financial Secretary and Deputy Protocol and Logistics Officer 2: North-Central; Treasurer and Assistant Financial Secretary: South-East; Auditor and Deputy Protocol and Logistics Officer 1: South-West; Protocol and Logistics Officer: FCT.

After the elections, the chair spoke.

"Irrefutably Select Ladies and Gentlemen! Words fail me. Growing and glowing emotions are blowing my mind. There's little doubt that all of us are similarly affected. Nevertheless, I congratulate all of us for being so positively chosen to represent our constituencies at this historic event and for the ways we've conducted business so far. I'm assured that our people will be pleased with the work we shall *all* do. I know that we are *all* aware of the challenges and the significance of our unprecedented tasks. Let's go to work!"

The election and the chair's speech were the only public activities. Word got out about the conference just before and during the two-week intermissions that followed every six weeks of sitting. All the intermissions started with a briefing of the president by the CSC.

As ACB became ACL, one clause slipped through to our pleasure—the provision that the government would implement decisions of the conference without stating when those decisions would be passed on to the government or when their executions would be. The ruling expression was 'at the appropriate time.'

Just before the first break, the conference secretariat addressed the country.

"In conformity with Affirmation Conference Law, the conference is about to take its first break to consult with you, all our people. All procedures for running the conference are in place, and the quality of delegates gives reason for optimism. The conference feels that splitting the country in any way will not serve us better; instead, we should further integrate some areas of our lives. The delegates will collect your reactions to these and other issues at the break. Kindly interact with all delegates in such ways that reflect that we are all equal to the tasks before the peoples' conference. Doing this ensures that we retain the level of control on the conference that we individually want to. That is what the ACL we all clamoured for is about.

"We have a tentative priority list of areas the conference will treat. Widespread corruption is top on the list. How should the country deal with corruption? How do you evaluate the tentative priority list? Make your contributions *now* so that you stay involved. The decisions of this conference shall be based on majority opinions. The final goal, we believe, is to transform Nigeria from a country to a nation. There are subtle, but important, differences between a country and a nation. Please, always remember that there are powerful internal and external parties that are not willing to let this transformation happen, because they benefit more from our present situations that cripple us as a country. These enemies can succeed only when they are aided by some of us. Thank you very much. Remain connected to the conference!"

TANNA was already initiating discussions on some issues the delegates were coming home to deal with. Thanks to ICT, our website remained attractive and active. The majority of the people endorsed the suggestions on the unity of the country depending, naturally, on how other critical items on the lists of ethnic groups were treated.

We maintained the alignments of our efforts while emphasising rural and other areas where the so-called ordinary people—people left outside opinion-making—lived. To them, TANNA was the redeemer. They had been waiting for the chance to do something, with mob action as the best option. We appreciated that, but we sufficiently discussed the powers of non-violent pursuits of the common good.

A report released by the Accountant General by the middle of the conference break indicated that the general levy paid significantly exceeded initial estimates. Hurray to the people! Who said the people didn't know what they wanted?

The next session passed by so quickly, it seemed, due to activities the break generated everywhere.

The conference secretariat announced the second break.

"The conference is going on its second break and there are important events to report. From your directives at the first break, the conference unanimously resolved as follows.

"The conference shall proceed with the mandate that the country shall remain united. This generates additional pressure, but that is your command. The people cried out that corruption is the primary issue the conference has to deal with *soonest*. A good starting point is the long-standing matter of the shamelessly increasing thefts of our common wealth by those who were supposed to protect us. Excellent auditors from within and outside Nigeria shall audit the affairs of the country from independence to date. This segment of the audit will be tackled from three fronts. A set of auditors begins its work from the present and tracks back to independence. Another set starts from independence and works towards the present. Both sets will finally produce two parallel reports. The third set is to devote its efforts to the private sector, starting from now and going back to independence. A fourth set tracks its work from independence to 1914, as is possible. They all target corruption.

"Special Corruption Courts, adequately empowered, shall be set up at federal and state levels before which living suspects are to appear. Prior to any suspects appearing before these courts, adequate opportunity for fully owning up misdeeds shall be provided for everybody. Any false information given by anybody in this regard will worsen matters for that person. In order to extend more of the people's fairness to suspects, Special Appeal Courts shall be provided for those wishing to use their services. The decisions of the Special Appeal Courts shall be final.

"The guilty shall be required to return what they had stolen in cash or kind, meaning that any assets they or their heirs possess shall be converted to cash to ensure that their thefts are made good to the people. If all that still falls short of the thefts, then additional prison terms shall be accordingly imposed on them. Where the suspects have died and left neither assets nor heirs, the occurrences shall be recorded for future reference, but the matter shall be reopened by new evidence.

"Hard labour prison terms, varying from one year to life, shall be imposed on the guilty in accordance with the impacts of the thefts. The conference has worked out the schedule of prison terms. The guilty shall be prevented from running away. Any one of them that manages to do so shall be brought back to face worse charges. The recoveries shall be lodged at the Central Bank and the Accountant General shall publish weekly reports on the account. A portion of the recoveries shall be equally distributed to all states to be used for enduring, landmark projects of the choice of the people in each local government area. The finished projects shall be so named as to serve as lasting reminders. The conference has produced detailed guidelines for the audits, trials, and the use of recoveries in formats that are easy to use in obtaining the people's final authority through quick referenda or for enacting enabling laws, as necessary.

"This break is devoted to your review of the work done so far in these areas. When the conference returns from this break, the first thing it will do is to incorporate the people's additional directives, as necessary, before forwarding the result for action. This transfer shall take place under a fortnight from resumption. The conference envisages situations where the executions of some of its resolutions are concurrent with its sitting, for good reasons. First, the combined package of these historic events will emphasise the true awakening of our country. Also, we need to act quickly, because we have all waited far too long for positive change.

"The conference appreciates the full-hearted support of the president and his government, especially by making all the materials on previous deliberations on the country available. Remember that fierce forces want to stop our dreams. Together, we shall overcome, because, as often said, we don't have another place to call our country. Together, the mission is possible. The delegates are truly your voices. Please speak through them. Stay connected! Stay involved!"

From the most remote to the most cosmopolitan areas, people cheered this address, as if they were one extra-large audience. The doubtful about the conference showed more interest, the lukewarm was revitalised, and the already hopeful became overjoyed. Through the break, delegates were inundated with suggestions on the corruption remedies—the revenge instinct pushing for the disproportionate, but the delegates were pacifying, an indication of their quality. Those who knew them best, from childhood to adulthood, had proudly selected them.

The more focused professional and social organisations and individuals had memoranda on other aspects of corruption ready for the delegates. Many people from all lifestyles were itching for action to begin, and to some of them, the looting of our common treasury was the beginning and end of corruption.

Lagos, the economic and social nerve centre of the country, was where protests broke out in support. Some other cities followed suit days later, but things generally turned out not too badly. When the Lagos protests broke out, TANNA quickly informed most Police Commands that we had nothing to do with the demonstrations and that we were willing to assist in bringing things under control, as we were nearly everywhere.

With the shaded nod of the police, we did, while fully subjugating our efforts to theirs. The chair and CSC members repeatedly pleaded with the people to keep the peace. Just as it all broke out, things quietened down rapidly. The more aware were glad that things stopped when they did, as they recalled instances in history when decadence had caused the spillage of much blood of both the guilty and innocent.

The conference resumed from the break and on the ninth day, its CSC presented its final resolutions on corruption and the unity of the country to the president in a brief ceremony. The president promised to implement the conference resolutions accordingly. The CSC eagerly departed; that was not the time to debate ACL's provisions. The term 'at the appropriate time' controlled proceedings, and the whole world watched.

The new-face Electoral Commission was ready to execute the referendum on the two resolutions within a fortnight with a yes or no vote setup. A near-unanimous vote was recorded for both resolutions. In correct anticipation of this, both the judiciary and the legislature had done some advance work.

The judiciary had structured the Special Corruption and Appeals Courts, while the legislature had completed preliminary discussions on expected bills. The president signed all resulting bills quickly, thereby setting the stage for the audits and trials. The engagement of the auditors was underway.

All these took the anticipatory moods to a threatening high, but many people were disposed to congratulating others close by on the general progress so far made. Corruption topped the agenda of discussions and, for once, was an issue beyond football that united a great majority of Nigerians.

The intermission of the conference arrived with reduced pomp.

"The conference will be on its third break in an hour from now. The agenda have been reconciled. The conference now has a clear-cut path. Discussions have remained spirited with many hard-fought disagreements ultimately settled. There are no resolutions for implementation. The delegates will interact with you on what the conference has done during the last sitting and other matters. Please meet with the delegates during the break; send your directives. Stay connected! Stay involved! Stay in control!"

The delegates were not surprised by the persisting, spirited discussions on corruption. There were many make-or-break items before them—exodus of youths and some professionals, resource control, equitable representation and distribution of outcomes and general insecurity. To complicate matters more, each topic had a relatively long history and was somehow related to the others, especially corruption. The solutions sought by delegates were sometimes considerably divergent.

Government hastened all actions on the audits and trials. The president often briefed the country on progress. The judiciary quickly created the Special Corruption and Appeals Courts. The public was told that all those willing to do so should file notices of voluntary admission to theft of public property. The consequences of doing so truthfully or falsely were explained.

Two weeks later, the auditors commenced work. The action had started, but TANNA was apprehensive, because there was no sure way of predicting the outcomes of executing such emotionally charged programs.

The president announced that all those with verifiable information on thefts from our common assets, in any sector, should send such information to the Auditor-General, while copying a special office at the presidency. He also directed those wishing to own up to their offences to send copies of their intentions to the same office. The purpose of the special office, he said, was for him to ensure that the appropriate parties acted promptly on every information received. The Auditor-General would send both information streams to the relevant auditors for spot audits, and that findings would be sent to the Corruption Courts nearest the suspects.

This meant that the auditors would initially work on transactions and that the result would be that the Courts would not have to wait for the auditors to complete work based on periods. Maybe, from his vantage points, the president had sensed some urgency.

Talk about failed dams spilling! Information on suspected thefts flooded the office of the Auditor-General and the special office at the presidency from every part of the country. The spot audits yielded a number of the accused that faced the Corruption Courts, and the Courts dispensed with their cases with incredible speed. All the confirmed guilty received the stiff penalties stipulated by ACL, and when the numbers of such people swelled almost everywhere, something else happened. People wishing to voluntarily own up and make good their thefts crowded some Special Corruption Courts. No mystery there; depraved thieves are not stripped of survival instincts.

The auditors' work produced a truly mixed group. There were suspects of both sexes from long past to the present, but one had to give it to the males; the young, the not-so-young, and the old; various pretenders; the visible and the low-profiled—a sampling from society's strata.

Pretty quickly, patterns began to emerge. Those at each other's throats in public had been secretly conniving to steal or corner our assets for themselves, their families, friends, and cronies. Those who noticed this kept a close watch and their anger increased.

The trials captured much interest, but many people paid attention to the conference; many hot issues remained unsettled. TANNA sustained its efforts towards informing the people that the best way to achieve the results everyone was after was to maintain peace, and that ACL had taken care of trial proceedings, including penalties.

The conference announced its break.

"The fourth break is here. As usual, the delegates will brief you and receive your further directives. The conference identified areas of our lives, especially our values, soiled by corruption and has made corrective resolutions. The recommended orientation is significant. Our economic affairs have gone beyond the thefts of our common wealth. A good set of resolutions realigns our economic development towards enduring paths. The voters' register goes to the Population Commission as a starter for adequately counting and categorising all Nigerians. Naturally, the Electoral Commission shall be upgrading it. All delegates endorsed this voters' register. The transformation of our country can only happen through our collective determination, participation, and support. We must all accept that no new, positive accord can result without compromises. Overall equity is the target. All delegates will be out there at your convenience during the break. Stay motivated! Stay hopeful! Stay in control!"

The first impression the delegates created was that they were itching to catch up on the corruption trials, but fortunately, none of them had been tagged so far. Recall that S&I cleared all of them. TANNA flaunted that as a tribute to the people, when enabled to act freely.

A good number of the people spent quality times with the delegates despite the corruption trials. Many people supported the use of the voters' register by the Population Commission, because it was the right step towards eradicating the scandals in our census activities. How could population inexplicably increase towards the desert, while decreasing towards the coastlines, and the growth in the numbers of physical evidence of human activities produced relatively fewer people, as vast empty landscapes depicted more people?

TANNA focused on making sure people were aware of the work that the conference had done, and that everyone desirous of doing so spoke freely to the delegates.

A day before the delegates went back to work, the president spoke to the country.

"The Affirmation Conference in progress is important in many ways. It is an outstanding product of the needs of all of us, highlighted in a unique manner. The challenge, therefore, is in being able to successfully build on this opportunity for better tomorrows for us as a *nation*. I use *nation* in line with the implications expressed by the conference. No matter where and how we find ourselves today, we have the remarkable prospects of vividly learning from our past so that the future will be much better. No doubt, the conference has become a powerful force that unites us; we cannot afford to even think about wasting any bit of this opportunity.

"We envisage the resulting liberation of our potentials such that the individual becomes more fulfilled and that we collectively take our rightful places in the world. Each of us is therefore obligated to do his or her part so well as to make the conference successful and to make the era it will bring endure. This administration will not be prompted to do the will of the people. We envisage the trials lasting beyond current estimates. We have therefore taken some proactive measures. However, we must note that our basic problem is gross indiscipline.

"The pension system, the Civil Service, workers' unions, security services, and others have all been engaged to rationalise and optimise services to become more responsive to our needs. In other words, this administration is doing all possible to remove the elements that encourage the corruption being addressed by the trials. We have initiated and, in some cases, finished talks regarding the trials with some countries. To reap the maximum benefits from these trials, we shall require their help and that of global organisations. This administration will not relent in its efforts to exhaust all available diplomatic options in pursuit of our goals. Some caution may be in order. Granted, the illegal and selfish appropriation of common properties, whether belonging to a family, extended family, community, state, country, continent, or humanity, is very wrong. It is also clear that two wrongs can never make a right. I therefore plead with everyone to go about the serious business we all have on hand in a peaceful and responsible manner. ACL is clear in all its provisions.

"I do not believe that there is any reason, whatsoever, for any of us to act in ways that detract from our noble objectives. I do not suppose that the goals before us now give any room for trivia. Let us therefore use the systems in place for abiding by the resolutions of the people's conference in dignifying ways. It is the duty of government to maintain peace, law, and order. This administration will not shy away from it.

"Finally, I hope that in the course of all activities, we can single out TANNA for special mention. Every time we invite them for a meeting, they usually send a committee related to the agenda. I have called them amorphous before because of the way they align their command chain. Regardless, we have been impressed by how they have operated. They truly raised the stakes for all the public service spirited among us. Thank you very much and may we live out our dreams peacefully to the greater grandeur of Nigeria."

That the president mentioned TANNA sent energising waves through our structures. He and his administration became the much-needed support for the realisation of the peoples' dreams. TANNA reasoned that the situation was getting closer to what the purpose of government should be. We gladly ignored Mr. President's moves to ratchet up his administration. Some of us felt that our successes could have been aided in some vital ways by unpublicised actions of Mr. President and his inner caucus. We had no proof. S&I had drawn blank on the matter several times.

The caseloads were so deftly controlled by the Auditor-General that all courts were busy without overloads. Judgments were swift, recoveries quick. Within months, the auditors began conventional time-period audits.

Patterns of collaboration in the infamy became clearer. Unsurprisingly, our former colonisers led the gang of external filchers or collaborators in the odium, with the rest of Europe next. External agents were emerging from other global regions. It became clear that some organisations and individuals were frequently featured in these acts of sleaze in other places. Their home governments had occasionally disowned some of them. Well, as we all know, they found some fertile grounds and eager hosts in Nigeria.

The trials didn't eclipse the conference, which retained the attention of many members of ethnic groups. This was fortunate because the delegates relaxed more, and key issues from ethnic groups were reasonably settled.

Initially, people were more attracted to those cases that emanated from complaints by the public, because they dealt with recent events whose impacts on their lives were easily remembered. However, the roll call at the courts still featured a mixture of the expected, the suspected, and the surprising. That added drama, but there were some common features at all the trials.

The courts regularly overflowed with observers who jeered the suspects even before conviction. Those convicted were roundly abused with unthinkable expressions. The journalists at the trials were responsible; they spread awareness about the gains from acting in ways that did not threaten due process. The accused often implicated others; and the people were in a frenzy of support for the trials.

Consider, for a moment, the tales and trials derived from the Railways, ECN-NEPA-PHCN, Nigeria Airways, P&T[20]-Nitel-Nipost, NPA, NNPC, police and other armed forces, PWD[21]-Works, FCDA[22]-FCT, banks, and the grit and grime of the private sector. Mr. President was right; the trials covered a prolonged period.

We were correct in being apprehensive about the trials. Seven events that occurred within two days in different parts of the country threatened to start serious mayhem. The convicts suffered more than verbal insults. The crowd overpowered security and jumped on them to administer what could be called 'jungle' or first impulse justice. You know, the type that's occasionally given to small-time purse snatchers in the markets—the general mauling and the final treatment of automobile tyres on the neck, dousing with combustible fluids, and burning. In these cases, however, the victims were not minor offenders. They had stolen large sums of money meant for critical services over long periods, while pretending to be the leaders of the people. They had also instigated some casualty-laden troubles among ethnic groups in their areas. Two of the victims were burnt to death, two others were beaten and

---

[20] P&T, Post and Telegraph.
[21] PWD, Public Works Department that became Ministry of Works after independence.
[22] FCDA, Federal Capital Development Authority.

stoned to death, while the fifth died later in the hospital.

Those incidents could not be avoided, because they happened in remote areas usually considered peaceful. Security was overstretched. Afterwards, security was much improved. Everyone concerned acted quickly and decisively to stop such actions from spreading. Thanks to ICT, TANNA responded to the lynching through our patented broadcasts in numerous languages to plead for due process. The government instituted vigorous enquiries, but no one could be charged for the mob-action killings. Curiously, all the cameras of the news crews at the trials didn't capture any of the incidents. Coincidence or conspiracy?

Nevertheless, the incidents served notice about how serious a business the trials were. The floods of evidence uncovered by the audits or presented by the public put to shame the vaunted long memory of the elephant. The past and the present were being re-examined in order to make room for much better probity for tomorrow.

The Population Commission prepared for a fresh census, using the same register as a starter. That census finally took place and threw up surprises. It was standard and provided most of the needed information for rationally growing the people and their environments. Making somebody personally liable for the figures made the difference. So, we got to know who and how many we were and all our ethnic components. It was quite an achievement, because the terribly disturbing uncertainties about our population were finally put to rest. The people were truly awake and into whatever promised relief.

The two auditing groups assigned to the affairs of the country from independence to now converged on the NNPC. Dung broadly hit the fan at sonic speed. Starting from the very first oil well to the present blocks handed out to companies or individuals, the two auditing groups went over everything meticulously. They received much cooperation from many quarters. The oil companies, for instance, obliged them with all the initial and current wellhead pressures and other parameters, all of which yielded fair estimates of the outputs of the wells from the time they were first tapped. Volumes of earlier petitions were made available to them by the authorities and the public. The infamous "bunkering" was fairly quantified and assigned perpetrators.

Many of the so-called rich and famous were tagged. Some of the holier-than-thou pretenders, impersonators of patriotism, the highly steeped in tradition, the specially empowered security guardians, the false activists, and a very large number of likely and unlikely others were flagged. It was all a much more shocking revelation than expected of how the country became a broiling hotbed of deprivation and anger. This audit was the most arduous and longest. It invoked much eagerness, and the people welcomed and guarded the opportunities of knowing it all. The audits concretised the solidarity of the people. The many attempts to scuttle either the audits or their attendant trials were quickly stopped by swift actions of the people.

"Yes, Oga, we'll do it, if your child leads the charge," became the expressions of former political thugs to their former masters.

As convicts emerged, the Accountant General issued mind-boggling reports on the recoveries. Remember that recoveries were from the public and private sectors. Those from the private sector were either returned to the rightful owners or deposited in the general account. Within three months, this general account hit the 106-trillion-naira mark and was growing rapidly.

Additional to the hugely colossal and raucously indexing regurgitations from the NNPC, a resolution of the conference had all our refineries working optimally within three months, and all subsidies removed. That stabilised the supplies and prices of finished petroleum products, with reliability as a super bonus. We gladly lost the hardly flattering distinction of being the only OPEC member importing finished petroleum products.

The ACL stipulated that the initial 500 billion naira of the recoveries should be equally shared among the states for the local government projects to be supervised by the states, with some provisions. The most critical of these were that the projects were to be identified by the people of the local government areas, and that the total overhead costs of implementing the projects were not to exceed 7 percent.

The special local government projects started almost simultaneously all over the country, and they didn't detract from the conference or corruption trials, but they served the very useful purpose of immediately demonstrating the benefits from the peoples' conference. It became harder not to participate in the countrywide transformation.

The federal government ordered emergency upgrading of all prisons and provided additional funds for the upkeep of the expected new inmates who were not to be "specially housed" this time around. The state governments prepared to provide transportation to and from the work locations for the same new hard labour inmates.

It was amazing to witness the value for money for these new government activities rise dramatically.

18

CONVERGENCE

"Shortly, the conference will be on its ninth break. You stayed with us all the way through your overruling directives during the intermissions. Thank you. After this break, the next is the three-month break during which you will deal with the first drafts of all resolutions. No issue has been so touchy as to require the extreme back-and-forth treatment in ACL. However, derivation formula requires your fair and honest input. In other words, how do you instruct that the net earnings from any mineral exploitation be distributed among the states of origin of the mineral, other states, and the federal government? This is important, because much of the dissatisfaction in our country arises from this issue. It is wise to project far into the future.

"We look forward to clearly hearing from you through every delegate. Stay with it! Stay in control! The best is in sight!"

Everyone eagerly awaited the drafts of the conference resolutions.

Many global initiatives of Mr. President were paying off. Some of the loot stashed offshore was recovered with fewer hassles. The exchange rate raised the naira values of those recoveries considerably. This increased anger, but ensured that positive things could be done at home.

The conference notched up another masterstroke by resolving that after the Internal Revenue Service had been audited, the new tax schedules it generated were to be applied. The schedules placed very heavy taxes on imported, outlandish items and induced more equity in society. The department was to specially audit entities it believed were acting beyond their means, but with restrictions to protect basic rights.

To identify entities to specially audit, the department started with reviewing tax returns against apparent assets and then asked for help from the public. Because the mood for such actions had been established, floods of petitions flowed in. Recall the multiple celebrations of birthdays, weddings, and burials at different global locations that required the transportation, feasting, and maintenance of a large entourage.

On buckled knees, some erstwhile "high-fliers" faced charges of tax evasion that invoked severe penalties. This exercise was long, but it increased the recoveries, gave more avenues for people to vent their anger, served as mopping-up operations to the corruption trials, and emphasised the transformation of the country.

The secretariat addressed the country at length.

"At last, the summary of the work of the conference. The three-month break is here. You made a few of our qualified compatriots from the diaspora delegates. This enriched discussions. Thank you. Every delegate is very grateful for being part of this conference.

"First, the conference honestly established mind-sets and goals. We reminded ourselves that the conference is truly that of the people for the renewal of Nigeria. The task of transforming Nigeria into a vibrant nation became the overriding goal. In reviewing our first drafts, we must *all* remember that in enduring relationships, the reliable binders are understanding and accommodation. Current concepts of development encourage the herd mentality, which promotes extreme individualism that shrinks humanity—take care of number one first! However, truly taking care of number one starts with ensuring enabling environments for others who are ready and willing. Then, to live well is to always uplift others around and self. The individual became a focus.

"The conference reviewed the histories of Afrika's interactions with the rest of the world and Nigeria's with the rest of Africa and herself to come up with remedies to the negatives of those interactions. We have three months for *thoroughly* going over the first drafts, but some areas need highlighting.

"A massive return to education is a priority. This is not limited to addressing the horrors in our formal education sector. Informal education from which we more strongly learn how to live received attention. There shall be special orientation classes that everyone must attend. For people under eleven years, new learning resources shall be created. Those between the ages of eleven and eighteen years shall spend a minimum of fourteen hours a week in these classes; those between the ages of nineteen and thirty years, twenty-one hours per week; those between the ages of thirty-one and forty-five years, fifteen hours per week; those between the ages of forty-six and sixty years, ten hours per week; and all those above sixty years, five hours per week. The outlines of materials for these classes have been specified.

"Then, 50 percent of the orientation classes for primary and secondary school levels are to be conducted at school and the other 50 percent at community locations. This ensures that the students get maximum interactions with varying groups of their peers. For higher institutions, 75 percent of the classes shall be held there, while the remaining 25 percent shall be undertaken during vacations. National, zonal, and state competitions on the materials from the National Orientation Agency are to be periodically held.

"With immediate effect, a body of linguists shall be set up to develop our *lingua franca* based on systems that capture most unique sounds in our various languages. The result of their work shall be tested on sample groups in each geopolitical zone in five years. The test learning shall last one year. Thereafter, they shall incorporate all the necessary changes and issue the first version for general learning within one year of test learning. A stream of at least five globally popular languages shall be taught in secondary schools, with students required to study a minimum of three, including the *lingua franca*. More global languages, complete with teaching laboratories, shall be taught in higher institutions.

"The conference spent some time on formal education because of your great concern. The six-three-three-four model is fully adopted as the framework from which to launch other remedies. This model will succeed only to the extent that the pre-primary and primary stages are well-grounded.

These beginning stages shall be free, with free lunches, and compulsory for all children in the age brackets. Stiff penalties await parents or guardians who fail to send their children to school. The state governments shall pick up the bill.

"Secondary schools focus on academic and vocational options. Starting immediately, secondary education shall be subsidised to the tune of 50 percent by the central and state governments on equal basis. It shall also define the minimum standard of education for all citizens in ten years of our new constitution, and shall become free, with the state and central governments equally paying the bill.

"Baselines, started from the census databanks, are to be established for pre-primary, primary, and secondary schools. They include such ratios as number of school types per number of area population, number of teachers per number of students, number of students per computer workstation, and travel distances. Deficiencies from global norms shall be eliminated within ten years of our new constitution.

"The Parents Teachers Associations for pre-primary, primary, and secondary schools shall be compulsory for parents or guardians. Each PTA is to become fully proactive and shall be chaired by a qualified parent and supported by the head of the school. The PTAs and their secondary schools shall immediately execute a program of homestay for students during vacations. This simply means that students are paired off to spend the holidays in the home of one of the pairs. This homestay shall be alternated so that the homes of each pair are reciprocally visited within a year. The pairing shall be reshuffled annually, as students go through secondary school. Secondary schools shall make provisions for capturing students from other zones and African countries. The present unity secondary schools shall be converted into four mixed, quadruple-stream boarding schools per geopolitical zone and one in the FCT, with class sizes not more than thirty-five students. These schools shall be run for the best of the best— and motivated students who shall be nurtured for leadership roles. The details of curricula for these schools are included. State governments and private parties can establish and run pre-primary, primary, and secondary schools, under uniform standards.

"Lengthy discussions on university education resulted from some delegates stating that the continental and global rankings for our universities give no cheer. Therefore, university education shall not be for all comers, but shall be reserved for those with proven ability. The federal universities shall be rationalised around the first-generation universities to two national universities per geopolitical zone and one in the FCT. The Central Government shall fund them beyond their capacity to generate resources. The resulting thirteen national universities shall be fully empowered to set standards in all aspects of university life. All state universities in each geopolitical zone shall merge with any remaining federal universities into one university system per zone and the FCT. They shall be equally funded by the central and state or FCT governments. All private universities in each geopolitical zone shall merge into a single university system in the zone, provided that the operators of such universities are able to upgrade the resulting union to specified standards. Private operators who show will and ability to open and run a university can do so, but its location shall be guided by the national necessity for equitable spread.

"To complement the six-three-three-four model well, two superb polytechnics, with their bias for practice further stressed, shall be located in each geopolitical zone and one in the FCT. They shall be equally funded by the central and state governments or the FCT. The diploma courses shall be brought at par with equivalent qualifications from the university. Each state is to run more advanced skills and vocational centres than what are offered in secondary schools, one in each of the three senatorial zones of the states and FCT, to offer options to those who miss higher education. Their programs are to emphasise practical needs of the country. Consequently, we shall have a minimum of six higher institutions in each zone and three in the FCT. Each one is to establish its current baselines from which to reform its academic, physical structures, and outreach programs for much improved carrying capacities. They shall devote a minimum of 40 percent of their efforts to research, starting with areas that offer solutions to critical challenges in the country and continent. Their postgraduate agenda must be strong. These institutions shall have the final say on their respective admission procedures within set standards, but free of discrimination. All students of higher institutions shall be housed on campus. The routes that extensive reviews of all curricula are to take are outlined.

"The National Universities Commission that oversees the university system has been empowered and shall be monitored to function properly. It shall have responsibility for Polytechnics and other higher institutions, meaning that it shall absorb the National Commission for Colleges of Education. Accreditation shall be more responsive to our needs. All nominees to councils of higher institutions shall be approved by the Commission to ensure enhancing contributions to the institutions. The appointments of top officers of higher institutions shall be free of unhelpful considerations such as ethnicity, quotas, and alumni standing. Merit shall determine such appointments. The head of an institution shall either be a proven manager or have such a person as his close assistant, for transparent use of resources. Funding shall be predictable, without needless prompting, for confident planning and execution. Institutions and their councils shall be guided by the restorative guidelines from the conference. Punitive actions for nonperformance, including the banning from similar positions for periods related to the magnitude of such failure, shall be taken against council members and the heads of institutions and their immediate subordinates.

"The conference provided a schedule of revised welfare packages for all teachers in the sector that will make teaching attractive, even to our qualified compatriots in the diaspora or foreigners. The retirement age for professors and lecturers has been raised to seventy-five years for the meriting, with the option, at the discretion of individual and institution, to continue for an additional five years, taken yearly. Each state is to upgrade or establish teacher training colleges, one in each of their senatorial zones, for training of teachers for the crucial pre-primary and primary levels, and children with special needs, including the gifted. Meriting teachers shall have development paths that lead to 75 percent subsidised higher education, to upgrade their careers. Adult education is reactivated; details of its implementation are outlined.

"Traditional rulers and their councils are the principal maintainers of our cultures that make us unique. The roles of Traditional Rulers shall be to keep our cultures thriving. Each ethnic group shall therefore overhaul how their

Traditional Ruler is selected to ensure legitimacy and peace. No longer shall they engage in activities such as roaming about in search of contracts. They shall no longer commercialise traditional titles to the detriment of the institution. They are to interact with all their community organisations as impartial and firm guardians, while ensuring that performing development associations flourish in their domains. To make their work easier, the conference standardised a few common cultural features for better integration. The vital institution of marriage is one such feature. To make it better, the conference placed a ceiling on the bride price to be paid by a prospective groom and reaffirmed that the guiding customs of the prospective bride's ethnic group shall dominate, while accommodating what obtains on the groom's side. The critical marriage ceremony shall take place in the applicable *village* of the prospective couple. Furthermore, for every state line crossed in going from one to the other of the villages of the new couple, the sum of 50,000 naira shall be paid to the couple by the central government, after five years of successful marriage. Similarly, 25,000 naira shall be paid by the couple's respective state governments to members of the union for every local government boundary crossed in a union within the state. These shall be one-time payments.

"Without exception, our cultural heritage forbids antisocial behaviour. Carefully authenticated and ranked listing of convicts from all formal law enforcement agencies shall be sorted out according to the ethnic groups of the convicts. These lists shall be forwarded to the relevant Traditional Rulers for their additional corrective measures. The lists become part of the criteria for evaluating the influences of Traditional Rulers. Appropriate national honours shall be awarded the Traditional Ruler whose subjects do not appear on them. There is also an award to the Traditional Ruler whose domain showed the best improvement within the periods between awards.

"Whenever practicable, Traditional Rulers shall be the first to attempt to settle serious disputes in their domains, but failing which, the disputants remain free to pursue the matter through appropriate law enforcement agencies. Inputs from the Traditional Council involved shall be allowed in evidence. Also, Traditional Rulers shall reach out to their counterparts for the same reason, when disputants come from different domains. This arrangement provides the possibility of settling differences in more friendly atmospheres, rich in culture, before they turn into lasting bitterness.

"Traditional rulers shall collectively make annual inputs to government at all levels. For this purpose, there shall be semi-annual congresses, rotated through the present geopolitical zones, for all traditional rulers. In line with the transformation of the country, traditional rulers shall ensure the accuracy of updates of data from their domains that are stored in all databanks. They shall ensure that cultural events, which strengthen the countrywide transformation, are suitably upgraded or introduced. Databanks shall be established at state, geopolitical zone, and national levels for all retired or serving professionals who are available and willing to give hands-on advice to worthwhile initiatives in the country. This new program shall be called 'Expertise Extension Services.' When such postings are to rural areas, the receiving traditional ruler shall be the chief host; likewise for the reviewed NYSC members and all service-oriented others so posted.

"Traditional Rulers duly enthroned through their domains' due processes shall be empowered to function well. The state governments concerned shall supply 50 percent of all their requirements and their subjects shall provide the balance through equitable contributions. This should make subjects appreciate and pay more attention to the institution. We shall return to values that serve our long-term goals best and with which we more readily connect. Ethnic groups shall be very careful in selecting their Traditional Rulers.

"Religion, the conference confirmed, shall be a *wholly personal matter*. The rights and liberties of everyone to practise his or her choice of religion shall be inviolable. However, newer religions that originated not more than 5,000 years ago have tended to splinter into sects at alarming rates, thereby causing tragedies. Our heritage in the matter received some educating reviews. Governments shall keep off all religious matters, such as sponsoring of pilgrimages, use of official resources for religious events, and making religion an index in governance. Practitioners shall abide by the codes guiding public peace and order. A specific is that the use of blaring loudspeakers or other loud noise generators for worship is banned; the practice infringes on others' rights to noise-pollution-free environments. Technology has provided alternatives that do not cause this problem.

"Sports received special attention in the areas of recreation, because of their global importance. The ministries of sports shall immediately commence a thorough overhaul of structures and operations for improved efficiency. Details stipulate, among others, the identification of promising talents and the nurturing of such talents to global glory. The focus shall first be towards those sports in which we have shown promise.

"There is also the creation of a countrywide, multi-location, cultural festival of tourism potential into the national holiday calendar.

"Law, order, and justice occupied the conference sufficiently. The country shall have only one legal system supremely applicable to everyone, but people who wish to add other sets of laws to their lives can do so, as long as the enforcement of such other laws do not overstep into any rights of others outside the group. This choice should not subject them or anyone else to any stress. The penal codes and court procedures of the country shall be quickly updated and harmonised to reflect the transformation. Our current maintenance of law and order was strongly discredited for its many omissions and commissions. It was noted that there is no country or nation in which crime is absent, but the differences are often related to how quickly criminals are caught and justly punished for their crimes. These issues require very urgent attention to improve general security of which they are essential parts. General security in society is measurably influenced by mind-set and psychology; both are often derived from reality.

"The conference found decentralising the police and the armed forces less desirable, in the context of our projections for Nigeria. The systems on ground, on paper at least, were found somewhat adequate. The resolutions here focus on improving those systems, such as ensuring that the judiciary and correctional institutions function more efficiently through upgraded infrastructures, and the adaptations of methods that drastically hasten the deliveries of justice, along with general improvement of policing. The existing Commission on Police Affairs and other commissions in this critical area of law and order have been merged and empowered for harmony and more efficiency. This is in addition to the increased duties of the assemblies on police and related matters. There is a two-year schedule for greatly improving staff and welfare matters.

"The armed forces have resolutions similar to those of the police, but a crucial additional resolution is that the armed forces, including the police, shall not have any role in governance beyond containing internal or external aggression, when duly directed to do so. The consequences of violating this provision includes that any injury or death occasioned by the objections of the people to any attempt of the armed forces to usurp governance powers shall be considered a crime of wilful injury or murder against all those behind the attempt. The armed forces and the police shall reactivate or create defence industries attached to them for research, development, and training that shall not only lead to sources of their hardware and methods but also serve as the pivot for our unique military-industrial alliances.

"The work on the economy was made easier by the materials made available by the president. The realignment of those materials with your directives led to a desirable plan for our economy. First, the healthy and well-fed is good for the economy. Rural farmers shall be immediately supported, including selected government subsidies to keep farming at this level attractive. Within a year of our new constitution, all state governments shall establish a minimum of 1,000 hectares expandable farms and processing facilities in every senatorial zone of the states. These farms shall first target 60 to 70 percent of their production towards local consumption and 30 to 40 percent for export. The threat of global hunger may be real, but we shall not be rushed into becoming the guinea pigs for genetically modified food. Those who produce these tinkered with foods should first test them on themselves. That commercial agriculture depleted the soil of some essential elements and that too many man-made chemicals entered the food chain through agriculture shall guide us.

"These farms shall be set up for later privatisation by selling 55 percent of their equity to private parties from their respective senatorial zones and the remaining 45 percent to private parties from outside the zones, who bring significant values to the farms. All available expertise shall be tapped to make these farms not only successful, but also the sources of driving knowledge on intensified, sustainable, and healthy agriculture to farmers, with 50 percent discount on transmitted information. If a farm fails, the land on which it is located shall revert to their original owners.

"After the audits, the ailing River Basin Authorities shall be reactivated and privatised, as in the 1,000 hectares farms, but localising them to their geopolitical zones, in two years of our new constitution. Nutritionists and related specialists shall be assembled and supported to identify the nutritional values of all the things we conventionally eat, the objective being minimum healthy diets tied to foods in season, our physiological profiles, and our dominant lifestyles. Their first full guidance shall be ready for circulation within three years of our new constitution, but they can be released in parts before then. Thereafter, they are to periodically update these guidelines. Food is a security issue. Our country should lead the effort to feed the distressed in Africa, always.

"Before it becomes too late, genuine outlets for our traditional medicines shall be immediately provided for those who wish to use them. Concurrently, all universities shall commence or intensify results-driven research in this area of medical science. We have many amazing solutions to offer humanity in this area. States shall immediately restart the dispensary system for providing first aid and basic healthcare to our rural areas. General hospitals that cater for maternity and other female and child healthcare services shall be located, one in every senatorial zone by the states and the FCT, within three years of our new constitution.

"Private hospitals shall be encouraged, but under strict standards and annual inspections, with prudent mergers in mind. Rural areas shall be emphasised for these private hospitals through incentives. Emergency and trauma centres shall be immediately and strategically located on our major roads, particularly those most prone to accidents, along with ambulances and communication.

"All rationalised universities shall improve or establish their teaching hospitals so that they focus on production of credible doctors, related specialists and practitioners, promote research, anchor to relevant global trends, and offer much improved services to their patients All specialist hospitals owned by governments shall be annexed to the teaching hospitals for cohesion. The cutoff date for these activities is within two years of our new constitution. To crown the healthcare area, one more national hospital shall be built at a strategic location that aids recovering. It shall be rationalised with the present one at Abuja by three years of our new constitution. Both shall offer many sets of specialist services, equal to most in the world. They shall serve as the epic outlets of our healthcare capabilities, uniquely attractive.

"In matters of healthcare, any purveyor of fake drugs or food shall receive severe punishment. All providers of healthcare procedures—practitioners and institutions—shall jointly be liable for any grave neglect. The national health insurance scheme is now more inclusive, enduring, and affordable.

"For our industries to prosper, the work force must be equal to the task. Employers, organised labour, and relevant others shall implement workforce training and retraining to improve production mentality and civic responsibility. Discipline, focus, reliability, routine and reiterative activities, studying, creativity, maintenance culture, and the wider pictures of sustainability, are pointers. Related curricula have been defined for learning institutions. These activities start now.

"Resolutions with timelines addressed production environments. Areas affected include physical infrastructure and power, minimum welfare packages, durable pension schemes, financial policies and institutions, growth of the private sector, labour intensive and local content-laden public works and projects, agro-based industries, and SME regimes. A wide-ranging development master plan has streamlined all available earlier suggestions with your directives that include global trends. In the troublesome power sector, the conference amended ongoing initiatives. Proper attention shall be urgently paid to extensive maintenance and upgrading of transmission and distribution systems. It would indeed be more laughable that on improving power generation, we are unable to amply transmit and distribute power to our people for their needs. Private operators brought on board shall be relentlessly monitored to safeguard expectations. The sources of energy for electricity shall be diversified to include renewable sources. Specifically, the hydroelectric power stations in Plateau state and the thermal plant in Enugu state shall be reactivated and upgraded soonest.

"When generation, transmission, and distribution have been reliably improved to meet growth demands, the current tariff regime shall remain in effect for five years. Thereafter, the subsidy shall be gradually removed over the next five years. This should be easy to do, especially if all the debts in the sector are recovered. The people and the economy have earned this courtesy over much time. The displaced due to the transformation shall be retrained and redeployed. Agriculture, education, public works, and entrepreneurships provide options. All employers on a national scale shall endeavour to post their staff out of their areas of origin in order to aid integration. Every citizen should be eager to contribute to the development of any part of Nigeria where his or her expertise will be most optimally utilised, without being disadvantaged. We want to all cherish the enrichment of every square metre of our collective real estate, Nigeria.

"Where not fully covered by the audits, all our past and current debts shall be quickly re-confirmed—meaning their validity, sources, borrowing governments, uses, current values, maintenance costs, and utilisation status. Thereafter, the central and state governments shall inform the people about our debts semiannually. The procedures for borrowing shall require prior approvals by the National Assembly before any government takes loans, to firmly insert the specific uses of the loans and the results achieved into the oversight of the Assemblies. Deficits by all governments are outlawed. Quarterly, governments shall make the status of their finances public.

"With the new constitution adopted, all annual budgets shall start from the people. Each ward shall identify, prioritise, and tentatively price what projects the people there want the government to execute for them. These requests shall next be collated at the local governments and transmitted to state governments. The national budget shall be derived from the reviewed and consolidated submissions of the states. Twenty and thirty percent of the budgets shall be left at the discretions of the state and central governments respectively. Easy to use formats have been produced for justifying every requested budget item. This way, the people shall be in better positions to evaluate yearly government performances that validate the presence of any government. The people are thus involved in budgeting, budget implementation, and monitoring.

"There shall be selected community projects that require matching funding by communities, so that community development associations sufficiently participate in project deliveries. All urban centres and their immediate environs shall be divided into neighbourhood associations for this and other purposes in environmental, social, economic, and political affairs. National services that require a great deal of independence to function properly, such as the Electoral Commission and special prosecutors, shall have dedicated budgets.

"Diversification of the economy attracted overwhelming consensus. Another body similar to the NNPC in the oil and gas sector shall be formed for solid minerals by rationalising the present mining corporation into an entity, with all lessons from NNPC and the past as guides. Government, with intensified oversight functions of the assemblies, shall relentlessly monitor both bodies. Whether in oil and gas or in solid minerals, all exploitation rights granted solely to individuals shall be immediately revoked. Any organisation owned by our citizens, fully or in part, shall be granted exploitation rights, if such ownership is equally spread over the present geopolitical zones, with the additional requirement that an owner shall come from the state in which the resource is exploited. From your directives, the net income accruing to us from minerals shall be shared as follows, on our new constitution: 20 percent to the state of origin of the minerals and, where more than one, shared out in proportion to production; 32 percent to the central government; 35 percent to all states; 10 percent reinvestment into the sector and reserves in appropriate yearly ratios; and 3 percent to the states from which the exploitation of minerals such as tin and coal had demonstrably contributed to our sustenance from 1914 to date, in proportion to such contributions. Also, 70 percent of the 35 percent allocated to all states shall be shared out equally to all states, while the remaining 30 percent shall be allocated to the states in proportions that reflect the needed yearly effort to bring the aggregated quality of life *per capita* indices in each state to global yardsticks.

"In arriving at these resolutions, there were some superior arguments. Mineral exploitation invariably degrades the environment and disrupts normal life in more or less permanent ways, depending on mineral type, methods of exploitation, and overall remedial attention paid to the undertaking. Rationally, such mineral deposits are finite and nonrenewable. Depending on technology evolution and prevailing global trends, the location and value of minerals can shift radically. Then, the combined requirements of enormous tangible and intangible inputs into successful exploitation of underground or undersea minerals are beyond an individual, family, community, or even a state to provide. Our performances in the general matter undeniably indict us for imprudence and grave acts of omission and commission.

"Schedules of remedial responsibilities go with these resolutions. In the spirit of the transformation, the central government, the states of origin of the minerals, and the rest of us must act quickly and decisively to correct these past mistakes and to ensure that they do not reoccur anywhere in our country. To properly focus our energies on the transformation of our country without the distractions of easy inflows of revenues from minerals, all net-earnings accruing to us from all minerals shall not be available to government for five years, starting from six months of our new constitution. Such net earnings, after allowing for operational needs, shall be securely invested onshore and offshore in equal ratios. The investments at home shall be in financial institutions whose boards and senior management shall also be responsible for them. The offshore investments require applicable guarantees from the home governments of the parties receiving them. These investments shall not be used as collaterals for loans by any government. The government shall monitor all the investments for strict compliance, and shall promptly act to secure them, aided by oversight of the assemblies.

"The six months from the adoption of our new constitution to the start of the embargo are to give government time to tidy up all matters before the embargo. After the embargo, an off-the-top allocation of 0.1 percent of all accruals, including capitals, from the embargo shall be used as matching awards to the top twelve states that show the most improvements in the quality of life of their people during the embargo. These assessments shall emphasise human capital development and verified adoption of the new national values. The embargo is expected to make us look more closely at who and what we are all about, especially our common obligations and destiny.

"Driven by all your clear directives, the conference may have accomplished the greatest innovation through our political affairs. Nothing short of clearing our political space of all pretenders, distorters, and opportunists would be good enough. Some of them, without performance or ethics and morality, had long forced themselves on our political space through unprincipled use of our common assets and overall circumstances. Returning to the old regional arrangements in order to allow each region to develop at its own pace was rejected, because that will stop our reaping the full benefits of our diversity, thereby leaving many calls of history and posterity ignored. We shall retain the tripartite governance arrangement of the judiciary, legislature, and executive, after some modifications, because of its checks and balances. The three shall be truly independent, yet act together for our common good.

"We shall have only two levels of government: one at the centre, led by the president and the other at the state level, run by the governor. We shall have only two assemblies of representatives: one at the centre called Greater Peoples' Assembly and the other at the states called Peoples' Assembly. The judiciary shall continue with its present set-up, after some improvements. The conference amended the present procedures for running the assemblies to properly reflect the transformation that calls for capable and dedicated people, mainly driven by the desire to serve as judged by the people who know them best. One such amendment is that committee duties shall be rotated every eighteen months with committees chaired by people who have the best backgrounds for the committees' work. At the end of each term of the assembly, each member would have served in four committees charged with different assignments in matters relating to our lives.

"National policies on such matters as orientation and education, agriculture and the economy, pension schemes, individual in community guidelines, and national cohesion shall become long-term. They shall be sustained through administrations so that their objectives are achieved and become regenerative. Support team sizes for the president and governors have been limited. With our new constitution in place, the annual cost of running any government shall not exceed 30 percent of its budget. This allocation shall decrease at the annual rate of 2 percent until the final figure of 14 percent is reached in eight years.

"The life of governments shall be four years, while that of the assemblies shall be six years. Whenever the lives of government and the assembly concurrently end in any year, the life of the assembly shall be extended by one year, for improved transitions. The president and governors are allowed two terms each, while the peoples' representatives have no limit on number of terms. The president and governors shall be free to select their teams, including deputies, subject to assent by applicable Peoples' Assemblies. Audited baselines shall commence and terminate every government. Government project management shall be automated with state-of-the-art facilities and techniques, while protecting project integrity and national security. These facilities shall be looped and based at the presidency. This tool should allow the president to know the status of critical projects even at ward levels. Government shall therefore make public the status of every project, quarterly for states and semiannually for the central government.

"Local governments shall become only administrative centres, answerable to the state governments alone. They shall cease to be direct recipients of national budgetary allocations. This means that the state governments shall be free to use any number of them that makes governance more effective. As administrative centres and the most visible links between government and the people, local government councils shall primarily focus on project deliveries. Every councillor shall therefore be capable of efficiently functioning as a project supervisor. The state governor shall appoint local government council chairs in his/her state, subject to the approval of the affected Peoples' Assemblies. The people shall elect other councillors.

"Explicit and fair provisions for removing the president or a governor from office have been clearly outlined. Any president or governor so removed shall go with his or her entire team, including local government chairs in the case of a governor. In the event of a head of government being so removed from office, the head of the relevant Peoples' Assembly, with the head of the judiciary as next choice, shall form an acting government for a period not exceeding six months within which a new government shall be accordingly inaugurated. The new government is free to return any member of the sacked government, following the normal approval by the relevant Peoples' Assemblies, excepting the previously removed president or governor or any member of their teams that had been found liable as well.

"The new face Electoral Commission shall become permanent. Periodic training and re-training programmes shall be conducted for the commission, to sufficiently impress on its members the critical nature of their work. Each represents people from whom they can hardly hide and therefore unwise to disappoint. The wards in any local government area shall be grouped into twelve so that a councillor comes from each of them. These groups shall be as equally populated as practicable. If the people return them, councillors shall have unlimited number of terms, with each term tied to that of the PA. The conference outlined the procedures for removing non-performing councillors from office in the sections on electoral laws and performance in office.

"The total number of support staff of any local government shall not exceed the number of wards in the local government. The remuneration of all workers, including chairs and councillors, shall be monetised in line with those of civil servants. A councillor's age shall be between twenty-one and fifty years, with the minimum educational qualification of SSCE or equivalent. The prospective candidate shall be credible in the judgement of the people of the wards, shall be of good physical and mental health, and shall be capable of supervising possible projects. All prospective candidates for political offices, starting with councillorships, shall first be so endorsed by their family heads, development associations, and the principal Traditional Ruler of his or her community.

"A committee shall screen down all candidates for councillorships to no more than three for the election of one of them. All staff of the Electoral Commission in the affected ward shall be members of this screening committee and shall be responsible for coordinating the committee's work. Six additional members of the committee shall be selected through the facilitation of the Electoral Commission as follows: two who are between twenty-one and thirty years old, two aged between thirty-one and fifty years, and two aged fifty-one and above. The chairs and secretaries of development associations, and the Traditional Ruler in the affected ward shall also be members of this committee. The procedures for screening all prospective candidates for political offices are clearly defined.

"In all cases, candidates shall conduct pre-election campaigns as follows. A series of meet-the-people rallies and debates in which all candidates shall participate shall be arranged and equally paid for by affected government and people. The candidates shall be free to conduct their individual campaigns, with the clear provision that they are forbidden to give any form of inducement to the people. The Electoral Commission and the security agencies shall monitor all campaigns. Any candidate found guilty of violating electoral laws by the electoral courts shall be disqualified and charged with violating those laws. Electoral courts shall conclude hearings within seventy-two hours.

"The state and FCT PAs shall each have twenty-nine members produced by proportional representation of the local government areas in the state or FCT. The local government areas concerned shall nominate or select from volunteers, three candidates from whom the people will elect one as their allotted representative.

"The screening down to three candidates for each allotted representative shall be by a committee of all the senior Electoral Commission members, chairs and secretaries of the development unions, Traditional Rulers, and six age-limited members as for councillorships. All local government chairs and secretaries shall be included. Members of the Electoral Commission shall manage this committee with the most senior member as chair. Candidates for the PA shall not be less than twenty-five years old and must possess a minimum educational qualification of a recognised university first degree. Each state shall have five, and the FCT three, representatives in the GPA through a scheme that assures equitable representation within the state or FCT. The procedures for allotting these representatives in rural and urban areas are provided. Candidates who want to serve at the GPA shall be thirty years and above, must possess a minimum of a recognised university first degree, and must have established credible records of accomplishments in the private or public sectors, or both. They shall be similarly screened as the candidates for the PA, to offer three candidates per allotted representative for elections.

"For the purposes of electing governors for the states and the FCT, each state and the FCT shall be divided into three zones, resulting from the amendments of current senatorial zones. Each zone shall produce a candidate for governor, resulting in three candidates for elections. Governorship candidates shall not be less than forty years old and must have proven management experience in either the public or private sectors, or both. The minimum educational qualification shall be a recognised university first degree.

"Each geopolitical zone shall produce an experienced candidate for president, and such candidates must not be less than forty-five years and must possess a minimum of a recognised university first degree. We shall then have six candidates from which to elect the president, after carefully arranged, executed, and monitored campaign appearances in all zones by the six. The screening committees in each zone shall include all state governors of each zone and shall otherwise be similarly constituted as those for the GPA candidates. Election activities shall commence six months prior to elections. The first activities are the selection and orientation of all screening committees. Every screening committee shall receive complete and timely security reports on all candidates from security agencies. There are provisions for run-off elections, if a winner does not emerge from the first round of voting.

"It is hoped that we will all appreciate the reengineering of our polity that moves us closer to our roots—the people have become the owners of our politics. The package that the conference is now issuing contains the drafts of our proposed new constitution in two formats: the first in legal language and the other, in ordinary language. Detailed schedules of the meanings of each section limit grey areas. The doctrines of necessity, efficacy, and consequences, which constitutional experts often use to interpret the words of constitutions, were sufficiently defanged in the drafts. We are all required to review this draft constitution and other resolutions thoroughly in the next three months. The delegates are all typically available for your information. You can reach the conference through its website and telephone numbers. The conference has opened temporary offices, one in each state capital and the FCT, until we approve the final draft of our new constitution.

"When the conference resumes from this three-month break, it shall amend this first draft of the constitution in accordance with your dominant inputs to produce a second draft, which shall be very widely publicised and commented on for a period of three months. After this, the conference will again make all necessary amendments, and the resulting third draft shall again be publicised for a period of one month. There shall be a referendum on our new constitution at the end of this one month. To approve the new constitution, it must receive approval votes of not less than 90 percent of all votes cast and not less than 45 of votes in each zone. The conference projects that by the time we cast our votes on this vital document, we shall be voting and thereafter living with conviction and no longer in ignorance or distortion. Please everyone should help make this happen by getting informed and by acting on this and other matters promptly.

"If the constitution is not approved on the first voting, the conference shall reconvene within a month of the voting to appropriately tackle failure points. Another round of voting shall take place thereafter. This process shall continue until the constitution is approved. When this happens, the new constitution shall be given legal backing within three months after the referendum. At that point, our country becomes NAIJA; each of us becomes a NAIJAN; our *lingua franca* becomes NAIJEN; and our general descriptive adjective becomes NAIJAN! The last lap is on! Stay involved! Stay on top of it all!"

19

PRICELESS EXCHANGES

Nigeria rumbled—draft constitution, the exciter!

Since change is inevitable and its successful management enviable, TANNA revelled in the ways people conducted themselves, while executing all directives, and in how well and quickly they adjusted to all results. All the false veils were off the peoples' eyes, hearts, and minds.

Mr. President and his team were great. With the possibility of investing part of the accruals from mineral exploitation offshore during the embargo, the international community listened more to him on the repatriation of stolen funds. Legal costs reduced significantly. Even the vaunted coded accounts of great secrecy were pounced upon. Then, the unbelievable amount the recoveries were adding up to daily were judiciously used to run governments, including conference-directed initiatives. Some amounts were used to leverage business loans to the clearly ready and capable, while emphasising agriculture and rural enterprises.

Mr. President harmonised and scheduled the conference resolutions. All areas needing immediate attention got it. Orientation, in all its forms, was first. Relevant economic boosters accompanied every step.

The conference-directed local government projects were completed with surprising efficiency. That gave more meaning to the conference and the transformation.

You should have seen what happened to the Niger Delta areas. It appeared that half of the people in the country, some global organisations and specialists had been assembled there on restoration activities. Special orientation programs were concurrently run there at a faster pace to lessen the anger and to otherwise empower the inhabitants. The North-East embraced peace and security, thanks to the peoples' awakened will. In these and all other activities everywhere, possible labour-intensive methods were used to create jobs fast.

One of the very first things that Mr. President did after that summary was to expeditiously put a faithful project management system in place. The completion of some of the local government projects were aided by it. The results of the census and voters' register projects were painstakingly updated and archived at surprising speeds.

The awesome system was basically a powerful stand-alone Wide Area Network with domestically created filters, blockers, and other security functions, which were all programmed to continually and randomly change their operating features. It was later embellished and called "naijacription."

Thanks to the recovery trials, four expansive residential estates, the types that competed with high-end five-star hotels or resorts anywhere, fell to the people: two in the northern and southern parts of the country respectively— great dispersion. They were remodelled into smaller residential units fully furnished for various types of efforts, cerebral and otherwise.

The people in the neighbourhoods of these estates gathered daily to watch the conversion work. Those of them lucky enough to participate did so with much relish. Many walked around with springing steps and assertive carriages. Earlier, they could hardly get close to the gates because of armed and fierce-looking guards, and the imported, huge, guard dogs just beyond the gates.

The first special guests to these work locations were from Mr. President. Without fanfare, dedicated teams he put together had seriously engaged some of our experienced people in the diaspora to take part in the transformation of the country. Some did so temporarily and others, permanently. A greater number of proven and experienced specialists, experts, and professionals, in many fields in the country joined them. This last group provided the additional advantage and settling contributions of current hands-on experience. The combination was dynamite.

Mr. President and his team truly showed that they needed no prompting to do their parts. They had succeeded, in a pioneering example, in converting a bit of the hurtful brain drain into some meaningful brain regain. This trend continued later. Some crucial projects connected with the transformation were driven by the intellect and hard work of the group.

After that summary by the conference, TANNA rolled on at a record pace. Our funds were still in good shape. We increased our facilities as required. Volunteers were there for the picking; many people wanted participation. TANNA poured out information that complemented the efforts of the media and government's actions.

Our most potent approach was direct contact with people. We capitalised on the new avenues: the orientation centres; the trial venues and work sites. We quickly translated the draft constitution into all languages and conveyed them to the field. TANNA was bombarded with the message that: "Because we can still do better, no success is final."

The delegates were also persistent. We sent harmonised and consistent messages to the people. The delegates were anxious about how people took the restructuring of the polity—the termination of party politics that harboured terrible waste, debilitating opportunism, debasing values, and wanton greed. They dwelt on the new political order being more in consonance with our heritage, the individual in community relationships of time. Those initiatives were well received by the people.

TANNA also worked on ensuring that people clearly understood every section of the draft constitution and that they were able to sufficiently capture, analyse, and appreciate the draft as a composite document, the total picture. Whenever any opposition was raised about a particular item or section, we used countervailing items or sections to broker equity and acceptance. We also paid attention to making sure that people understood all the resolutions pertaining to the new political order, which gave a lot of work to the people. We drummed in what had to happen at every stage of implementing the new system that returned political power to the people through repeated reminders.

Perhaps, due to the commissioned local government projects, the recoveries, and other activities going on simultaneously, some people became a little smug by being less inquisitive or adamant. We countered the development with considered hints to the principal officers of the National Orientation Agency.

Long after the new constitution, TANNA still had much work in support of the new political order—screening of candidates, campaigns, elections, the PA, and the GPA needed unrelenting support.

As the resolutions of the conference came into effect, the atmosphere of change became more stimulating with time and events, and beset nearly everybody. In the manner of that veritable evergreen that drops off its worn leaves at the end of the season to again sprout back to luscious life so irrepressibly at the beginning of a new season, the entire country took on new, vibrant, communal life.

Internal and external rings of exploiters and oppressors, imperialists all, ossified and dropped off. The intra-ethnic opportunists abandoned their monopolistic and dog-in-the-manger attitudes to correctly queue up for prospects, as were available to all. The individual returned to the community and the community again counted the individual as its own. The transformation, like a potent dispersant, was clearing off the unconscious fog of forced multiple personalities that had been unsettling us, as each person started finding the path to the true self—the Afrikan self. Ever more, we turned to being the keepers of our sisters and brothers; the action-packed focus on reducing differentials between parts of the country told the joyful stories.

There was the widely accepted stipulation that, if one continuously resided in any part of the country, different from one's place of birth or prior residence, for five years, one qualified to run for any office at this new location. Everywhere, the indigene-settler brouhaha turned into fraternity.

The return of general security was very empowering. Almost everyone experienced unbelievably elevated self-esteem. That made it easier for a focused, common outlook, including the defusing of global negative images of us, to prevail. The newly enshrined probity propelled activities and restored confidence in governance and society. Afrika was regaining bits of her glories.

The referendum approved the new constitution by 93 percent. Mr. President signed it into law a month later. Every square metre of the country was highly electrified and vibrated with excitement. "Naija! Naija! Naija!" resonated everywhere. Quite a few people came up with spontaneous melodies and original jigs.

The day the new constitution came into being became the new national day, but October 1st remained a strong reminder of our encounters with the British, their cousins, and their other co-travellers. That day was declared a national holiday and Mr. President signed the new constitution into law at midday, after a splendid, landmark speech. He did not fail to strongly emphasise that there was still much work to do. He invited 650 members of TANNA to a national reception he hosted later that week.

During the last address by the conference before they dispersed, we learnt that even though it was not specified in ACL, the conference had used other powers conferred by ACL to further enable the political transformation. Mr. President and the governors were to remain in office for four years of the new constitution, but they would be bound by the new order. They were to reconstitute their teams accordingly and were to ensure that the GPA and PA took off according to the new provisions, for examples. After their four-year tenures, the next set of government executives would then be elected as stipulated by the new order. At this point, the people could not say no to the conference.

§ § §

To give notice to Africa, our portion of the long-stalled transcontinental highway was quickly completed above specifications. We headed the drive that created an efficient AU taskforce that completed the rest of the highway similarly. Multilingual communication across and within all regions improved incredibly. Dedicated satellites made news, entertainment, and business contacts prevalent and affordable. Flights linking major cities of the continent exploded in their number and variety from the upgrading of airports everywhere in Africa and from activities of African and global airlines.

These channels, layered and uninhibited, allowed the profusely cross-fertilised essence of Afrika to naturally crest and ebb everywhere in Africa. The transformation of the country received firmer footing.

§ § §

Instructively, a few of the delegates became local government chairs and members of the PA or the GPA. Remember how they became delegates. That was part of how Naija was created. Nigeria and Nigerians became Naija and Naijans respectively—*priceless exchanges.*

The conscious create and alter the subconscious, but often, the subconscious prevail.

Indeed, events naturally vent the advent of wisdom.

"We must become the change we want to see." – Gandhi.

Create or sign on to a TANNA!

ACKNOWLEDGEMENT

Welugewe and Mulubwa, my daughter and her husband, who reposed driving confidence in me, remain indispensable. From Zambia, Nonde Munkanta recommended stressing the pan-Afrikan postures. Repeatedly, Amankekwu, Chidume, and Uzobuenyi, my sons and nephew respectively, decried the outcomes from the *status quo*, especially for Nigerian youths. Bim and Edwina Salako never stopped encouraging the project. Arize and Egele Nwobu stood tall with multifaceted facilitation. I'm truly grateful to you all.

HIS ROYAL HIGHNESS, IGWE Tom A. Inyiama, The Ogwugwu Ebenebe I of Ogwofia Owa Kingdom, reviewed and gave the first copy grace. Then, Professor Richard C. Okafor authoritatively gave the book enriching insights and recommendations through the foreword. Extra-esteemed gentlemen, I thank you both very much, and I also thank Chief Theo Okechukwu for making both events possible.

Oyofo Oghe, my community, gave me identity and early personality, both of which eventually led to this writing project; may you overcome the challenges of change to remain magnificent, as an Afrikan community.

Government Secondary School Afikpo, "The Campus on the Cross," so called then because of its high standards of facilities, programs, and from its location close to Cross River, carried on from my community to nurture me. The environment constantly screamed, "Question, further confirm, evaluate impact, and then aim for the far stars, but FEAR GOD, HONOUR THE KING!" May your true model amply resurrect everywhere in Nigeria and Africa.

The African-American Institute allied with the University of Wisconsin,

USA, and made me a beneficiary of the trailblazing ASPAU (African Scholarship Program of American Universities) to study mechanical engineering at the Madison, Wisconsin, campus, where I got so broadly "tooled up" as to be able to contend with the challenges of this writing project. It was all interesting, international, learning centre and times. Thank you!

Rita Ann, my dear wife, found her own ways of coping with all my slacks and abrasive edges, while the writing was in progress for a long time, challenged and urged me on in compelling ways. Hey, I love you!

Amankekwu Joseph and Welugewe Monica, my parents, made and taught me to live. From my earliest memories, Amankekwu has remained that empowering source of strength and guidance. Decades after he physically departed this life, I still "perceive" his presence whenever a cowering challenge confronts me. From her centenarian command at 104 years before bowing out, Welugewe still radiated impregnable willpower couched in imperatives for forgiveness, peaceful coexistence, cascading progress, and love. To both of you, I owe too much; more than words can convey. Thank you, thank you very much for the privilege; what else is possible to say?

Polgarus Studio – http://www.polgarusstudio.com – called to mind the poem, *Time-Square-Shoeshine-Composition,* by Maya Angelou. Therapeutically to a newbie, they gave me timely editing, other services, and encouragement, all affordably and with great cheer. Uplifting touch; thank you so much.

May the spirals of all your wisdom and charity remain on ascending trajectories always, and with abundantly joyous fallouts and spin-offs surfeiting each of your days and ways, my multidimensional and omnipresent support team.

I'm truly much obliged.

Chukwuajalike
Email: ccaningoboox@gmail.com
Blog site: http://www.beamnaijadream.com

About the Author

Born in Oyofo Oghe, Enugu state, Nigeria, author Chukwuajalike C. Aningo studied mechanical engineering at University of Wisconsin as an ASPAU (African Scholarship Program of American Universities) scholar. He served in various capacities in residential, commercial, industrial, and government projects on six continents.

After returning to Nigeria in 1980, he led the Technical Division of Benue Cement Company, PLC, which set the production record of ninety-three percent annual capacity utilisation in 1985. He also was the pioneer chief coach of the company's football team, BCC Lions FC, which ultimately "roared" to capture both African and Nigerian club championships.

In between setting production records, coaching a company soccer team, and launching his own engineering company, Aningo has published *The Nigerian Engineer by and after the Year 2000* (1997), *My Cry for Nigeria: A Challenge to Our Essence* (2011), first edition, and several articles and poems on engineering, social, and environmental developments. A collection of his poems is in progress. He writes that "Everyone is a library; each book, bestseller. /Tweak stories – how truly one we all are." And that "we all come naked then go portfolio-less; /medical science ceaselessly choreographs alliance."

Aningo believes that any artificial curtailment of the full expression of an individual's talent is the first sin against humanity.

Work, football, and pleasure allowed him to travel the length, breadth, and all in-between nooks and crannies of Nigeria. To hear him expound on the potentials of Nigeria is to have your mood frozen, because of jarring underuse of opportunities everywhere in the country. But he believes that options still exist for mending Nigeria.

Chuks Aningo currently resides in Enugu, Nigeria, where he enjoys growing fragrant flowers, tomatoes, okra, and others; listening to highlife, reggae, and jazz; watching soccer, boxing, cricket, and American football; and pontificating with his dear wife and three adult children. He spends quality time with members of his Oyofo Oghe community's UCA (Umu-ogba Chukwuajalike Aningo) Age Grade he mentors as the traditional "Father" of the Age Grade.

Email: ccaningoboox@gmail.com
Blog site: http://www.beamnaijadream.com